'I thought you wanted me off the case,' Jess reminded him.

His fingertips skimmed her cheekbones, the pad of his thumb her mouth. 'Wanting is dangerous, Detective. I learned that a long time ago. I want my daughter back. That doesn't mean she's standing here. A smart man deals in reality.'

She grabbed his wrist and pulled his hand away from her face. 'Play your games with someone else. They won't work with me.'

'I'm simply saying you've got as much on the line as I have. You can't afford to take the easy way out, because if it turns out Emily's in trouble and you didn't help, you'll never be able to live with yourself.'

'I don't need to be bullied by you to do my job,' she said. 'I promised you I'd bring your daughter back, and I will. We both want the same thing.'

A faint light glimmered in his eyes. 'Then let's stop wanting and make it happen.'

His choice of words, the low tone in which he uttered them, sent an unwanted sizzle through her. He'd done it on purpose, she knew. He always did.

Available in May 2004 from Silhouette Sensation

When Night Falls

JENNA MILLS

SILHOUETTE®
SENSATION™

*Silhouette, Silhouette Sensation and Colophon are
registered trademarks of Harlequin Books S.A., used under licence.*

*First published in Great Britain 2004
Silhouette Books, Eton House, 18-24 Paradise Road,
Richmond, Surrey TW9 1SR*

© Jennifer Miller 2002

ISBN 0 373 27240 5

18-0504

*Printed and bound in Spain
by Litografia Rosés S.A., Barcelona*

JENNA MILLS

grew up in south Louisiana, amid romantic plantation ruins, haunting swamps and timeless legends. It's not surprising, then, that she wrote her first romance at the ripe old age of six! Three years later, this librarian's daughter turned to romantic suspense with *Jacquie and the Swamp*, a harrowing tale of a young woman on the run in the swamp and the dashing hero who helps her find her way home. Since then her stories have grown in complexity, but her affinity for adventurous women and dangerous men has remained constant. She loves writing about strong characters torn between duty and desire, conscious choice and destiny.

When not writing award-winning stories brimming with deep emotion, steamy passion and page-turning suspense, Jenna spends her time with her husband, two cats, two dogs and a menagerie of plants in their Dallas, Texas, home. Jenna loves to hear from her readers. She can be reached via e-mail at writejennamills@aol.com, or at PO Box 768, Coppell, Texas 75019, USA.

This story ended up having a lot to do with fathers and daughters. It seems fitting, then, to pay tribute to the men in my life—my father, James Aucoin, and my precious grandfathers, Cloyd Allison and the late Milton Aucoin—who guided, inspired and protected me, even when I made that difficult!

And, as always, for my husband, Chuck, who accepts me just the way I am and loves me anyway. May fatherhood come your way someday, as well.

Chapter 1

"**O**pen the damn door!"

William Armstrong pounded his fist against pitifully thin wood, surprised his hand didn't smash right through. He wished it would. He wanted inside.

Instead, he stood on the neglected front porch of an old frame house. A bitterly cold wind ripped through the surrounding oaks, while somewhere in the distance, a dog bayed. The muted light from a dirty porch lamp just barely filtered through the darkness.

"I mean it," he growled, "open the goddamn door." Almost anywhere else in town, someone would have called the cops by now, but here, in this run-down south Dallas neighborhood, late-night shouting was nothing unusual. "If you don't, I'm coming in anyway."

The laugh track of a late-night sitcom leaked through the rotted wood siding, but no hushed voices, no muffled cries.

Liam's body tightened in frustration. She could be in there, he knew. With Braxton. The chances of the punk opening the door were slim. What would he do if he found them in there? Liam wondered. Together.

The thought made his blood run as cold as the freezing rain that had delayed his flight back from Chicago.

Liam crushed the ugly possibilities before they became even more sickening images. She wouldn't do that. She'd promised. She'd looked at him with those beseeching blue eyes and told him she never wanted to see Adam Braxton again.

And Liam had believed her.

Then he'd come home to find her gone.

He pounded once more against the door, then crossed the rickety porch. The cops hadn't listened to him. They hadn't cared. They never did. If he wanted her back, he had no one to rely on but himself.

Through a grimy window, Liam squinted to see inside. Filth, was his first impression. A lamp illuminated clothes strewn everywhere, fast-food bags, CD cases. A sitcom blared from an old TV, but the couch sat empty. Milk crates on either side of the ratty structure served as tables.

Frowning, he wiped his hand across the dirty glass pane, leaning in for a better look.

She smiled back at him from a large, elaborate silver frame. Wearing only a black tank top and a short leather skirt, she lay on some sort of velvet settee. Thick, black hair cascaded over the beautiful skin of her shoulders and arms. Her smile lit up the whole room, full and beckoning, shockingly provocative.

He'd never seen any of it, not the photo, the risqué outfit or the smile. It was the kind of ensemble a woman chose for her lover, not one that a seventeen-year-old girl modeled for her father.

Liam's heart kicked up another notch. Blood thundered through his veins. Adam Braxton had no business owning a picture of Emily. The two had broken up after she had caught him getting it on with some piece of trash. He had needs, Braxton had tried to explain, and if Emily wouldn't fill them, he had to take care of them elsewhere. That didn't change the way he felt about Emily.

Like hell. Liam thanked God his daughter was smart enough to recognize that line of garbage for what it was. Still, she'd been crushed. He'd held her while she cried, doing his best to soothe her broken heart.

And now she was gone.

His first hint at trouble had come in the form of a voice mail from the high school, informing him Emily hadn't shown for homeroom. Concerned, Liam had tried unsuccessfully to reach her. By the time he arrived in Dallas, six hours later than planned, it had been past midnight, his daughter and her car nowhere in sight. No lights or music in the house, no voice mail message, no note.

Kids missed curfew all the time, he knew, but not Emily. Not ever, not even once. Trust was an implicit bond, he'd taught her. Once shattered, the fragile pieces could never be fully repaired. He'd worked hard to forge a relationship with his daughter where she could tell him things he didn't necessarily enjoy hearing, so that he would never find himself at a moment like this.

If Emily was missing, he knew it wasn't by her own choice.

She flat-out wouldn't do that to him.

Liam scanned the semilit room again, this time noticing Emily's letter sweater and a pair of painfully familiar ribbon-laced running shoes. Fury almost made him see double. She could be in there. Braxton could be trying to get her to fill those *needs* of his.

''Emily!'' Something dark and punishing tore through Liam. A father's rage. He glanced around wildly, his attention narrowing on a broken section of the porch railing. He grabbed a piece of wood and drew back to shatter the glass.

"You don't want to do that, Mr. Armstrong."

The authoritative voice stopped him midswing. He pivoted and found a woman standing halfway up the steps to the porch. Even the dark night couldn't hide the steely determination in her eyes. Moonlight glinted off the pistol she held pointed toward him.

"Keep your hands where I can see them," she said in that steady voice.

A sense of vertigo closed in on Liam. The woman cut a striking figure standing there in a long leather coat, her thick auburn hair pulled back from her face. Not an ounce of fear shone in her eyes or her stance.

He blinked, but she didn't fade into the night as her breath did. A vague familiarity nagged at him. "Who are you?"

She mounted the next step. "Detective Jessica Clark, Dallas PD."

The revelation surged through him like a shot of whiskey straight up. Aside from those unyieldingly sharp eyes, she looked more like a runway model than a cop. Her coat flapped open, revealing the attractive taupe pantsuit she wore beneath. Silk, he noted. The brushed fabric draped over curves a cop had no business sporting. Her heavy-lidded, almond-shaped eyes conjured images of long, athletic afternoons in bed. Her thick auburn hair was mussed and pulled back with combs, her skin flushed and flawless.

What the hell was she doing here? He hadn't even heard her approach.

"Step away from the window, sir."

"I'm not breaking any laws."

"No, but you were about to." She nodded toward the piece of wood still clenched in his hand. "You should have stayed at home and waited for me, like Commander McKnight told you to do."

Liam swore softly. *This* was who the commander had

sent to find Emily? Clearly, the doddering old fool hadn't taken him seriously. Rather than the panther Liam needed, the skilled hunter, Commander McKnight had sent a kitten.

The temptation surfaced to turn toward the window and smash his way inside, but something about the way she looked at him, the cool challenge in her eyes, held him in place.

Or maybe it was the gun in her hands.

"Waited on you?" he demanded instead. "While my daughter is missing? Sorry, Detective, but I learned a long time ago the danger of trusting cops with my life. I've got better things to do than twist in the wind."

"So do I." She motioned with the gun. "Now turn around and put your hands against the side of the house."

"*What?*"

"You heard me."

He did. He just couldn't believe it. "For crying out loud—you can't be serious."

That faint smile all cops had down to an art form played with her lips. "I don't owe you any explanations. I'm not the one about to break into someone else's house."

She had a point, damn it. "My daughter is missing. This is her ex-boyfriend's house. They had a bad breakup. She could be in there. You know that's the only reason I'm here."

"And if you'd found her inside, then what? You'd just take her by the hand and lead her home?" She advanced to the top step. "Let me tell you what I see. I see a man who's decided to take the law into his own hands. It's the middle of the night. You're prowling around a house where you clearly don't belong. You have a piece of railing in your hand. If I hadn't stopped you, you would have already committed a crime. You're damn straight I'm going to make sure you're not packing before we take this any further.'' Fire flashed in her eyes. ''Now turn the hell around.''

Liam swore under his breath. He didn't know whether to be furious or to admire a woman not afraid to stand up to him. She had more guts than most men he knew.

Realizing the faster he got this over with, the faster he could find Emily, he dropped the wood and did as she asked.

Detective Jessica Clark stepped onto the darkened porch. Adrenaline surged so hard and fast she was surprised William Armstrong didn't hear the pounding of her heart. She was also thankful.

Grimy windows hoarded most of the light oozing from inside the house, leaving only a muted glow to cast the large man standing against the door in shadow. Despite the scene she'd intruded upon, she didn't think he'd been drinking. There was no smell of alcohol, and his eyes were sharp. Still, she moved cautiously. She doubted he'd try anything more foolish than he already had, but she also knew enough about William Armstrong to know how easily he could prove her wrong.

Missing daughter or not, the man had already disobeyed a direct order from her commanding officer.

That's why she kept her .38 trained on him.

The creak of old wooden planks announced her progress, but he didn't so much as flinch. He just stood there with his feet shoulder-width apart and his ungloved hands pressed against the rotting siding. He seemed to know the pose well.

Yet for some odd reason, he looked more like he was bracing himself.

Mild curiosity sharpened into intrigue. When Commander McKnight called less than an hour before with instructions to pacify the big bad wolf, she'd envisioned herself sitting on a sofa in William Armstrong's fancy living room, asking questions about his daughter, jotting a few notes. She'd imagined politely explaining procedure and discussing all the reasons a teenager might not come home on time.

She hadn't once pictured herself holding a gun on one of Dallas's most notorious citizens while the brutal north wind slapped at them both.

But she should have.

William Armstrong never made anything easy.

For a fleeting instant, Jess wished she didn't know so much about the self-made Internet mogul. That way, she might be able to feel sympathy for a man who didn't know where his daughter was. But she couldn't. She knew too much. About the man and the fortune he'd amassed, his trouble with the law, the dark allegations that never seemed to die. Many believed he belonged behind bars.

What would Armstrong do, she wondered, when he realized exactly who *she* was?

Somewhere in the neighborhood, a dog barked rambunctiously. Another answered. Jess listened for her partner's approaching car, but hearing only the sounds of the night, she took one last step and positioned herself behind a waiting William Armstrong.

He still hadn't moved.

The faint light cast his face in shadow. He wore expensive tailored gray slacks, but instead of a matching suit coat, a well-worn leather jacket covered the expanse of his back and shoulders. It was an odd combination of backstreet tough and big-city refinement. His past and present personified.

"What's the matter, Detective?" he asked, glancing over his shoulder. Mistrust sparked in his eyes. Blue, the light from the window revealed. The dark, threatening blue of storm clouds gathering on the horizon. "Having second thoughts about putting your clean hands on my body? Think I might contaminate you?''

Jess offered a tight smile. ''Eagerness doesn't become you, Mr. Armstrong.''

''Eagerness?'' He almost growled. ''Don't you understand what's going on here? That my daughter is missing? She could be in trouble. Scared. I don't have time to stand here playing mind games with you all night long.''

The very real worry in his voice scraped against training. ''I understand your frustration,'' she said levelly, ''but you can't just take the law into your own hands. You would have saved us both considerable time and frustration if you'd stayed at your house, like Commander McKnight asked you to.''

''If I'd thought you would actually show up and listen to me, I might have.''

''I showed up, Mr. Armstrong. I showed up just in time to see your car tearing down the street.''

''You followed me.''

''And it's a good thing I did, otherwise you might be spending the night in jail.''

A muscle in the hollow of his cheek thumped. ''I was tired of waiting.''

''Mr. Armstrong,'' she said, stepping closer. ''Your daughter has only been missing a couple of hours. Her car is gone. In all likelihood, she's with friends or—''

''She's not,'' he said emphatically. ''Go ahead and do what you have to do. Frisk me. Maybe then you'll listen to what I have to say.''

Jess recognized a gauntlet when it lay glimmering at her feet. At this point, if she didn't carry through, he'd take that as a sign of weakness. She needed to reestablish the order of things, even if that meant putting her hands all over this coldly furious man's rigid body.

She'd rather touch a lightning bolt.

''Turn around.'' She didn't want to feel the heat of his eyes as she put her palms to the hard planes of his body.

Surprisingly, he obeyed.

Jess tucked the .38 in her waistband. Her heart rate revved up another notch. She drew a deep breath, the cold air stinging her lungs, then pressed on tiptoes and lifted her gloved hands to the soft, well-worn sleeves of his leather jacket.

He stiffened at her touch, as though she were the lightning bolt, not him.

The reaction surprised her, but she ignored it, patting from his wide shoulders down the length of his arms, then along his sides to where the jacket ended and his slacks began. Before going any lower, she shifted her hands and ran one up the length of his back, the other along his stomach and chest.

As she suspected, she found nothing but hard muscle and angry male.

Jess frowned. The harsh north wind battered her, but inside her leather coat, she felt as toasty as though she'd just stepped onto the equator. The night air seemed to thicken, and she grimly realized she'd chased armed and dangerous suspects down darkened alleys without feeling this winded.

Biting back an oath, she put her palms to Armstrong's hips and worked her way down the soft fabric of his slacks. His legs were long and thick, obviously the product of rigorous conditioning.

The thought jarred her. She'd patted down more suspects than she could remember. It was routine, part of the job. Male, female, young, old, it didn't matter. Never had the bodies she touched caused her pulse to surge. Never had her palms started to sweat. Never had she thought about the body beneath the clothes. What all that hard muscle would look like—

"What the hell is going on here?" A startled male voice came from somewhere behind her.

Armstrong jerked beneath Jess's touch and pivoted toward her partner, leaving Jess on one knee, awkwardly facing his groin. She abruptly stood and turned toward a scowling Detective Kirby Long.

"Armstrong hassling you?" he asked.

"It's a long story," Jess answered. "I thought you were right behind me."

Kirby frowned. "Caught the lights wrong."

It was just as well. Had he been on the scene, Armstrong would be sporting cuffs right now. Her hard-line partner would have gladly let the man smash the window and commit a crime.

"This is the boyfriend's house," she told Kirby. "Armstrong thought she might be here."

He nodded. "Wouldn't be the first time a girl chose the thrill of a lover boy over Daddy's curfew—"

"I'll finish up with Armstrong." She cut him off. "You go check around back, see if you can tell if anyone's home."

Kirby's eyes took on a cautious glow. "You sure you don't want me to finish up with Armstrong?"

She knew what he was really asking. Was she okay? Did she feel threatened? Had Armstrong finally crossed the line?

After three years of partnership, Kirby still acted like she was a delicate flower someone could step on.

"I've got it covered," she told him.

He hesitated before heading around the house, glancing at Jess one last time before turning the corner.

"Why didn't you tell him?"

She swung around to find Armstrong watching her with eyes as hard and dark as cobalt marble. "Tell him what?"

"How you found me. What you and I both know to be

true, that if you hadn't been here, I would have smashed that window and been inside? Something tells me he would have watched and waited, then pounced.''

"Half the force would have." The lingering resentment ran that deep.

"Then why didn't you? And why not tell your partner?"

"It doesn't matter."

"It does to me."

An unsettling current ran through her. The whisper-fine blade of compassion made as much sense as taking a water gun to a three-alarm fire.

"Maybe I was protecting you," she said, more for shock value than anything else. "Maybe I know my partner. Or maybe I'd like to put this incident behind us and get on with discussing your daughter. Believe what you like."

The words hung between them. She thought he would make some sarcastic retort, but he didn't. He watched her a moment, then looked toward the grimy window.

Jess welcomed a blast of brisk wind against her face. After an unbearably long, hot, dry summer, winter had hit Dallas with a vengeance. Extremes, Jess thought. The very definition of William Armstrong. Poverty and fortune, disgrace and celebrity. Famine. Feast.

"There's no sign of anyone inside," Kirby said several minutes later. "No car, either."

Armstrong strode to another window and peered inside. "He could be hiding her in there."

"He could be," Kirby acknowledged, "but I don't think he is. Neighbor says Braxton left shortly before ten. Said the guy is in a band and they had a gig or something."

"We'll send a black-and-white," Jess added. "When Braxton arrives, they'll let us know and we can talk to him." She knew her answer wouldn't please Armstrong, but at this point nothing indicated the need for a search warrant. Everything they knew so far suggested his daughter had left home of her own free will.

"I'd like to head back to your house now," she said, "ask a few more questions, look around."

He nodded. "You think she'll be there?"

It wouldn't surprise Jess. Teenagers were notorious for putting their parents through the wringer, sometimes intentionally, sometimes without even realizing they were doing it. "We can hope." She gestured toward the street. "Come on."

Kirby waited until Armstrong was several steps in front of them before lowering his voice. "I'll ride with him."

"Your car is here," she replied.

Her partner glanced toward the street, where William Armstrong slid a key into his car door. "The man got away with murder once, Jess. I'm not letting him get away from me, too."

The wind whipped up, cutting through the leather of her long coat. "Where would he go?" she asked, fighting a shiver. "His daughter is missing." Despite Armstrong's shady past, she'd seen real worry in his eyes. They had to treat this case separately and objectively. "I'll lead the way, Armstrong can follow me, and you can follow him."

Kirby caught up with her. "What's the matter? Don't trust me alone with moneybags?"

Not for a heartbeat. Kirby hadn't been on the force seventeen years before, but Armstrong's brush with the law was the stuff legends were made of. *Bad* legends. "McKnight sent us for a reason. Police brutality wasn't it."

Surprisingly, Kirby let her comment go. Several minutes later, their little caravan left the run-down Dallas neighborhood and headed north, toward the exclusive subdivision Armstrong called home. If his daughter wasn't there, the next few days promised to be a minefield of trouble.

Seventeen years was long enough for the shadow of a

high-publicity investigation to fade, but not vanish altogether. A young mother's mysterious disappearance. No trail left behind, no trace ever found. Armstrong claimed his girlfriend ran off, but her father, a state congressman and hunting buddy of the lead detective, cried foul. The police had investigated, but with no body, not even a mountain of circumstantial evidence could prove he'd committed a crime.

Jess merged her car with traffic and floored the accelerator. The air coming out of the heater finally warmed, but the chill deep inside her remained.

After all this time, suspicion lingered. Nobody had forgotten the way the press had shredded the department over Heather Manning's disappearance. They didn't understand how a nineteen-year-old nobody could outsmart the entire police department. To this day, accusations of ineptitude and shoddy police work lingered.

Unless Armstrong could miraculously provide proof of his innocence, his name would forever be mentioned with those suspended in that hazy place between guilt and innocence. High-profile cases never completely dissipated.

Innocent until proven guilty sounded well and good, but most cops couldn't let go that easily.

Lead detective turned chief of police, her father certainly hadn't. He'd gone to his grave believing William Armstrong guilty of the perfect crime, one he'd walked away from scot-free.

The low rumble of a car engine snagged Liam's attention. In a heartbeat he was at the window across his study and fixated on headlights cutting through the darkness. Emily—

The car drove right on by.

He exhaled a ragged breath. He wanted to believe his daughter would stroll through the door any minute, laugh-

ing, full of light and energy. He wanted her to smile and
melt his heart, just like she always did. He wanted the chill
in his blood to go away.

It didn't. It couldn't. Not even the blazing sun could
warm frozen tundra.

"Mr. Armstrong, did you hear me?"

Liam pivoted toward the smoky voice and found Detective Jessica Clark watching him with those intelligent, inquisitive eyes of hers. She'd shed her gloves and coat, revealing the tailored silk pantsuit beneath. A strand of curly
auburn hair against a well-defined cheekbone lent her a
softness he knew better than to trust.

"I heard you," he said.

"And?"

"And nothing. I've told you all I know. It's after four
in the morning. No one has seen my daughter since I left
for Chicago yesterday morning at six. She didn't show up
at school. Her friends haven't heard from her. But for some
crazy reason, you don't seem willing to believe she's in
trouble."

"Mr. Armstrong, we need to consider all the possibilities. Teenagers turn up missing every day. Rarely is something sinister involved. Is there anywhere else your daughter might be?"

"Like with her mother?" Detective Long added from
across the room.

Liam didn't flinch, didn't let himself react. "Emily
wouldn't know her mother if the woman walked up to her
on the street."

"Could that happen?" Long prodded. The man looked
entirely too sure of himself, his dark hair neat and tidy, his
sports coat and pressed slacks more suave than professional. The hard lines of his expression said he wasn't here
for fun and games. A hint of cruelty lurked in his eyes.

"Would it be a flesh-and-blood woman walking up to Emily, or a ghost?"

That was the heart of the matter, Liam knew, the disappearance of Emily's mother. No one believed she'd left of her own volition, leaving nineteen-year-old Liam to raise an infant daughter. No one believed a spoiled coed would simply walk away, leaving all her clothes, her jewelry, her favorite albums, even her car, right where they belonged. Tests studied for, but not taken. Classes unfinished. A package still on order.

No one believed a mother would abandon her child.

Heather's father, a blustery former state congressman, still preferred to hold Liam responsible. It was easier for Carson Manning to cry foul than to look in the mirror.

The higher Liam's star had climbed, the deeper the resentment had grown. Carson had used his influence with the police department to keep the waters muddy—he had practically turned it into a sport. For seventeen years, the boys in blue had hassled Liam every chance they got. For going one mile over the speed limit. For a rolling stop in a residential area. For a burned-out taillight.

Now they had him just where they wanted him.

On his knees.

"I have no idea where Heather Manning is," he told the closed-minded detective, not even trying to convince him.

The jackal narrowed his eyes. "That's not what Chief Clark believed."

Liam started to tell him where he could go but went very still instead. Vague familiarity sharpened into a nasty suspicion. *Clark.* The most determined, dangerous of all Liam's persecutors. The man who let his friendship with Carson Manning blind him to anything Liam could say.

All the hope he'd momentarily heaved Detective Jessica Clark's way, all the trust she'd skillfully built, shattered into shards of ice.

The realization hit Liam hard. Rarely did he miss something so obvious. Adrenaline shot through him. His heart pounded. He gazed into her fascinating amber eyes, but saw only the eyes of the man who'd done his best to nail Liam to the wall.

"Son of a bitch," he growled. "You're the daughter."

Chapter 2

Detective Jessica Clark smiled like a barracuda. "Pardon?"

"Wallace Clark. You're his daughter."

"You're damn straight she is," Detective Long answered.

She lifted her chin, an odd glitter in her eyes. "I take it you remember my father."

Liam swore under his breath and reached for her hands. He took them in his, noting the coolness of her smooth flesh, and slid the sleeve from her wrist.

"You can't touch her like that!" Long barked.

"What are you doing?" she demanded.

He offered a cutting smile. "Looking for those infamous kid gloves, of course."

She snatched back her hands and glared at him. "Now who's playing games?"

Liam wondered what her angle was, what game her father had taught her to play. He'd hoped Wallace Clark's passing would usher in a new era. He'd hoped the past would be dead and buried right along with the bullheaded chief of police.

Now he realized the fallacy of that hope.

"I've heard about you," he told the man's daughter. "The department's golden girl. Smooth as silk, tough as nails. Daddy's little girl straight down to the core. That's why you're here, isn't it, Detective Clark? To keep me in line, keep me quiet. To pacify the big bad wolf."

She squared her shoulders, the defiant effect ruined by that strand of curvy auburn hair, now flirting with her lips.

"I'm here because your daughter is missing," she said with perfect diction, "and you claim to want her back. If you can tear yourself out of the past, I'd like to see her room now."

She turned and strode from the study.

Liam watched her go. Frustration burned through him. The commander hadn't taken him seriously. Instead of sending over his best men, McKnight offered up a hothead and a debutante. Wallace Clark's daughter. Another slap in the face. It was like ordering aged whiskey but receiving a cheap beer and a goblet of lush red wine instead. Whereas one left a bad taste in his mouth, the other was deceptively benign, leaving him dangerously thirsty.

Swearing under his breath, he left the study and took the stairs two at a time.

A sprawling loft opened before Jess. A game room, she quickly surmised, with an old-fashioned jukebox, a pinball machine, a battered pool table, even what looked to be antique sports pennants. The massive big-screen TV and cushy sofas represented the only hints of the twenty-first century.

Two long hallways ran off from the room. All the doors stood closed. Jess had no idea which room belonged to

Emily Armstrong but had no intention of waiting for the father. He'd already given her permission to look around. She didn't need him breathing down her neck.

Her job pertained to the daughter, the innocent, not the tall, isolated man with the hard eyes and angry words.

Looking for kid gloves, of course. The taunt matched her step for step. She should be used to the reaction, the snickers behind her back, the insinuations that she was more of a figurehead than a real cop.

Still, the jab burned. She'd made detective on her own merit. She wasn't her father's puppet, his clone, his anything. Just his daughter.

She stopped at the first door she came to. An odd jolt went through her, no doubt the result of endless hours of training about caution and closed doors. But she was in a posh residential home. Nothing sinister lurked on the other side.

"I don't think you want to go in there."

The overly confident masculine voice revved through her. She turned toward it, found William Armstrong towering behind her. His tailored gray slacks and black button-down shirt should have made him look civilized, but putting fleece on a wolf didn't make the animal a sheep. The expensive clothes were wrinkled, as though being so close to Armstrong could exhaust even fabric.

He seemed taller up here where the ceilings weren't so high. She hated the fact she had to look up to see his face, hated the odd vulnerability it sent stabbing through her. But even more, she hated the shadows lurking in his gaze. The pain. She didn't want to see either, knew better than to notice the man behind the case, certainly not the bereaved father.

Facts and theories, clues—they were her stock-in-trade. Every cop knew emotional involvement equaled a surefire formula for disaster.

"What's the matter?" she asked, tearing an insolent page from his book. "Got a skeleton in there you don't want me to see?"

"No, just my big, unmade bed."

She released the knob as though it was a hot coal, not cool glass. She didn't want to see William Armstrong's bed. Didn't want to think about him in the context of rumpled sheets and carelessly tossed pillows. That made him too real.

Too much of a man.

"I need to see your daughter's room." While she checked out the interior, Kirby would look over the perimeter.

"Then follow me." Armstrong turned and led her across the plush carpet and through the game room to the second hall.

Jess wanted to ascribe some cold motivation to the fact the father separated his room from the daughter but found she couldn't.

He stopped beside the second door on the right. "Here you go."

Another tingle of anticipation zipped through her, but she squelched it and entered the room, flicking on the overhead light. She wasn't sure what she'd been expecting, but that didn't stop her surprise upon seeing the teenage girl's room. The freshness of it, she supposed. The innocence. William Armstrong commanded such a forbidding presence, she'd expected equal gloom from his child.

But the daughter's room was like a breath of fresh air, an intriguing combination of little girl and young woman.

The subtle aroma of jasmine invited her in. All the typical accoutrements greeted her, the bed, the nightstand, the dressers, the stereo. But the abundance of color lent them a vividness Jess hadn't expected.

A smile worked its way free, an instant liking for the

teenage girl. Then a blade of worry cut in, reminding Jess why she was here, what she had to do.

"Seen enough?" Armstrong asked. "Ready to call it a night?"

"Is that what you want?" She turned to find him practically guarding the doorway, the hard lines of his face muted by whiskers. "That would be easier, wouldn't it? You could hang the department out to dry like you so clearly want to. But your daughter would still be missing, wouldn't she?"

His expression darkened. "Don't talk to me about what I want."

"Then don't make idiotic assessments about how I do my job." She turned to the heart of the surprisingly neat room before he could comment further. His fear was easy to see and one hundred percent human, but for some reason, the man chose combativeness over cooperation. Jess wanted to feel anger and resentment but instead found herself fighting an unwanted twinge of compassion.

What was it about strong men that made them isolate themselves from those in the best position to help?

Since the question had no answer, Jess focused on Emily's room, noting the tray of perfume on the dresser, the cluster of picture frames. She moved in for a closer look, ignored the sharp impact of seeing Emily and her father in every single picture. The photos chronicled the girl's childhood, from pigtails to party dresses. They featured Armstrong, as well, beaming a razor-sharp smile of love and pride.

The sight added to the growing number of surprises.

Jess hated surprises.

But William Armstrong ranked right up there with the worst of them. Meeting the man in the flesh was like opening a door and expecting to find a small dark closet but discovering a whole new world instead. A world of uncertainty and danger, but intrigue, as well.

She'd been so intent on Armstrong's name, his identity, his past, she hadn't thought about the father whose only child was missing. But she should have. She, Jessica Clark, daughter of former police chief Wallace Clark, should have.

Crows, after all, always came home to roost.

She remembered being an impressionable sixteen-year-old, listening to her father rant about Armstrong. She remembered hearing about the infant daughter. But now, seventeen years later, she had a hard time seeing this rugged-looking thirty-six-year-old man as the father of a teenage daughter. A child he clearly loved. If Jess ended up proving the girl had left of her own volition, Jess feared she'd break the man's heart.

The thought gave her pause, surprised her even more. She had no business thinking about William Armstrong and broken hearts.

The violent man about to break into Adam Braxton's house, that's who she needed to remember, not the way he'd practically run across his study when a car engine rumbled somewhere down the street. She needed to forget the crazy little stutter step her pulse had done, the ravaged look in his dark blue eyes. And above all else, she needed to forget the feel of his rigid body beneath her steady hands.

"So is this how you like to spend your nights, Detective?"

She spun toward him, biting back a laugh. It was one of those rare frigid nights in Dallas that made a woman dream of snuggling against a lover's warm body and feeling strong arms hold her tight. Instead, Jess faced a man many believed guilty of murder, and it was her job to determine if his little girl had been kidnapped or if she'd simply walked out on him.

Oh, yeah. This was *exactly* how she liked to spend her nights.

"Look, Mr. Armstrong. I know you've had trouble with law-enforcement officials over the years, but turning everything into a battle won't bring your daughter home any faster. I'm not the enemy. I'm here to help. That's my job."

"You want me to believe Wallace Clark's daughter takes the protect-and-serve oath seriously? To trust you with my daughter's life? Your father wanted nothing more than to see me rot in jail."

"I'm not my father," she said, "and I don't really care what you believe. I care about your daughter, the young girl who should be tucked in this bed right now. I care about getting her home safe and sound. You can be an obstacle in my path, or you can help me. The choice is all yours."

A curious light glinted in his eyes. "Are you always so tough at four in the morning?"

"How I am when I'm usually in bed is really none of your business." Enjoying the moment of shock on his face, she crossed to the adjacent bathroom.

A quick survey revealed no makeup, no hairbrush or dryer, no curling iron. Jess frowned. While kidnappers weren't renowned for taking time to pack, young girls didn't often leave home without their styling accessories.

In the bedroom, Jess made a similar discovery at Emily's dresser. Most of the drawers were empty.

She turned toward Armstrong. "From the looks of this room, your daughter could be on fall break." Or somewhere on the streets, intending to never see her father again. "Her clothes are gone, her makeup, everything a teenager needs for a trip."

He glanced toward the center of the room. "The bed is made."

Jess followed his gaze and found the comforter sporting

an underwater ocean scene pulled tightly over the mattress. "Is that unusual?"

"She never makes it unless I'm standing here in a staring contest. The fact she did so now has to mean she was trying to tell me something. She wanted me to know something wasn't right."

The theory sounded far-fetched, but Jess made a habit of discarding nothing. "Maybe she made the bed as a last favor to you."

Armstrong winced. "You really are your father's daughter, aren't you?"

"Pardon?"

"You go for the low blow, just like he did. Must run in the blood."

An unprecedented splinter of guilt cut through her. Cruelty wasn't her style. "Just considering all possibilities."

In Emily's closet, the pattern continued. Pink hangers dangled without clothes. No shoes lay scattered about. She turned toward the doorway, but Armstrong no longer stood there. Instead he sat on his daughter's bed, staring at a tattered stuffed donkey in his big hands.

The sight hit Jess like a swift punch to the stomach. Seeing this darkly dangerous man in this fresh-and-innocent room, the way he clutched the battered, patchwork donkey, spoke to her on a level she didn't understand. Didn't like.

Sure as hell didn't trust.

Too easily, the woman in her responded to the man's anguish. She had the crazy desire to join him on the bed and put her arm around his wide shoulders, to assure him everything would be okay.

But the cop in her held her rooted in place. The notorious William Armstrong didn't need comfort from her. And she had none to give.

"I won this for Emmie at the state fair when she was

six," he said. "I can still picture the excitement in her eyes."

Jess smiled faintly. "I bet she was an adorable little girl."

·"From the day she was born, she's been the light of my life."

The pain in his voice, his eyes, nicked at the shield of indifference that kept Jess strong. "The father-daughter relationship is special," she found herself saying. "Most little girls grow up thinking their father can conquer the world."

She certainly had. Sometimes, it was still hard to believe her father was gone. She'd thought him too tough even for cancer.

Armstrong's smile turned brittle. "Emmie thought I hung the moon."

"For her, I'm sure you did."

He stared at the tattered animal in his big hands. "I just wish she never had to learn the truth."

Jess moved closer. "And what truth is that?"

He looked up from the stuffed donkey. His expression was remote. "That I'm a man, not the hero she once believed me to be. That I've made mistakes. That I have regrets."

The admission stopped Jess cold. With painful intimacy, she knew the land mines growing up the daughter of a prominent father introduced to a young girl's life. "You've done a good job keeping her out of the spotlight," she commented. Despite Armstrong's notoriety, she'd rarely heard mention of the child.

"She's an innocent. I don't want her to suffer because of my mistakes."

"You think that's why she's missing? Because of your mistakes?"

What little light there'd been in his gaze vanished. He clenched his eyes shut for a heartbeat, then turned to gently place the donkey on a pillow. It was almost as though he was tucking the stuffed animal in bed. Then he stood and looked down at Jess, long and hard.

"My daughter didn't run away."

"I didn't say she did."

"Not with words."

She stepped back from the bed, realizing she'd let herself get too close. "The investigation is wide-open right now, Mr. Armstrong."

"It's Liam."

"I prefer to keep—"

He stepped closer. "Don't lecture me about protocol, Jessica."

She tilted her head to avoid staring at the chest hair curling in the open V of his black dress shirt. He did it on purpose, she knew. Stood within her personal space.

The man was a master at leveraging his advantages.

But she knew how to play the game. She knew how to handle men like Armstrong, like her father, powerful, driven men with no time for anyone or anything but their agenda.

And again, she felt an odd kinship with a seventeen-year-old girl she'd never met.

"We both know you were sent here to appease me," Armstrong said silkily. "Fine. I'll overlook who your father was, what your motives are, so long as you find my daughter."

Jess slid her hands into the pockets of her suit jacket. They'd become oddly damp. "What does that have to do with using your first name?" she asked coolly. "We're working on a case together, not having tea."

"I want you on my side, but it's hard to believe you're there if you keep calling me Mr. Armstrong. Only the IRS uses that."

The urge to laugh didn't sit well. "I see."

The blue of his eyes hardened into cobalt. "If you were sent here to appease me, Detective Jessica Clark, do it. Call me Liam."

Her heart strummed harder, sending heat to every nerve ending. Standing in teenage Emily's room, that was exactly how Jess felt. Years of training and experience melted away, leaving her feeling like a freshman alone with the school bad boy, worried her parents would come charging in, hoping they wouldn't.

And she hated it. She'd hated it sixteen years before, hated it even more now.

"Liam." She didn't know why, but she stuck out her hand.

He took it in his, curling his long fingers around hers. His grip was warm and strong, not crushing like so many others she'd encountered. "Find my daughter, Jessica. Don't make me sorry I trusted you."

The words sent an unwanted jolt through her. So did the feel of his palm pressed to hers, the heat of his fingers encasing her flesh and bone. "That's my job."

And she intended to do it, no matter what this man did to her in the process.

Because of Emily, she reasoned. The missing girl who reminded Jessica entirely too much of herself.

Liam watched the enigmatic detective head down the dimly lit walkway. After the way she'd outlined her strategy, he wanted to believe she was eager to get started finding Emily, but he suspected her brisk departure had to do with the father, not the daughter.

He couldn't say he blamed her. He'd pushed hard, determined to discover if her mettle was as strong as she conveyed. He needed to know who he was dealing with.

An odd tightening in his gut warned him the lady detective possessed all the traits her gutsy demeanor promised.

Intelligence and confidence, conviction. She didn't back down when most people did. She stepped forward when most people ran.

Her ill-tempered partner strutted to his car, while she slid into hers, the streetlight giving Liam one last glimpse of those stunningly long legs. The engine roared to life, headlights cut through the darkness, and just like that, Wallace Clark's daughter vanished into the bitter early morning.

"What do you think?" Liam asked the sad-eyed Labrador retriever sitting obediently by his side. He rested his hand on her head. "Will Wally's daughter come through for us? Or will she be like all the others?"

Molly gazed at him. Not even she had escaped Emily's fashion fetish. The black dog wore a light brown bandanna with orange and red maple leaves embroidered on it. Emmie had selected the fall-themed scarf from her collection just a few nights before.

The sight of it tied around Molly's neck, the memory of his daughter securing the cloth there, sliced at Liam like a knife to the heart. Needing to do something, anything to help find his daughter, Liam crossed to his desk and grabbed the phone.

"I'm all over it," Vega St. Clair said moments later. The private investigator was one of the most renowned in the southwest. "We'll find the son of a bitch who took your daughter. We'll get her back."

The first few rays of optimism pushed through Liam. "There's one more thing, someone else I need you to look into."

"Shoot."

"Detective Jessica Clark. Daughter of former chief Wallace Clark." Liam picked up a picture of Emily and Molly, remembering how the detective had studied it just a few minutes before. There'd been something curious in her heavy-lidded, intelligent eyes, a sliver of sorrow, a shadow of regret. A flash of familiarity.

She was the key. Any hope of the cops finding his daughter rested squarely on Detective Jessica Clark's shoulders.

"I want to know how she did in the academy, how fast she made detective, what her track record is. I want to know what makes her tick, what makes her hurt."

St. Clair laughed. "Looking for a little insurance?"

Liam appreciated minds that worked as fast, as strategically, as his. "A puzzle can't be put together until all the pieces are identified."

And if he wasn't careful, the beauty with the badge could easily shift from being a piece of the solution to the heart of the problem.

Chapter 3

"That man belongs behind bars," Carson Manning barked. "Isn't it obvious he's a menace to society?"

Jess put down the heavy-duty coffee she'd picked up on the way to the station. Operating on less than an hour's sleep, she held her frustration with Emily's grandfather in check. She'd known the quick-tempered man all her life, still remembered those brisk fall weekends when he and her father had taken off in search of deer. She'd hated it then, hated the memory now.

The former state congressman had been waiting when she arrived ten minutes earlier. They sat in one of the small interviewing rooms while she attempted to keep him calm enough to take his statement. "Mr. Manning—"

"I warned Judge Donovan that man had no business raising a daughter. I told your father something like this would happen."

She frowned. Loss and death changed people, she knew. Twisted them. Turned them inside out. Carson Manning hadn't been an easy man to begin with. "Something like what?"

The older man surged out of the small wooden chair like an oil well gushing out of control. "I tried to get custody of Emily. After what that bastard did to my Heather—"

"He was never charged with a crime," Jess reminded, standing. There hadn't even been a body, just a mountain of circumstantial evidence—brand-new clothes still in the closet, suitcases under the bed, a hair appointment for the following day, never kept. Money in the bank, never withdrawn. Credit cards never used again. A history of loud arguments.

A baby left alone, hungry and crying.

"That doesn't mean he isn't keeping secrets, Jessie, only that he's smarter than the cops are."

Smarter than a lot of people, Jess knew, based on the money he'd made writing and selling code for Internet companies. He'd amassed a fortune seemingly overnight, much to the chagrin of her father and Carson Manning.

"Heather was a happy, loving girl," he went on. "A bit of a free spirit, but with a good heart. We always thought she'd marry the boy next door. Heather went to college and forgot all about poor Kale the second she met Armstrong. He used her. Knocked her up. Then got rid of her."

Jess found herself glad Kirby had yet to arrive—the last thing her father's protégé needed was more ammunition for his intense suspicion of William Armstrong. She already worried about his ability to investigate the case objectively.

Of course, that could be said for half the force.

"I'm sorry about your daughter, sir, but there's nothing to suggest William Armstrong was involved in his own daughter's disappearance. He wasn't even in town at the time."

"A man with his money doesn't have to be in town."

Jess reached for her coffee, trying to reconcile the man

Manning described with the father she'd seen clutching a tattered stuffed donkey in his big hands. What must it be like, she wondered, to live with so much hatred directed at you?

"By all accounts Armstrong dotes on his daughter. Why would he want her gone?"

"Who knows what goes on in that man's mind? Maybe she was cramping his style. Maybe he just got fed up with her, the fact she wasn't daddy's little girl anymore. Now that she's older, she doesn't always do what her father wants."

"So you think he got rid of her?" Jess asked incredulously. She'd encountered equally heinous crimes, but Carson Manning's allegations sickened her in a way she didn't understand.

His eyes took on a fevered glow. "It's called a pattern, Jessie. A pattern your father would have seen. If you can't see it, I'll find someone who will."

Liam slammed his fist against hard leather. The punching bag swooshed back, swung forward for another jab. He pounded the abused surface, sending the hundred-pound mass of high-impact foam swaying violently. Right then left, right then left. Over and over, harder each time.

The exertion sent jolts of satisfaction spearing through him.

Sweat poured down his face, ran down his chest. He blinked it from his eyes but kept right on punching. The impact cleared his focus, reinforcing the fact he was awake and not living in some nightmare.

Damn, but he wished that seeing his daughter's smile again was as simple as waking up.

On a low oath he stepped back and kicked up his right leg, the bottom of his foot slamming into the heavy bag. His trainer would curse him for not bothering with shoes, but Liam wasn't seeking comfort. He needed to take the edge off before he trusted himself around others.

Heaving in another breath, he kept fighting.

Liam was a man accustomed to making things happen. If an obstacle blocked his path, he moved it. Sometimes negotiation worked. On those rare occasions when it didn't, he employed more severe tactics. Whatever it took to produce the desired outcome.

"Damn it," he said, then landed another vicious blow to the innocent punching bag. Rather than leather, he envisioned the person responsible for taking his daughter.

"Oh, Liam, honey, don't hurt yourself."

The feathery voice took him by surprise. He stepped back from the swinging bag and turned to find Marlena Dane posed in the training-room doorway. As always, she was dressed to the nines, her bottle-blond hair and bright blue suit a stark contrast to his mood. His housekeeper must have let her in.

"What are you doing here?"

Her smile was tentative. "How can you even ask me that?"

"Easily." He grabbed a white towel and scrubbed it over his face. Other than Emily, the only person he cared to see was the enigmatic detective who'd promised to find his daughter. Certainly not his former lover.

The click of stiletto heels against ceramic tile warned of her approach. He slung back the towel and draped it around his shoulders. "This isn't a good time, Marlena."

"There never is with you, William. When are you going to admit you're not indestructible and let someone help?"

"Unless you know where to find Emmie, there's nothing you can do."

Marlena made a breathy clucking noise and stopped mere inches from him. "I suppose that's why you're down here punishing yourself? Look at you." She surveyed the length of his body, from his bare chest where sweat still glistened to his shorts, then his feet. "If ever there was a man who needed someone, Liam, it's you." She moved in for the kill. "Why don't you—"

"Stop."

"You don't have to be alone," she said, resting a hand on his forearm. "I'd like to be there for you."

He knew what kind of comfort Marlena had in mind, what she *always* had in mind. And it sickened him. "This isn't about me," he said flatly.

Something hot and hurt flashed in her eyes. "I'm sorry, Liam. I'm sorry this had to happen."

The memory of coming home to find the house dark and quiet erupted. "It didn't *have* to happen, damn it. Someone took my daughter, and I wasn't here to stop them."

"William, you have a company to run. You can't be with her every second."

"She's my daughter. She comes first."

"But she's also a big girl. You know how independent she is. You can't keep her locked away from the rest of the world."

The rage he'd been trying to control bucked up against threadbare confines. "She didn't run away, damn it."

"Of course, she didn't," Marlena backpedaled. "I was just saying you shouldn't feel guilty for leaving her alone. This isn't your fault. You had no way of knowing she needed you."

The passive-aggressive jab scored a direct hit. "Marlena, I told you now wasn't a good time. Don't make me say it again."

"You just won't admit it, will you?" she whispered, lifting a hand to his face. "Won't admit you're human, that you need other people."

"How I live is my business." Even if many didn't call it living at all. A beautiful woman stood inches from his body, her hand stroked his cheek, her soft green eyes made promises most men would find irresistible.

He felt nothing.

"Liam, let me—"

"Don't you get it, Marlena? You can't. No one can." Because inside, in that place where promises lived and the future seduced, he felt nothing.

She stepped closer, angling her mouth toward his.

"Excuse me."

The urgent words echoed through the quiet room. Liam swung around to find Detective Jessica Clark standing just inside the door. Like the night before she wore a pantsuit, this one tailored. The light beige fabric showed off her curves in way too much detail, emphasized the length of her long legs. Her thick auburn hair was pulled into a twist, a few stray squiggles drawing Liam's attention to her face.

The expression he found there kicked his heart into over-drive. Her mouth was hard and grim, her whiskey eyes flat. "My, God." He could barely breathe. "Emily—"

Liam released Marlena and all but ran to Jessica. "Have you found her? Is she all right?"

"I'm sorry—"

He reached for her. "What? What is it?"

She stepped back, raising a hand as if to ward off an attack. "I don't have news on your daughter. That's not why I'm here."

Adrenaline swirled away like rainwater down a storm drain. An intense relief that the detective wasn't here to deliver devastating news battled with the knowledge Emily was still out there. That she could be hurt.

He pushed the thought aside, refused to go down that path.

How long had statuesque Detective Jessica Clark been standing silently in the doorway? Why hadn't she an-nounced herself?

The answers took on a disproportionate importance. Over the years he'd learned to launch his own attack before someone could beat him to the punch. He'd learned to answer queries with cutting questions of his own. He'd learned success came from going for the jugular.

"What are you doing here?" he asked. "Shouldn't you be out looking for Emily?"

Jess resisted the urge to narrow her eyes. First Carson Manning, now William Armstrong. She didn't need either man telling her how to do her job.

"Well, that answers that question," she said, scanning the well-appointed weight room. The housekeeper had yielded to Jess's badge, but she hadn't given any indication that Liam wasn't alone. Just what had she walked in on? she wondered. A lover's quarrel?

"What question?" Liam asked.

She offered a cool smile, not about to yield to his domineering tactics. "After last night, I was curious to see if you'd be more cordial without the cover of darkness to hide behind." With her father's trademark shrug, she added, "Guess not."

His eyes went a little wild. "My daughter is missing, and you're worried about manners?"

Before Jess could respond to the dangerously soft question, Liam snatched her hand and drew it to his mouth, keeping his gaze on hers as he brushed his lips across her knuckles. "Is this better, detective?"

Shock streaked through her. She noticed how fine-boned her pale hand looked engulfed in his, the hard line of his mouth, then the challenge in his cobalt eyes. The anger. The pain.

The breath whooshed right out of her. "Mr. Armstrong—"

"For God's sake," the woman in the peacock-blue suit interrupted. She slipped between them and grabbed Armstrong's wrist. "Pushing me away, I can understand, but the cops? Do you want Emmie back, or not?"

Armstrong went very still. The change came over him like a wild animal shot with a stun gun. One moment he was alive and fighting, in the next he completely shut down.

Fascinated, Jess pulled her hand from his. "Maybe we should start over," she suggested. She realized Armstrong had no reason to trust her, especially after her flippant comment about manners. "I'm not here to antagonize you."

For a moment, he said nothing. Did nothing. Then slowly his eyes met hers, and Jess sucked in a sharp breath. She'd never seen so much turmoil in a man's gaze, not even in the eyes of the newlywed husband whose wife was found strangled near the airport.

"I'm sorry." He shocked her by saying it. He imparted a charged stare at the woman in the blue suit, then looked at Jess. "You'll understand if I'm a little leery of your type. You know what they say about wolves in sheep's clothing."

Yes, she did. Entirely too well. Instinctively, she glanced at her tailored suit and said a silent thanks she wasn't wearing wool. Then she glanced at Armstrong, who was hardly wearing more than a sheen of perspiration.

Her pulse did an unwanted little stutter step as she took in yet another dimension of this complicated man. The man her father believed guilty of murder. The man whose hard body she'd run her hands over last night. His broad shoulders, narrow waist and long powerful legs were the stuff of the classic male physique. Jess saw plenty of those around the station. But his chest... My God, she thought. Broad and well-muscled, it sported a thick spattering of dark hair tapering down to his ratty gray gym shorts.

Her mouth went as dry as West Texas.

"Detective Long is checking airports and bus stations," she said matter-of-factly, trying to focus on the case, not on the barely dressed man. But again she wondered about the woman watching them with speculative eyes. "I spoke with Carson Manning this morning and—"

"I suppose he thinks I'm responsible for Emmie's disappearance."

"What he thinks doesn't matter, not unless we find corroborating evidence."

Armstrong clenched his hands into tight fists. "That man would give his firstborn to prove me guilty of something. He had his little girl's cozy life all planned, even who she was going to marry. A nobody with a small bank account and big dreams wasn't included. For all I know, he took Emily himself, just to pay me back for his daughter. It wouldn't be the first time."

No, it wouldn't. Twice before Emily's grandfather had picked her up from school without permission. Once, they'd been halfway to Mexico before Armstrong had caught up with them.

"Kirby and I swung by Manning's house earlier. It's clean now, but we'll keep him under surveillance. If Emily's with him, we'll get her back." Jess opened her satchel and pulled out a notebook and pen. "I'll be talking with her friends shortly, seeing what they know, but I wanted to see if you've thought of anything else."

"Information that might help find my daughter, but I didn't tell you?"

She bit back a sigh of frustration. "Mr. Armstrong—"

"Liam."

"Why do you insist upon making this so difficult?"

His cobalt eyes took on a peculiar glint. "Is there any other way?" he asked grimly. "My child is missing, and to get her back, I have to rely on the daughter of the man who made locking me behind bars his lifelong mission. I don't see how this can be a walk in the park for any of us."

The truth of his words hung between them. "I know you don't have any reason to trust me," she acknowledged, and again, regret nicked at her. "But you're a smart man. You have to realize every second you waste arguing with me is a second I'm not looking for your daughter. I'm not the enemy. How can I make that any more clear?"

"Find my daughter. That'll be clear enough for me."

In the end, Jess figured, it really was as simple as that. "Okay," she said, opening her notebook and readying her pen. "What more can you tell me about this boyfriend—"

"*Ex*-boyfriend."

"He never returned home last night. Do you know where else he might be?"

"The Braxton boy?" The woman in the blue suit gasped, rushing toward Liam. She'd been silent since Liam had hushed her with a hard look. "I knew he was trouble the minute Emmie brought him home. Emmie did, too, you know. That was part of his appeal."

Jess noted the way Liam stepped away from the woman's touch. "Can you elaborate, please, Ms.—"

"Dane. Marlena Dane. I'm Liam's—"

"Friend," he finished for her, "and there's nothing to elaborate on. Braxton wrote a song for Emily, and like most young girls would, she fell hard. It's as simple as that."

"Oh, Liam." Disappointment riddled Marlena's expression as she again laid a hand on his arm.

He jerked from the possessive gesture, forcing Jess to wonder about the nature of their relationship. Clearly some type of familiarity existed between them, but rather than intimate, it seemed strained.

Jess made a note to follow up with Ms. Dane, find out what Liam didn't want her to say. "I take it you didn't approve of your daughter's association with Mr. Braxton?"

Liam frowned. "Emmie's not the first smart girl who got involved with the wrong guy. There were no ulterior motives,'' he said, moving toward Jess. ''She was just star-struck. His band plays the local club scene.''

That Jess had already learned. Braxton's band frequented the renovated warehouse district adjacent to downtown Dallas. ''Detective Long's headed to Deep Ellum this afternoon.''

''If that punk has laid one hand on her—''

''We'll take care of it,'' Jessica said levelly. The ex-boyfriend topped the list of acquaintances she and Kirby still needed to talk with. ''We'll find Adam Braxton. If your daughter is with him, we'll bring her home. If she's not, we'll keep looking.'' She flipped her notebook closed. ''You have my word on that.''

He moved closer, stopping mere inches from where she stood. ''Is that supposed to make me feel better?''

''I'm not responsible for how you feel, only finding Emily.''

''You're asking me to trust Wallace Clark's daughter.''

It was a two-sided coin. ''I'm asking you to cooperate,'' she corrected, ready to find the leads that would bring his daughter home. ''I'm asking you to let me do my job.''

''Counting on others doesn't come naturally to me.''

She heard what he didn't say. Not just counting on others, but counting on cops. ''I understand, but you don't have a choice this time. You have to trust me to do my job. I'm good at it. I won't let you down.''

His eyes took on a heated glitter. ''And if I hold you to that?''

''Then you're as smart as my father said you were.'' Because there was nothing else to say, she slid her notebook into her satchel. ''Now, if we're done playing cat and mouse, I'd like to head over to the high school.''

He nodded. ''You do that.''

''Call me if you think of anything else.'' She hesitated,

fascinated by his oddly seeking gaze. It was almost as though he didn't want her to go.

But that was crazy, and she knew it, so with a tight smile she turned and headed out the door.

Liam watched her go. The weight room seemed ominously quiet without her, as though she'd taken his energy with her. For the few minutes she'd been there, her huskily spoken words and courageous amber eyes had kicked his adrenaline into high gear. Damn, but she made him feel alive.

That reality stung worse than an army of hornets.

He had every reason in the world to distrust the statuesque detective—not just a cop, but Wallace Clark's daughter—but Liam couldn't squelch the uncanny notion that if anyone could find his daughter, it would be Detective Jessica Clark.

"You should head on out, too, Marlena."

His former lover frowned. "You never learn, do you, Liam? I just hope this time the price isn't too high." That said, eyes glittering, she made her typical overdone exit.

Hours passed before Liam realized his mistake. That afternoon, he looked up from the report Vega had faxed him and felt a bitter disappointment churning in his gut. "Son of a bitch," he swore.

He'd let an attractive, gutsy facade blind him to a truth he should have realized all along. Counting on Wallace Clark's daughter to find Emily was like a fugitive turning to a bounty hunter for sanctuary.

The beauty with a badge harbored a past as questionable as his own.

Jess dragged a hand through her hair. Her body ached. Her stomach growled. Too many hours had passed since she'd slept or eaten, but she couldn't pull herself away from the kitchen table. She sat in the darkness, only a single lamp burning, trying to make sense of all she'd learned.

A young girl was missing. Emily Armstrong could have left of her own will, but instinct warned something else was at play. Something sinister. The possibilities chilled Jess, increasing her resolve to crack the case before time ran out.

Thoughts of the girl's father crept into her mind. The isolated man was dangerous to Jess in ways that extended far beyond his haunted eyes and curt words. She knew his type too well. Driven and domineering, singularly focused, men like him wreaked havoc on the lives of anyone who crossed their paths. Her father had taught her that.

No matter how deeply William Armstrong intrigued her, affected her, she absolutely could not let herself think of him as a man, or even a bereaved father. That made him too human.

She could only think of him as a case.

Across the room, the lamp in her aquarium revealed a small school of angelfish flitting through the greenery she'd added a few days before. The sight normally relaxed her, but tonight even the graceful fish didn't work.

Jess pushed the hair from her face and picked up her tape recorder. She'd managed to talk to three of Emily's friends today, and from them, she'd learned a wealth of information. To their young, impressionable minds, Armstrong ranked right up there with Tom Cruise and George Clooney.

Pencil in hand, Jess began reviewing the interviews. Close to an hour passed before the telephone jarred her from her introspection. She stood, finding her foot asleep, and hobbled to the phone. "Detective Clark."

"Did you find him?" barked a gruff masculine voice.

"Who is this?"

"You have to ask?"

No, she didn't. The commanding tone struck a chord of familiarity, even though she'd known its owner less than twenty-four hours. "How did you get my number?"

"That's not important."

"It is to me." She shot the words back. "I'm unlisted for a reason."

"I called the station, but you weren't there. I wanted to know if you found Adam Braxton."

Earlier in the day she'd thought she and Armstrong had called a truce. Now she realized white flags were hardly his stock-in-trade. "I don't give play-by-plays of my investigations."

Armstrong muttered something unintelligible under his breath. "You just turn in when you get tired, is that it?"

"And you just attack."

"It's a simple question, Detective. Can't you give me a simple answer in return?"

Jess reined in her illogical response to the man. He wasn't talking to her as a woman, but as a cop. He wasn't her friend or lover. He was a man whose daughter was missing. A man her father thought capable of murder.

"I talked to several of Emily's friends," she told him, knowing it was only right to update him, even if he was deliberately trying to goad her. "But I didn't find Braxton."

She carried the phone into her living room, but didn't sit. That was too casual. Just talking to the man while wearing pajamas felt oddly intimate. Too easily she remembered the sight of him more nude than dressed. Those clingy gray shorts had cupped in all the wrong places, revealed a physique more impressive than she could have imagined.

Jess had a vivid imagination.

"I plan to follow up a few leads first thing in the morning," she told him.

"That's what I thought."

The disappointment in his voice hit like a rock. "What?"

"Nothing. Good night, Detective. Dream well."

Yeah, right. Long after she hung up the phone, the hollow words lingered. They crawled into bed with her, tossed and turned, accompanied her into a fitful sleep.

Bone-tired, she fell into a trap she avoided while awake and alert. She did just as William Armstrong commanded. She dreamed.

The images were hazy, the sensations acute. Heat and urgency, need, recklessness, bliss. A lover's arms holding her against his chest, the steady strum of his heart. Sensual words of pleasure and fierce promises of forever. Strength and warmth, intensity. A touch that ignited a fire deep within her. A seductive tangle of fulfillment and hunger.

She awoke abruptly to the cold. Alone.

Jess pulled the covers closer. "Stop it," she admonished the darkness. Around her, the familiar sounds of the night tried to work their magic. The rhythmic ticktock of her bedside clock, her neighbor's two Australian shepherds who thought they'd been born to serenade the moon, the steady January wind blowing through the shivering branches of a red oak. But they weren't enough to steady her choppy breathing.

Resigned, she accepted the truth. Sleep would not return.

She rolled out of bed, taking the covers with her, and moved to stand before the window. Despite the thick comforter, the bone-deep cold radiating from the glass pane cut right through her. The temperature had to be well into the teens. No wonder Thelma and Louise wouldn't stop barking. The mutts had to be freezing. She understood.

Demons crept out of the shadows to jeer at her. Strong Jessica Clark. Daddy's fierce little warrior princess. Independent. Capable. Brave. Didn't need anyone.

The words had been intended to rally, and rally they had.

But like many calls to arms, they also lingered. And wounded.

What was it about the cover of night, she wondered, that left her raw and exposed, vulnerable to daggers she could avoid during the light of day?

"Damn it," she growled, then headed downstairs. She was adding cocoa to warm milk when the phone rang. "Detective Clark," she answered.

"Jessie, it's Margo."

Her heart beat a little faster. A patrol cop didn't call late at night, not unless something had gone down. *Emily.*

"What's happened?" she bit out.

Margo laughed. "Nothing yet, but I'm betting that's going to change."

"What are you talking about?"

"Your man. He's down here, looks like a panther on the prowl, too."

"My man?"

"William Armstrong," Margo clarified. "You'd better come get him, hon, before someone else does."

Chapter 4

"Hang on there, lady."

Already scanning the crowded nightclub, Jess glanced at the burly young man barreling toward her. "Excuse me?"

"Need your ID," the bouncer said.

Jess gritted her teeth, tempted to flash her badge instead. The punk looked so proud of himself; little did he know she could take him out in less than a minute.

With an overly sweet smile, she obliged his request and handed over her driver's license.

He shone a flashlight on the small plastic card, then on her, from her face down the length of her body. Her long leather coat hid her figure, but it didn't stop the gleam suddenly radiating in his eyes.

Again, she indulged the fantasy of showing the cad one or two of the lessons she'd learned in the academy.

"Sorry, but you're a bit young for my tastes," she drawled. "I prefer a man who knows what he's doing."

She enjoyed the flare of his eyes, then turned and wove

her way deeper into the chaos. Laughter and music mixed. Alcohol flowed like honey. She'd always heard the best place to hide was in a crowd, and this club definitely verified the old adage.

But she had an ace.

Find Adam Braxton, find William Armstrong.

A stage occupied the far wall, but no band played there. Dancers contorted their bodies to the sound of recorded music.

Grateful for her height, Jess was surveying the crowd when she heard a collective gasp. She spun around, then fought her way through the cluster of tables and stools toward the ruckus. A circle began to form near the far corner of the darkened bar.

"Where is she?" a masculine voice demanded, and her heart kicked harder.

She broke through the crowd like a runner bursting through tape at the finish line, then stopped dead in her tracks.

Near the far wall, two figures stood squared off like boxers. The dim lighting stole detail but didn't hide the hostility in their stances, the tension radiating off them in hot, suffocating waves.

Jess eased closer. The aggressor towered over the second man, a bear ready to attack. He stood at an angle to her, allowing only a glimpse of the black knit cap hiding his hair. Whiskers darkened his jaw. A leather jacket and dark jeans covered his powerful body. He looked like he belonged in a back alley or seedy port—she almost expected him to pull a switchblade, toss it from hand to hand.

Then she heard his voice.

"So help me God, you lowlife. You give her back to me or you're a dead man. Is that clear?"

The fierce growl struck an all-too-familiar chord. Before she could react, Armstrong charged, throwing Braxton against the wall. The younger man struggled but was no match for him. Armstrong grabbed his T-shirt and twisted, got right up in his face. "Start talking."

"She's not with me," Braxton seethed. He stood a few inches shorter than Armstrong, his body more wiry. His dark hair was long, his moody eyes narrow and filled with contempt.

"She tells you to hit the road, then vanishes herself?" Armstrong countered. "I don't believe in coincidences."

"You don't believe in anything, Slick, but cold hard cash."

Jess saw Armstrong's body gather force, knew Emily's father was about to make a huge mistake. Knew she had to stop him. She broke through the crowd and rushed forward. "William, stop!"

He stiffened, spun toward her, flat-out stole her breath.

Rarely had she seen a man look so capable of violence. She barely recognized him as Emily's father. The black knit cap completely changed his appearance, made him look like a street fighter rather than a corporate executive. The bohemian look accentuated the intensity of his blue eyes, the whiskers on his jaw, the hard line of his wide mouth.

And the earring. She hadn't noticed the diamond stud before, but now it winked like a beacon.

For some inane reason, her heart took on a rhythm as hard and sensuous as the rock music blaring through the bar. His look may have done a one-eighty, but William Armstrong still emitted power and authority, this time of a sexual variety, pure male animal.

She fought his impact on her, stepped closer. "You don't need to do this," she said steadily.

Hope lit his eyes. "Have you found her? Is she safe?"

"Don't get your hopes up," Braxton snarled. "I'm betting Daddy never sees his little girl again."

Armstrong swung toward the punk. "Shut the—"

Jess rushed forward and grabbed his arm. "This isn't the answer, Liam."

"Leave me alone, Detective."

"You don't want to do this," she warned.

"I want my daughter back, damn it!"

"That's what I'm for."

Braxton laughed. "Well, hot damn, Slick. Looks like you're in business. You get a new babe as fast as you run 'em off. How long till you lose this one, too?"

Jess stiffened, but Armstrong ignored the taunt. "Last I knew, you were crawling into bed, Detective. How is that going to bring my daughter home?"

She tightened her grip on his leather-clad arm. "You've got to stop undermining—"

Adam Braxton sprang to life. He took advantage of Armstrong's turned head to break free and throw a mean punch to the man's cheek. Armstrong staggered but quickly righted himself and swung toward Braxton. Egging him on, Emily's ex deflected a nasty hook and launched one of his own.

Armstrong ducked out of the way.

Jess did not. She didn't have time to. The blow caught her in the jaw and sent her slamming to the concrete floor.

"Jessica!"

She fell hard, her head bouncing off the leg of a bar stool. Shards of pain shot through her. Splotches of white clouded her vision. The room blurred. She heard a man swearing savagely, heard the crowd erupting.

She thought she saw a man lunging toward her, but then the world went dark, and she saw nothing at all.

Liam saw black. The crowd erupted and surged, but he could discern nothing but the woman out cold at his feet.

He dropped to his knees and reached for her. "Jessica?"

The fearless detective didn't move, didn't make a sound.

She lay crumpled on the dirty concrete floor, still and un-moving, all that gorgeous red hair spilled out around her. A knocked-over bar stool lay by her side.

He crawled closer, saw the blood.

Rage pulsed through him. The bastard had hit her. In the mouth. ''Get me a damp rag!'' he called to no one in par-ticular, then glanced at the woman lying next to him. ''Jes-sica? Can you hear me?''

A moan this time, soft, groggy.

He reached for her, touched a finger to the corner of her wound. The flesh there was already turning darker. He hated thinking of the bruise that would mar her lush mouth. ''Jessica?''

''She all right, Mister?'' someone asked from his left.

''If you'd like someone to kiss that mouth and make her feel better,'' asked another, this one drunk and amused, ''I'm game.''

Liam caged the urge to surge to his full height and teach the loser about respect and decency.

''Give us some room!'' he shouted. The whisperings and laughter, the raucous music, fueled his temper. This woman was hurt, and everyone just zipped along with their lives, paying attention only out of mild curiosity, for the drama, the spectacle, like gawkers at a freak show.

Liam wanted to gather Jessica close, scoop her into his lap and shield her with his body, keep her away from the prying eyes of the crowd. Instead, he ran his hands through her thick hair and along her scalp, checking for injuries. He felt the small knot immediately, the stickiness, and pulled his hand back to discover blood.

''Where's that damn rag?''

''Here you go.'' One of the bouncers handed him a wet cloth. ''Braxton's long gone, you know. You lost your chance.''

''There'll be other chances,'' Liam growled. He wasn't

done with the boy, had a few more lessons to teach, but instinct had taken over the second Jessica hit the barroom floor. No way could he leave her there, hurt and alone, in trouble.

"Detective?" The formal title tasted bitter on its way out, but some hazy part of him recognized the wall he was trying to erect, the barrier. The way he touched the damp cloth to her parted lips was entirely too intimate.

"Can you hear me?" he asked.

Her eyelids fluttered, another soft whimper.

"Easy does it." Blotting away the blood, he resisted lifting her into his lap. He needed to discern the severity of her head injury. Pushing back her hair, he dabbed the cloth to the wound. "You're okay, Detective. Just open your eyes for me."

Slowly, she did. Her eyes were as dark and swirling as always, but dazed, unfocused.

He leaned closer, stroking his hand along the side of her face. "How do you feel?"

She winced. "L-like a truck just slammed into me." Her voice was soft and throaty, gravelly, like she lived on cigarettes and whiskey.

"You took a nasty blow. Can you see me okay?"

"F-fine."

"How many fingers?"

She squinted at him. "Three."

"Good. Who am I?"

A weak smile curved her lips. "Sir Lancelot?"

He almost laughed. "Sorry, rescuing damsels in distress is hardly my style."

"Good," she whispered, "because I'm hardly a damsel in distress."

Her flippancy brought a surge of relief. Her mind was clearly connecting the dots. "Do you always try to be so tough, Jessica Clark?"

Her gaze focused. "With men like you, there's no other way."

Encouraged she wasn't suffering a concussion, he eased her into his lap. He wanted her off the cold sticky floor but found himself unprepared for the feel of her lithe body so close to his. Those smooth curves and long legs, the heat. Just the sight of her watching him with those wide, cautious eyes, of auburn hair spilling over his thighs, was enough to send a weak man running for cover.

Good thing Liam wasn't a weak man.

He leaned down and fingered the corner of her mouth. Her skin was soft, the feel of her breath warm.

"You caught a pretty brutal hook," he said, "but I don't think anything's broken."

Frowning, she worked her mouth, opening it, shifting her lips to the right, then the left. Pain flashed in her eyes.

"Don't overdo it."

"No, I'm okay," she said. "I've been through worse."

The matter-of-fact words stirred something deep inside. Something dark and primitive. Something he didn't like. He knew the danger being a detective entailed, but when he looked at her in his lap, her flawless skin and provocative eyes, he saw a woman of silk and lace, not a cop. The reality of her putting her life on the line, of getting hurt in the process, didn't sit well.

She struggled to pull herself upright, then pushed the hair from her face and cupped her forehead. "Tomorrow won't be any fun."

For either of them.

He gently inspected the nasty bump on her head, but the feel of all that luxurious hair, the kind a man liked to twine in his hands, undermined his good intentions. "The bleeding's stopped."

"Everything okay here?" asked a voice from his right.

Liam glanced at the club's manager. "If you call assaulting an officer okay, then I suppose we're right as god-damn rain.''

The man's jovial face went ashen. "Assaulting an officer?"

"It's okay," Jessica said, trying to stand. When she swayed, she cut Liam a smile. "Okay, anti-Lancelot, here's your chance to redeem yourself. You going to help me up, or what?"

Liam didn't understand how easily she made him want to laugh. He'd be a fool to forget what he'd learned about her that afternoon, an even bigger fool to let misplaced chivalry distract his focus. But that didn't mean he wanted her hurt.

Wallace's daughter or not, Detective Jessica Clark possessed a core of courage he wasn't used to seeing.

He stood, took her offered hand and gently helped her to her feet. When she reached her full height, he held her waist to make sure she didn't sway. "Okay?"

She drew a shaky breath. "Okay."

Because he didn't quite believe her, because her smile was too tight, he didn't release her. "Let's get you out of here, see if it's true what they say about fresh air." He reached out and secured the sash of her long leather coat. Didn't the woman realize how she looked in the damn thing? Not the least bit like a cop, but chic and mysterious.

Focus, he reminded himself. Just because Detective Jessica Clark took a punch for him didn't change what he knew about her. Neither did her intelligent but strangely vulnerable eyes, her curves. They only made her more dangerous.

He needed to remember his investigator's report, the cutting sense of reality. He hadn't realized how badly he wanted to believe her claim to be on his side until he learned she wasn't. That she couldn't be. That she was no different than anyone else.

She glanced toward the dance floor, where people of all ages gyrated to the sounds of classic rock.

"Where's Braxton?" she asked. "I need to question him."

He kept a hand at the small of her back, kept her close. So she could hear him above the blaring music, he told himself. That was all. "That coward doesn't have her."

"How do you know?"

"Father's intuition. Something I saw in his eyes. The enjoyment, but not the guilt. Not the fear."

The question slipped from her gaze, replaced by something dangerously close to compassion. "I'm sorry, Liam."

"So am I."

She held his gaze a moment longer, then started pushing her way toward the door. "Let's go look for him."

He didn't know whether to laugh or lecture her. He doubted either would do any good. "I don't think you're in any shape to go after anybody," he said as he caught her arm.

She tossed a cocksure glance over her shoulder. "I'm fine."

Liam stepped in front of her and parted the matted hair concealing her wound. He touched it lightly. "This hurt?"

"Yes, but—" When his fingers left her hair and found her mouth, she stiffened. "W-what are you doing?"

"Either you're concussed after all, Detective, or you don't have the sense God gave a goose."

She stepped back from his touch. "Trust me, I don't have a concussion."

"Then apparently you don't have any common sense, either. What—" He took her arm and pulled her toward him before a lumbering giant spilled his beer all over her. "What were you trying to prove back there, anyway? Don't they teach you better than that at the academy?"

She squared her shoulders. "I'm a cop. I was doing my job."

"But you're also a woman, and you inserted that lush body of yours between two angry men." The memory of her fearlessness made his blood run cold. "Didn't you realize what could happen?"

She cut him an overly sweet smile. "I didn't know you cared."

"My concern has nothing to do with me caring." He bit the words out quickly. Too quickly. "You're a cop, you're hurt. I have no desire to be charged with assaulting an officer because you don't know when to back off."

He didn't know where the blunt accusation came from, but for the first time since she'd broken in on him and Braxton, he stood on familiar territory.

She looked at him like he was stark raving mad. "Why would I levy charges against you?"

"You're Wallace Clark's daughter, aren't you?"

From her, even aggravation sounded sexy. "You have to quit dwelling in the past. I'm my own woman. I was simply doing my job. If I bring charges against anyone, it's Adam Braxton, not you." Without giving him a chance to respond, she pulled away and vanished into the throng of partygoers.

Liam suppressed a growl and took off after her.

Wallace Clark was going to have his revenge yet.

The cold bit into Jess the second she walked outside. She lifted her chin and turned down the sidewalk, appreciative of the revitalization of her senses. She needed to be sharp like the wind. She needed air. She needed space.

She needed away from the swarming crowd pressing her against Armstrong's hard body.

Irritation flashed through her. Her head pounded and her stomach roiled, but through the haze, she remembered a low masculine roar as she hit the ground, the sight of Armstrong dropping to her side, the feel of him cradling her in his lap.

For such a hard man, he had unbearably gentle hands.

The memory burned.

The lethargic way his touch made her feel burned even more.

She was a cop, damn it. Hard, focused, objective. He was a man whose daughter was missing, a man her father went to his grave believing belonged behind bars.

Jess knew the danger of thinking of him in any other light. She wished she hadn't seen him this afternoon in nothing but ratty gym shorts. She wished he hadn't forfeited his chance of going after Braxton in favor of tending to her. She wished he hadn't touched her, showed her a seductive glimpse of a compassionate man behind the hardened exterior.

God help her, she wished she'd stayed in bed.

"Running from me, Detective?"

The rough-hewn masculine voice revved through her like a bolt of raw electricity. She kept her stride brisk, her gaze focused on the antics of three young men at the end of the street. "Don't flatter yourself, Armstrong."

He surprised her by laughing. "Ah, there she is," he mocked, settling his hand at the small of her back. "Welcome back, Jessica."

She flinched at his touch, the use of her first name. Picking up her pace, she glared at him. "What are you doing?"

An overly gallant smile touched his mouth. "Making sure you don't take another tumble."

"I'm fine," she said, this time with more conviction. Damn it, where was the stone man from the night before?

"I'll be the judge of that."

Jess drew a deep breath, enjoying the affirming sting of

the cold air. She eased it out, noting the cloud of vapor. Below freezing, she guessed, despite how warm she felt.

Armstrong fell into step beside her. He still wore the knit cap, still sported the diamond earring, a dark trench coat still covered his body. Odd that he could appear bohemian and dangerous at the same time.

She tried not to look at him, didn't want to see his profile, but the cop in her couldn't stop assessing. In William Armstrong's penetrating blue eyes she saw intelligence. In the set of his jaw and hard line of his mouth, she recognized determination. In the broad expanse of his shoulders, she found strength.

What must he be going through? she wondered, then berated herself for doing so. He was a case; that was all.

Emotions didn't enter the equation.

She turned abruptly down an alley between two nightclubs. The sudden movement sent her head reeling, but she blocked the reaction, not wanting him to spring to her aid once again.

Too late. "Jessica?" he asked, reaching out to steady her.

She ignored the feel of his hand on her shoulder, the question in his gaze. Instead she imagined herself in an interrogation room. She saw herself standing before a table, leaning forward with her palms down. She pictured Armstrong seated before her, a single lightbulb glaring down on him.

Familiarity flowed through her, and she felt a slow smile touch her lips. She flinched at the pull against tender flesh, automatically raising her hand to the corner of her mouth. But she didn't back down.

"It's just you and me now, Armstrong."

He cocked his head to the side and narrowed his eyes. "That it is," he said. "What are you going to do about it?'' he asked darkly, but there was a hint of amusement, as well. ''Frisk me again?''

Surprise flickered through her. Not bloody likely, she answered silently. A woman didn't touch lightning unless she had to.

''I'm going to take supreme advantage,'' she said instead, ''like any good cop would.''

An enigmatic light glinted in his eyes. ''Wallace Clark's daughter is going to take advantage of big bad William Armstrong? This could be interesting.''

''Not you,'' she corrected, irritated with herself for enjoying the game. ''The situation. You put on a good front. All that bluster and belligerence, that I-don't-give-a-damn look in your eyes.'' She braced a hand against the cold brick wall. ''But tonight you proved you might have a sliver of humanity beneath that tyrannical facade, after all.''

The possibility intrigued more than it should have.

''If you're approaching a point,'' he said softly, dangerously, ''feel free to make it.''

''My head hurts like hell, and my vision is blurred. I'm not sure I even remember where I parked my car. You could leave me here, alone, or you can keep playing hero.''

His gaze took on an assessing quality, one reminiscent of a cop on the prowl. But he said nothing. Just stepped closer, using his body to crowd her against the wall.

''Walk away,'' she invited, intrigued by his reaction, ''and prove to me you're the heartless bastard you want everyone to think you are.''

Surprise registered in his deep blue eyes, but again, he said nothing. Just watched.

Her heart kicked a little harder. While he had her against a wall literally, she had him against one figuratively, and they both knew it. He could walk away from her and her questions, but in doing so, he'd leave an injured woman alone. If he took her up on her offer, he proved he was as cavalier as he wanted the world to believe.

If he didn't, he admitted he wasn't.

"Or stay," she invited. "And face the music." Face her. Prove what she was beginning to suspect about the kind of man he was.

Armstrong swore under his breath, triggering a glimmer of satisfaction. She knew he wanted everyone to think him a dark, sinister force, she just didn't understand why. He'd demonstrated an altogether different side tonight in the bar, and the cop in her wanted to understand the dichotomy.

She refused to think about what the woman in her wanted.

He leaned closer, bracing a hand against the wall near her face. "I didn't think games were your style, detective."

"You don't know me well enough to know my style."

A low light gleamed in his eyes. "Tell me, then. Tell me what you want."

The breath backed up in her throat. She was a trained cop. Tough, seasoned, prepared. She'd chased suspects down darkened alleys and up multiple flights of stairs, but she couldn't recall feeling so winded while standing absolutely still.

"I want to know what you were doing down here in the first place," she said. Maybe Kirby was right, after all. Maybe playing with William Armstrong was a little like playing with fire. "Deep Ellum hardly strikes me as your scene."

"Like you said. You don't know me well enough to know my scene."

"That's not an answer."

"No, it's not. But I could ask you the same question, couldn't I? What are *you* doing down here? Following me? Last I knew you were calling it a night."

She'd been in bed, all right. And she'd done as he asked. She'd dreamed. Of a man. Heat, intensity—

Jess broke off the thoughts, tempted to unfasten her leather coat and let some cool air in.

"Tell me something, Detective. If I found Braxton so easily, why didn't you and your partner? Face it. You don't want to help me."

"Detective Long knows what he's doing." But damn it, Jess thought. How *had* Kirby missed this? Or had he? "You really think a kidnapper would come down here and play with his band if he's got Emily tucked away?"

He lifted his free arm to the other side of her face, caging her in. "You're the detective. You tell me."

She met his gaze, didn't shrink or cower like most people would. Power and games were nothing new to her. She'd been raised with them, knew how to recognize and use them herself. What she didn't understand was the disappointment cutting through her.

Just because his touch was surprisingly gentle, just because he'd forfeited his chance to go after Braxton in favor of helping her, she couldn't let herself start thinking the man was something other than what he was. Driven, isolated, dangerous. His ministrations to her had nothing to do with the woman she was and everything to do with the fact she was his best chance of bringing his daughter home.

Thinking anything else only invited trouble.

"That's right, William. I am the detective. It's my job to find your daughter. You need to let me do it, too, not stir up trouble on your own."

"Looking for leads is hardly stirring up trouble."

"But confronting Adam Braxton is." She pushed the hair from her face. "I know you're worried, but you have to trust me. I see cases like this all the time. Statistics say in all likelihood, Emily will come back on her own."

"Statistics?" he growled, and she almost felt remorse.

"You think Emily's disappearance is just a ploy? Her way of teaching me a lesson?"

"Teenage years are a scary time. She could be confused, trying to sort some things out."

"You don't know my daughter," he barked. "Just because you went to extremes to get your daddy's attention doesn't mean my daughter has done the same."

Everything inside her went very still. "Pardon?"

"You heard me. Extremes." He skimmed his finger along the tender corner of her mouth. "Just because the almighty Wallace Clark didn't care, didn't notice, doesn't mean I don't."

She stepped back from his touch, but the cold brick wall of the nightclub halted her retreat. She couldn't move without touching Armstrong, couldn't breathe without drawing in the scent of sandalwood and smoke.

She lifted her chin. "My father was a good man."

His finger moved against her lips, and for a moment regret flashed in his gaze. Then it vanished. "But being a good man doesn't equal being a good father, does it? Was the sainted Wallace Clark both, or is that why his only daughter felt the need to live on the streets for over three months?"

The point-blank question almost knocked her flat. In the space of a heartbeat an unwanted chill replaced the heat of Armstrong's nearness. Deep inside, she started to shake. He couldn't know. No one did.

She glanced around, realized he had her completely caged in. She had no choice but to meet his gaze, where the light of a predator glittered in his dangerously dark eyes.

Her heart rate kicked into high gear. William Armstrong was renowned for his ruthlessness; when he felt threatened, he attacked. But she hadn't expected him to turn on her.

She should have.

"Just what is it you think you know?"

"*Everything,* Jessica. I know everything."

Chapter 5

He saw her eyes widen then blink in denial, the blood drain from her face. Shock, he knew. That cloudy moment when the body shut down while the mind struggled to comprehend. He wanted to take satisfaction in the intensity of her reaction, but found splinters of remorse instead.

Despite what everyone believed about him, William Armstrong wasn't a man to terrorize a woman.

He knew he should back away, back off, but couldn't bring himself to move. Not his body, not the fingers at the corner of her swollen mouth. The cool flesh was already turning a nasty shade of purple.

He hated seeing perfection marred.

The dazed detective blinked at him. "What did you say?"

He ignored the way the question puffed out in a breathy cloud of vapor. Even more, he ignored the sudden urge to draw her into his arms and stop the shaking she was trying so valiantly to hide.

He stepped closer. To emphasize his point, he told himself. Not to share his body heat. "I'm a cautious man. I don't trust easily or blindly. Do you really think I wouldn't learn everything I could about the woman in charge of finding my daughter?"

"My personal life is none of your business."

"When it affects me and mine, you better believe your life is my business. I know why you think Emily ran away, Detective. Because that's exactly what you did. You preferred the streets to Daddy dearest's roof."

The light sparked into her whiskey eyes, the defiance and intelligence he'd come to expect. A hint of color brought her cheeks to life. "So this is how you operate?" she asked, and God help him, she almost sounded disappointed. "Crowding? Badgering? Is that how you crushed and gobbled up all your competitors?"

So he wasn't the only one who'd done his homework.

"For such a smart man—" she pushed on, and he could feel her words against his cheek "—you're not acting very smart. Even hoodlums know better than trying to press their advantage with an officer of the law."

Back off, he warned himself. Don't push it. He couldn't find Emmie if he was behind bars and knew Wallace Clark's daughter wouldn't hesitate to put him there.

But he could no more ease up than he could heal the wound at the corner of her mouth with a kiss.

"You going to press assault charges against me?" he asked softly, extending his pinkie to stroke her cheekbone. "I bet that would make Daddy proud."

Betrayal flashed brilliantly in her eyes. Anger. He readied himself for verbal retaliation, received physical instead. She slapped his hand away and ducked under his arm, gracefully spun out of his reach.

Liam was admiring the athleticism of her move when he saw her sway.

Instinct had him reaching for her; the warning in her gaze stopped him cold.

"I'm not a man who trusts anyone with my life," he said instead. "Or my daughter's. Nor am I a man who just stands on the sidelines and waits for results."

She pushed the tangled hair from her face. "And that's why you felt the need to have me investigated?"

"A smart man learns all he can about his opponent."

"That's what you think I am? Your opponent?"

The thought, the disappointment in her voice, burned. "You think my daughter ran away. I know she didn't. How would *you* describe our relationship?"

She narrowed her eyes, held his gaze long enough for him to see the debate in hers. Then she sighed and glanced toward the street. Music still blared from the various clubs, laughter and animated conversation still carried on the cold wind. He didn't know what exactly held her gaze, didn't want to look away from her to find out.

"I wanted to be your friend," she said, turning to him. "I wanted to help. Has no one wanted that before? Is that the problem? Is that why you hold me at arm's length rather than letting me in?"

It was his turn to go very still. Her words kept rushing through him, like a sip of exotic wine. Unexpected, jolting, dangerously seductive.

"Sorry, Detective—" he forced himself to speak "—but my daughter is missing. I don't have time for friends and intimate midnight liaisons."

Didn't have time for her to pick him apart, didn't have time to fight the desire to silence her questions by answering one or two of his own. Just how would that smart mouth of hers taste? How would it feel? Was it possible to kiss a wound and make it all better? To make the hurt go away?

And whose hurt would it be? Hers? Or his.

What would she do if he tried?

Jessica frowned. "Hate to break it to you, tough guy, but chasing you around and making sure you don't get into more trouble is hardly a good use of my time, either. If you want your daughter back, you need to let me do my job."

"No one is stopping you from doing your job. I'm just taking out a little insurance."

"By having me investigated? By picking a fight with Braxton? Sounds to me like you're wasting that time you value so highly."

"I know what I'm doing."

"Then why don't you tell me."

He ignored the provocative sight she made with defiance in her eyes and leather on her body and focused instead on the desperation tearing around inside him. "A smart man learns, Detective. A smart man realizes a brick wall is a brick wall, and no matter how many times he slams against it, nothing changes."

She angled her chin. "But if you hit it often enough, with enough force, after a while, the mortar crumbles."

God help him, he laughed. "You really are your father's daughter, aren't you?"

Her eyes flared wide. Resentment marched in. "I'm my own woman, Mr. Armstrong. Not my father's daughter. Not my partner's partner. I'm on your side. If you'd quit compartmentalizing, if you'd quit drawing lines, maybe you'd realize you don't have to."

Liam looked at her standing in the puddle of a lone street lamp, a tall woman wrapped in a long leather coat. The sharp wind whipped her auburn hair about her face, keeping her color high. Her intelligent eyes were narrowed in challenge, her swollen mouth in a mutinous line. Too easily he remembered what the flesh there felt like beneath his fingertips, the soft fullness of her lips.

It was one memory he wished he didn't have.

"It's late, detective. Braxton is long gone, and I'd like an early start in the morning. What do you say we postpone round three until tomorrow?"

A small smile played at the corners of her mouth. "Retreating?"

"Maybe I'm just allowing my forces to regroup."

She eyed him a moment longer, then sighed. "Very well then." She stepped toward the street, but when she turned left, Liam again took her arm. "My car is that way," he said, gesturing to the right.

"But my car's not."

He slid his hand from her arm to the small of her back and tried to steer her down the street. "You won't be needing your car, Detective. I'm taking you home."

She didn't budge. "The domineering routine may work with your employees, but it doesn't work with me. It's late and I'm tired—"

"And you took a blow meant for me." After tonight, he vowed to forget all about the sight of her sprawled on the floor, the feel of her in his lap, her lustrous hair between his fingers. "You shouldn't be driving. I'll have someone bring your car to you."

Her smile was a little too quick. A lot too sweet. "I thought rescuing damsels in distress wasn't your style."

"Are you in distress?" He fired right back, stepping closer. "Let me know if you are. Maybe I can help, after all."

She stiffened. "Touch me again, and you won't have to wonder anymore about whether I'll press assault charges."

Liam resisted the cutting urge to laugh. Detective Jessica Clark sure as hell wasn't the answer to his prayers, but he couldn't help but admire her style.

Curiosity nudged him closer. "You just lectured me about accepting help, but you're no more willing than I am." He turned the tables. "What are *you* so afraid of?"

"Just because I don't want you to take me home doesn't make me afraid of accepting help, Mr. Armstrong."

Mr. Armstrong. Her continued use of his formal name emphasized the barriers she denied. "If it's not help you're afraid of, it must be me. Again, my question is why?"

"Afraid of you? Haven't I just spent the past thirty minutes alone with you in a darkened alley?"

"Yes, but you're refusing to let me give you a ride, and you're shaking."

She pulled the sash of her long leather coat tighter. "It's below freezing," she reminded him. "Why all the questions? Why are you so curious about me? That credo about knowing your enemy as well as you know yourself?"

"I thought you said we weren't enemies," he reminded silkily. "Change your mind?"

A hard laugh broke from her throat. "Always the tough guy, aren't you?"

"Quite the contrary. I've been told I'm amazingly tender."

For the first time since he'd known her, Detective Jessica Clark faltered. Her swollen mouth tumbled open, and color rushed to her cheeks. Disbelief sparked in her always-assessing eyes.

Enjoying her reaction, the fact he'd finally caught her off guard, Liam pressed his advantage and put his hand to her back. "See?" he said as he did so. "Gentle as a lamb."

She glared at him. "You heard what I said about touching me." But the long strands of auburn hair blowing across her face softened the strength of her words.

"I heard," he said, easing the hair from her face. She stiffened but didn't bat his hands away or step from his touch. "If you want to press charges against me because I don't want you walking the streets alone, because I don't like the idea of you driving home in your current state, then go right ahead."

"I'm a cop. I've walked alone more times than I can count."

Liam frowned. Her words conjured a solitary image he found oddly unsettling. He made note of it, then pointed to the sleek black convertible parked a few feet away. "Fine then, but my car is right here. At least let me drive you to yours. It's cold outside. No point in you walking more than you need to." He raised his key chain and depressed a small button. Three answering beeps just barely sounded above the strains of classic rock spilling from a nearby club.

But Detective Jessica Clark didn't move.

"What's the matter?" he asked. "Afraid I'll bite?"

She lifted her chin. "Maybe I'm afraid you won't."

The heat of battle wasn't the time for laughter, but Liam came dangerously close. "Ah, come now, Detective. You insist that I need to trust you, but you won't give me the same courtesy? It's either a two-way street or it's a dead end." He opened the passenger door. "Which is it?"

The fiercely independent detective glared at him, and for a moment, he thought she meant to shove him against the car and slap cuffs around his wrists. But then she mumbled something unintelligible and slid into the passenger seat.

The way she eased her body onto the low seat drew his attention to her unbelievably long legs. He wondered what they would look like in a short dress designed to show off her curves, rather than the tailored pants she favored.

Liam couldn't help it. He had nothing to smile about, but his lips curled anyway. Every little victory, he supposed, counted for something.

Wallace Clark's daughter would be no different.

A pair of low headlights stayed with Jess the entire way to her uptown condo. She wove through the high-rise-crowded streets of downtown and accelerated onto the toll road; all the while Armstrong remained right on her tail.

She was tempted to press the pedal to the metal and give him the ride of a lifetime, but in truth, he was right.

Her head throbbed. Her stomach felt like she'd just disembarked from a twisty-turny, deep-dive roller coaster. Her nerves were no better than a frayed rope. She was in no shape for a high-speed chase through the streets of downtown Dallas.

The thought of sitting next to Armstrong in his sleek little sports car had even less appeal. Too intimate, a steadfast voice of caution had warned. Too little distance between them, too much time to fill. Too little to say.

They'd already said it all.

You preferred the streets to Daddy dearest's roof.

Jess zipped down an exit ramp and blew through a yellow light. No matter how fast she drove, though, Armstrong's bombshell announcement stayed with her. She had no idea how he'd found out about the three darkest months of her life.

After the way he'd tended to her in the bar, she hadn't expected him to attack. But she should have. All the research she'd compiled on the man described him as clever and cunning, not one to pussyfoot around. If you weren't on his side, you were against him, and Armstrong had a reputation for crushing opponents.

Apparently he saw Jess as an opponent.

Why then, she wondered, had he dropped to her side on the cold barroom floor? Why had he chosen to help her rather than go after Braxton? And why had she seen flickers of concern in his eyes as he'd inspected her injuries?

Despite the subsequent animosity, the shockingly intimate feel of his hands on her body lingered. She wouldn't have guessed the stone man could be so gentle. Her father hadn't been, not even at the end, when his body had been riddled with the cancer that claimed his life. A man's man, he'd called himself. Not cruel, just not sensitive.

But Armstrong was different, a veritable study in contradictions.

I've been told I'm amazingly tender.

She wished she could forget the wicked promise, the dangerous curiosity he'd stoked. That had been his intent, she knew. To throw her off balance, distract her, gain the upper hand. The man was nothing if not clever.

He was also right behind her. The rearview mirror displayed the headlights of his sleek little sports car hot on her tail. She didn't understand his insistence on following her home, figured he probably didn't want anything happening to the one cop who might actually listen to him.

Jess gunned the engine to match the revving of her pulse and wheeled onto the entry street to her neighborhood.

Armstrong did the same.

An unwanted rush pulsed through her, and again she had the surprising urge to see just how far she could push him, just how far he'd follow.

Dangerous, she knew. After the night she'd had, in all luck she'd get pulled over—not the kind of publicity the department needed. She didn't like leading Armstrong straight to her house, either, thought about taking a detour down to the station, but if he'd found out about her days on the street, finding out where she lived would be a piece of cake. He already had her unlisted phone number.

In all likelihood, he had her address, too.

Simultaneously frowning and wincing, Jess turned onto her street and activated her garage door opener as she approached her driveway. She'd always thought of her home as her sanctuary, but never more than now as she zipped up her driveway and eased into the semidarkened garage.

She sat a minute, engine running, not wanting to turn around. When finally she raised her eyes to the rearview mirror, she found Armstrong's car blocking her driveway.

He emerged from the driver's side and walked to the sidewalk.

Her heart took on a low staccato rhythm.

Jess lifted her hand to the garage door remote, but stilled when she realized Armstrong wasn't coming any closer. He slipped his hands into the pockets of his leather jacket and stood with his feet shoulder-width apart, watching her sitting in the garage. She could feel the heat of his gaze, though in the darkness he was nothing more than a shadow. Form and substance with no detail. She couldn't see the expression in his intense eyes or the salt-and-pepper whiskers on his jaw, only that he still wore the funky knit cap.

And like before, she wondered how the hell the bohemian look made the man appear so damn sexy.

The rhythm of her pulse changed, thickened. Her breathing deepened. She was tempted to charge down the driveway and demand he get the hell on his way, but a little voice inside warned against getting that close to the man again.

There'd already been enough intimacies for one night.

Gritting her teeth, Jess jabbed the right button of the remote and smiled at the familiar hum. Armstrong didn't move a muscle. Didn't try to hurry up the driveway before she shut him out, didn't turn to leave. Just stood there still as stone and watched.

The heavy door slid downward, stealing first Armstrong's darkly handsome face, then the chest she'd had the dangerous desire to touch, his lean hips, taking last his long, black-jean clad legs.

Jess didn't understand the stark sense of loss she found alone in the darkness of the garage.

But she knew it was for the best.

Her growing fascination with William Armstrong could only lead to trouble. He was a dangerous man, an island, a man with no time for anyone or anything that didn't fit into his preconceived agenda. She would be a fool to let a misguided attraction override that knowledge.

Firsthand, she knew the pitfalls of living with a driven man. Not only did she have a daughter's perspective, but she'd seen the toll on her mother. The disappointment, the loneliness, the knowledge that she didn't come first, not even to the man who'd promised to love and cherish her all the days of his life. Jess loved her mother, but never understood why she settled for being second best. Jess wanted more than stolen moments. She wanted the sun, the moon, the stars.

She would settle for nothing less.

And Liam was more like the sky itself, vast and endless, seductive but dark, the kind of man a woman could lose herself in and never find her way back to where she began.

Jess went very still, then let out a humorless laugh. The sun, the moon, the stars? The sky itself?

"Give me a break," she grumbled into the darkness, then swung open her door and headed for the house.

Clearly that bump on her head had muddled her more than she'd thought.

"Jessie, there you are! It's about damn time—" Kirby stopped by her desk and looked closer. "What happened to you?"

Instinctively, she lifted a hand to the swollen, bruised corner of her mouth. The flesh had been stiff when she awoke, the sting sharp. "What makes you think something happened? Maybe I had a late-night rendezvous that got a little out of hand. You know," she said dryly, "passion marks."

Kirby laughed. "And you don't think that would be something? Lady Daring letting someone close enough to bite would be more newsworthy than the latest football scandal."

What's the matter? Afraid I'll bite?

Maybe I'm afraid you won't.

Jess tried for a smile, but winced at the pull on her sore mouth. "Braxton's band played Deep Ellum last night. How the hell did we miss that?"

Kirby shrugged. "Who says we missed anything? That punk doesn't have the Armstrong girl. Mr. King-of-the-World is just grasping at straws." He leaned closer, easing the thick hair from her face. "He do this to you? Is that what happened?"

"Did you even talk to Braxton?" she asked.

"Of course I talked to him. You will, too. Later today."

"See to it that I do." She stood. "You're not looking so swell, either," she commented, steering the conversation away from last night. She knew he'd find out but wanted to put off the lecture about partners working together and covering each other's backs for as long as possible.

She didn't want him to suspect her trip to Deep Ellum had been more personal than professional.

"Everything okay with Ms. Twenty-seven?" she asked. Kirby had long since quit telling Jess the names of the women he dated. That made them too real, she figured. Too personal.

He frowned. "It's…complicated."

"With you, it always is." Her partner didn't talk about it much, but Jess knew someone had all but shredded his heart. Gently, she touched his arm. "If you ever want to talk, I'm here."

"Talk about what? Why women always walk away? Why the grass is always greener?"

Rarely had she heard him sound so overtly bitter. "Kirby—"

"Don't worry about it, Jess," he said. "Everything's cool. If nice guys always finish last, then maybe I shouldn't be so nice anymore."

"Who says nice guys finish last?" And for that matter, who said her partner was a nice guy, she thought wryly. He had an edge to him, that volatile streak women loved to try and tame.

"Just look at William Armstrong," he drawled. "He either killed or ran off the mother of his child, then he trampled his way to the top of the business world, but has he ever had to pay the piper? Atone for his sins? Hell no. He's come out on top, despite everything."

"His daughter is missing, maybe kidnapped. I'd say that's a pretty steep payment."

Kirby cursed under his breath. "Now he's even got you defending him. Maybe you'll change your mind after you talk to his lover."

Jess went very still. "What?"

"Follow me," Kirby said, walking toward one of the meeting rooms. "She's scared about being here, says there's no telling what Armstrong will do to her if he finds out, but she's got something to tell us."

Jess swore softly and hurried to catch up with her partner. She had a bad, bad feeling all hell was about to go down.

Chapter 6

History Repeats Itself As Internet Mogul's Daughter Turns Up Missing. Tragedy…Or Pattern?

Liam scanned the offensive article that just barely passed for journalism. He'd already called his lawyer. This time Heather's father had gone too far.

A cold fist of rage worked its way through him. His daughter was missing. In trouble. But for some asinine reason, people seemed more interested in a spectacle, a scandal, than a child. Innocent until proven guilty had become nothing but a bad joke.

He threw down the article and strode across his office to a wall of windows overlooking the city. Twenty stories above street level, he had a sweeping view of the skyscrapers downtown, the snarled roads snaking between the congested buildings, the crowded suburbs beyond.

A sleek jet zipped through the intermittent clouds, easing toward the west. Liam tracked its progress against the cold gray sky, remembering all too vividly his trip only days before. When he'd kissed his daughter goodbye while she still slept. When he'd called all over town trying to find her. When his blood had turned to ice with the chilling awareness something terrible had happened to his baby girl.

"Damn it," he growled, jerking his gaze from the western sky. She was out there somewhere. His little girl.

Teenage years are a scary time. She could be confused, trying to sort some things out.

The words grated at him, but he knew Detective Jessica Clark was wrong. Emily hadn't run away, and it wasn't too late. He knew that just as surely as he'd ever known anything. He could feel Emily in his heart, strong and sure and deep, where he'd cradled her since the moment he learned of her existence.

Liam drew a hand to his chest and rubbed. Each breath cut like a dagger. He swallowed against the tightening of his throat and again glanced toward downtown. He couldn't make out details but picked out the area where he and Jessica had squared off the night before.

He still didn't know what to make of Wallace Clark's daughter. Fiercely independent, strong and courageous, she was clearly a woman of conviction, and yet he could still see the stabbing vulnerability in her eyes when he'd mentioned her troubled teenage years. Clearly, he'd prodded a wound that hadn't healed. One that might never heal now that her exalted father had gone to his grave.

He didn't know why the thought disturbed him so.

"He's a hard man," Marlena Dane said. She sat across from Kirby and Jess, her small, fine-boned hands clasped tightly.

Jess waited for her to continue, all the while studying the woman she'd found touching William Armstrong just the day before. The woman who'd once shared his bed. Maybe still did.

Marlena's tailored pale pink suit looked just as elegant as the one she'd worn the day before, but the way she wore her hair twisted behind her head lent her a pinched look. Her cheeks were pale, her eyes anxious. So far she'd responded better to Kirby than Jess.

"He's not a man you want to cross," she said. "When William decides you're the enemy, you better take cover."

Kirby jotted something in his notebook, then glanced at Marlena. His compassionate smile almost hid the glitter in his eyes. "Take cover? What do you mean by that? Does he become violent?"

The woman laughed. "Violent? Liam? Heavens, no. He doesn't need violence. If you get too close, or even just when he decides he's had enough of you, he simply cuts you out, no questions asked."

"Is that what he did to you, Ms. Dane? Cut you out?" The questions slipped out before Jess could stop them. Others she held at bay. Like why Marlena was really here. To help Emily? Or hurt Liam?

The woman frowned. "This isn't about me."

Jess had her answer. "Of course it's not about you," she said professionally. "It's about a missing young girl."

"She's only missing because she chooses to be," Marlena blurted.

"So you think she ran away?" Kirby asked.

"William couldn't accept her relationship with that Braxton boy. He was always breathing down her neck, taking her car keys and such so she couldn't see Adam. Poor Emily was heartbroken."

Jess jotted a few notes. She had grown up with such a father, knew how restrictive that kind of parenting could feel. More like a glove than a blanket.

"From what you're saying, Emily didn't appreciate his protective nature, but did she understand it?"

"She's not here anymore, is she?"

Jess started to reply, but a knock interrupted her words, and one of the secretaries popped her head in the door. "Detective Long? I've got a call for you."

Kirby didn't move. "Take a message."

"I tried, but the guy says he really needs to talk to you."

Kirby grumbled something unintelligible as he rose. "I'll be right back," he said, then strode from the room.

Jess looked at Liam's former lover and tried to ignore the sharp blade of dislike. "About Emily—"

"Not now," Marlena said, leaning closer. "I know I haven't told you anything you don't already know about William's overbearing nature, but there is something… something I didn't want to say in front of your partner."

Jess went on full alert. "Go on, then."

The woman glanced at her diamond-laden fingers, hesitated, then lifted her gaze to Jess. Uncertainty lurked in the pale blue of her eyes. "I've never known another man like William Armstrong. He's got that edge to him, you know? The kind a woman is drawn to, even though she knows how far she'll fall if she steps too close."

Jess lifted a hand to her mouth, trying not to remember the feel of his arms around her the night before, the gentle way he'd tended her wounds. "And?"

"He's dangerous. Deceptive. I just thought you should know."

"That's why you think Emily ran away?"

"In all likelihood, but I'm not telling you this because of Emily. I'm telling you this because of you."

Jess sat a little straighter. "Me?"

"I saw the way you looked at him yesterday—saw the way he looked at you."

Heat surged through Jess, as though the beam of a searchlight had just discovered her streaking through a dark alley. "I don't know what you're talking about."

"It's okay," Marlena said. "I understand. I fought it, too. That's why I'm here. I hate to see another woman get tangled with a man like him."

"I'm not another woman," Jess corrected. "I'm a detective investigating his daughter's disappearance."

Marlena shook her head, loosening a strand of pale blond hair. "I'm afraid what you're really doing is wasting your time, another William Armstrong specialty."

Jess put down her pen. "In what way?"

"Don't let that wounded facade of his fool you, Detective. Don't get sucked in. He knows why Emily is gone. He's the one who has to live with himself day in and day out."

"Sounds like you're saying Liam chases everyone off except the one person who does the most damage." She fought the regret welling within her. "Himself."

Marlena tucked the stray hair behind her ear. "Be careful, Detective. If you get too close, you'll be next."

"I'm sorry, ma'am," the serious-looking secretary said. Her name plate read Louise Hatcher. "Mr. Armstrong is in conference right now and he doesn't wish to be disturbed. You'll just have to wait."

"Tell him Detective Clark is here. He'll want to see me."

Skepticism shadowed Louise's expression. After Marlena Dane's assassination of Armstrong's character, Jess found the secretary's loyalty refreshing. Of course, she also detected a hint of fear mixed in with the respect. Regardless, she hadn't made it all the way to the lion's den to let this woman stand in her way.

She put a hand to her purse. "Are you going to make me pull my badge?"

The woman stiffened. "No, no. Of course not." When she reached for her phone, Jess made a split second decision and headed for the double doors to the right of Louise's immaculately neat desk. She was in no mood for protocol.

"You can't go in there!" the secretary screeched, but before Jess could reach for the knob, the door swung open, and Armstrong strode out. His features were tired and tight, but hope lit his fierce blue eyes.

Jess almost thought he didn't see her. He just kept right on coming. "What is it?" he asked, taking her shoulders in his strong hands. "Have you found her?"

Her heart sank. She hadn't thought about what her presence might signal to him, and now, even though she had no real news to deliver, she felt like she was about to yank the carpet from beneath his feet.

"No," she said gently. "I'm afraid that's not why I'm here."

The light drained from his eyes, the energy from his body, but his hands remained on her arms.

"Oh, Mr. Armstrong," Louise said, moving closer. "I'm so sorry."

He stiffened. "Let me know the second Vega calls," he growled, then took Jess's hand and pulled her into his office. The door closed securely behind them.

Jess readied herself for a battle, but Armstrong released her and strode across the plush carpet to the wall of windows overlooking the city. There he simply stood, feet shoulder-width apart, back tensed, head bowed.

And Jess realized what had happened. William Armstrong was a strong, private man. The second his secretary expressed sympathy, moved to comfort him, he'd shut her out, just like Marlena had predicted. He didn't want his employee to see him wrestle with Jess and the disappointment she represented.

That was why he stood with his back to her.

Jess tamped down the insane urge to go to him, to lay

her hand against his tense back and ease his burden. She could only imagine the hell he was going through.

Uncomfortable watching the private moment, she did a quick survey of his office. The massive room fit him. She could easily see the man in the leather chair behind the distressed mahogany desk, his long legs propped against the credenza. A desktop computer and a laptop sat on the surface; both were on. Several files lay open. A wood-grain pen lay atop what looked to be a contract.

Jess moved closer, drawn by a large picture frame to the far side of the desk.

"She's not here, Detective."

She spun toward the deceptively soft voice and found William Armstrong had abandoned his post at the window and stood mere inches behind her. He looked edgy, restless, like he hadn't slept in days. He wasn't wearing a suit, only khakis and a black golf shirt. His salt-and-pepper whiskers were thicker and darker than the night before.

The diamond earring was gone.

"Pardon?" she asked, battling the unwanted rush of his nearness.

"The way you're studying my office, me, I just thought I'd save you some time and let you know Emily's not here."

Frustration tightened through her. Disappointment. The second Armstrong felt threatened, he attacked. "And you're not wearing your earring, either, but pointing out the obvious doesn't accomplish anything, does it?"

"Quite the contrary, Detective. Sometimes the obvious is the most overlooked. Most denied. I've always found it useful to call a spade a spade."

Awareness flashed through her. The man had more facets than a prism. So far, she'd met at least three—the warrior, the businessman and the father. From Marlena, she knew there was also a lover. "Who'd have guessed you're a philosopher, too. So is that how you keep your opponents off balance? Change your skin as often as most people blink?''

''Are you calling me a snake?''

She smiled sweetly. ''Just asking a question.''

He gave her a smile of his own, but his was sharp, cutting. ''Tsk, tsk,'' he chided. ''Feeling nasty this morning, aren't we?''

''Just curious.''

''Well, now. You know what they say about curiosity.''

His deceptively soft voice seeped through her. He did it on purpose, she knew, to rile her. Refusing to take the bait, she glanced around the office, this time noting the wet bar and stereo system to the right. She wondered what kind of music a man like William Armstrong listened to. Pulsing rock and roll? Mournful blues? Sensuous jazz…

''I was surprised to find you here,'' she commented, battling the distracting curiosity, ''thought you'd be at home or in a back alley somewhere.''

He took a step toward her. ''And why did you think that? Didn't you read the paper this morning? Isn't this exactly where coldhearted William Armstrong should be? At his office, making another buck, while his child is God only knows where?''

The taunt stung. The fact everyone she knew believed what he'd said replaced the sting with an ache.

''An attitude like that isn't going to help,'' she said.

He held her gaze a moment, then shoved a hand through his hair. She could almost pinpoint the moment the change came over him, the shadow, like a solar eclipse at high speed.

''What do you want me to say?'' he rasped. ''That the walls of the house were closing in on me? That everywhere I turned, I saw Emily? In every sound, every creak, I heard her laughter?''

The rough-hewn admission did cruel things to the walls

of the professionalism Jess relied upon. Everything inside her that was female reached for the man, wanted so badly to touch him, help him. She hadn't meant to hurt him like that. Didn't want to pick him apart piece by piece.

Never had she seen a man so alone.

Never had she wanted to just put her arms around someone and find a way to make it all better.

"If that's the truth," she said, "then yes."

His gaze prodded her. "Would that make you happy, Jessica? To know I'm finally where your father wanted me?"

She swallowed against the emotion thickening her throat. "It breaks my heart, but that's not what you want to hear, is it? For some idiotic reason, you want to pick a fight."

Armstrong winced. For a moment she thought her candor might return them to calm waters. But this was William Armstrong, the man who'd pulled himself up from nothing and turned himself into everything. "Why are you really here? Because of last night? To find out why I didn't follow you into your garage?"

Jess stiffened. Her breathing hitched. She knew what he was doing—trying to muddy her objectivity by reminding her of the unwanted physical attraction that had flared the night before—but awareness didn't dim its power. She'd stepped too close. Prodded too deeply. Forced Liam to voice a truth he wasn't ready to admit.

Too bad Jess wasn't a woman to roll over and play dead. She'd come here for a reason, and it had nothing to do with last night, the dangerous desire he'd stoked, the wicked dream she'd awoken from, the one in which he'd followed her upstairs....

"Tell me about Marlena Dane," she said matter-of-factly.

He laughed. It was a purely masculine sound, dark and

wicked, amused. "I wondered how long it would take you to get around to her."

"Get around to her?"

"After what you walked in on yesterday, I knew sooner or later my inquisitive little detective would want to know more."

My. "You two were an item for a while, yes?"

He turned toward the wet bar, poured two fingers of mineral water, threw it back. "My involvement with you, detective, pertains to my daughter. Not my love life."

His choice of words scraped. She recognized the defense mechanism but refused to yield.

"My job is gathering facts," she said tersely. "Stringing them together." She wanted a drink of that water herself. Either that or an ice cube down her blouse. "Since you only tell me what you want me to know, I have to look where I can."

He poured another finger of water and threw it back. "Not anymore."

"I'll believe that—"

"I've got a call into Commander McKnight. I want you off the case."

Jess went very still. "You what?"

"I want a different team of detectives on the case. I want someone who can be objective."

Shock winded her. Disbelief and something dangerously close to regret spurred her closer to the edge. "So you're going to shoot yourself in the foot," she said softly. Sadly. "Guess Dad was right about you, after all. Too bad he's not alive to see the day."

He didn't move a muscle, didn't flinch. "A man doesn't crawl from the gutter to high-rises by shooting himself in the foot, Detective. But he does learn to cut his losses."

"What are you so afraid of?" she asked, because for

some reason, she had to. "Don't you realize I'm your best chance?"

"Best chance for what?" He stepped toward her, so close he had to look down to meet her eyes. "Counseling me why my relationships never work? Why I run through women faster than a jet tears through the sky?"

"Damn it," she said, grabbing his forearm, "you've got some kind of nerve—"

His eyes sparked. "Playing by Daddy's double standard, Detective?"

She felt his muscles bunch beneath her fingertips. "Excuse me?"

"You can touch me, but I can't touch you?"

Jess wasn't quite sure why, but she laughed. "Good try, but I know what you're doing."

"Oh? Why don't you tell me then?"

She didn't release her grip on his arm, noticed that he didn't pull away, either. A crazy energy buzzed around them. "I'd rather tell you what *I'm* doing," she told him bluntly. "My job. A job I take seriously." She paused when she felt her beeper begin to vibrate, but didn't check it. "I'm exploring every angle because I want to help you. I want your daughter back. I want to see you hold her again. It's obvious how much you love her. A blind man could see it."

Those hard, cobalt eyes of his bore down on her. "Just last night you told me she probably ran away."

"The two aren't mutually exclusive. Sometimes love can be suffocating. Just because you love your daughter doesn't mean she agrees with how you show it. I sure didn't."

"Just what's wrong with how I show my love, Detective?" The words were silky, the way he lifted a hand to cup her cheek shockingly intimate. "I didn't realize you'd seen it."

Jess's heart beat so hard and deep she could barely

breathe. She abruptly released his arm and backed away from his touch. "I was talking about my own father."

"Ah," he said. "Then you need to learn to be more specific."

"And you need to learn to pay attention."

He laughed. "So that's why you ran away?"

She lifted her chin. "My father was a good man," she said, tired of the cat and mouse game. "But he was also a hard man. Focused. He defined himself through police work—"

"Runs in the blood, huh?"

"He loved his family but didn't know how to show us. He thought by working hard, climbing the ranks, making a good living, he would be filling his role as husband and father." She paused, surprised by the words falling from her mouth. They applied to her father as easily as they applied to the man she was coming to know.

She wasn't sure who needed to hear them more.

"I never realized how much he loved us, how hard he tried, how difficult emotion was for him, until he lay in his hospital bed, a shell of his former self."

Liam held her gaze, each breath he drew thickening the air around them. Jess tried to move away, look away, couldn't. She was too drawn to what she saw in his gaze. In other men, she would label it compassion, but she knew better than to entertain that dangerous notion with the stone man who didn't allow himself human traits like emotion.

The odd glitter more likely stemmed from the formulation of some plan, the cataloging of the information she'd just handed him.

"Detective?"

"What?" she asked, blinking back the painful memories, the even more painful realities.

"I wasn't sure you were still with me. Thought you might have run away again."

She squared her shoulders. "I don't run away anymore, Mr. Armstrong. That was a lesson I learned well enough the first time."

"Oh, I'm not so sure about that." He stepped closer to her.

Recognizing the tactic, Jess held firm.

But God, how she wanted to back away. To breathe.

"What you're sure about really doesn't matter, though, does it?" She slid the pager from her pocket and saw that Kirby wanted her down at the station. Something about a big break. "Look, I'm needed downtown."

Armstrong streaked a finger down the side of her face. "What was it you said about not running away, Detective? We've just barely scratched the surface."

Heat rushed through her. "Funny." She forced herself to speak. "That's all it took to get rid of my itch." Proud she'd kept the breathlessness from her voice, she turned and walked out the door.

"That man belongs behind bars," Adam Braxton snarled. The punk had called Kirby, said he needed to talk. Seated across the interrogation room table from him, Jess took a moment to study the boy to whom Emily Armstrong had given her heart. With his moody eyes and angry mouth, it was easy to see why the teenage girl had fallen hard and fast.

Jess had no such problem. She still felt the sting of his fist on her jaw.

"You sure your accusations against Mr. Armstrong have nothing to do with the fact he opposed your relationship with his daughter?" she asked point-blank.

Braxton leaned across the table. "You saw him last night—he's out of control."

Kirby turned to look at her. "Last night?"

She lightly touched her injured mouth. "Later." Slapping the punk with an assault charge appealed, but Jess wasn't interested in the scandal doing so would invoke, particularly with William Armstrong's involvement.

"As I recall," she said to Braxton, "you were the one out of control."

"That lunatic attacked me. No telling what he would have done if you hadn't come along."

The punk was wasting her time. "What does all this have to do with Emily?"

"She's scared of him, too. Her mom couldn't take it and cruised, and now Emily has, too."

"You sure she isn't with you?"

"I wish she was," he said with great drama. "Then, at least, I'd know my girl's safe." He leaned across the table. An odd light glittered in his eyes. "Just look around. No one stays in that man's life for long. He's got a track record. The clues are all over the place, if you can get past your hots for him and see the truth."

Jess stiffened.

"Hots for him?" Kirby echoed.

"I saw the two of you," Braxton went on. "Huddled in that alley. You couldn't keep your hands off each other."

Jess pushed to her feet. "Need I remind you what happened inside that barroom? Perhaps you'd like an overview of what happens when someone assaults an officer."

Kirby stood, as well. He glanced from Adam Braxton to Jess, and Jess knew the second he put two and two together.

"Later," Jess growled again, then focused on Braxton. By the time she finished with him, she was confident he understood very clearly the potential consequences of her swollen mouth.

"What happened to my by-the-books partner?" Kirby demanded the second Braxton left the station. "Forget to mention a few pertinent details?"

"My personal life is just that," Jess retorted. "Personal." She was tired, and her head hurt. She wasn't about to get into this. "I can spend my free time as I choose."

Kirby blocked her path. He was exceedingly tall, and when he got up close like that, she understood why he'd made more than one suspect wet his pants. "Is that really what Daddy taught you?"

Jess frowned. She was darn tired of everything relating back to her father. "Dad taught me a lot, Kirb. Keep pushing and maybe you'll find out just how much."

He shook his head. "You're my partner. I don't want to see you fall under Armstrong's spell. The man is dangerous. I—"

"There you two are."

Jess swung around to find Commander McKnight striding toward them. Her chest tightened. She knew what was coming. Her dismissal from the case. "Commander—"

"Just got a call from the boys out in Irving," he said gruffly. The planes of his dignified face were unusually grim. "We've got a break in the Armstrong case. There's been a discovery in a field by the airport."

Dread almost sent Jess to her knees. She could hardly breathe, much less form the question. "Emily?"

The commander nodded. "They've found her car."

Chapter 7

Liam took the street hard and fast. He ran with the focused determination of the sprinter he'd been in college, pumping his arms and keeping his stride long. His feet pounded the cobblestone. Sweat dampened his body, despite the arctic wind blowing from the north. He wore only ratty gym shorts and an old tank top, but he barely felt the sting of the cold.

It was the most alive he'd felt in entirely too long.

By his side, Molly matched his pace. His daughter's dog ran full throttle, like a retriever chasing her latest prize. Her ears were back, her eyes fevered. She missed her mistress, appreciated the exercise.

Man and dog turned from the main boulevard onto a quiet street in Liam's neighborhood. Waiting at a stop sign, a young mother with a minivan full of children lifted a hand in greeting.

Liam couldn't bring himself to wave back.

The realization of how normal he and Molly appeared,

man and dog out for an afternoon jog, tore through him. Illusion, he knew. One of the most seductive narcotics known to mankind. The belief that appearances equaled reality.

Not even a man like Liam was immune. He'd been seduced by the fantasy when he built a home for his daughter in one of the most elite areas of Dallas. He'd naively thought the prestige and dignity, the privilege, would rub off on him, clean him, and he'd be able to give Emily the normal, unencumbered childhood she deserved.

He'd never been more wrong in his life.

Violence and tragedy, greed, callousness—they didn't discriminate based upon address. Beauty often masked ugliness; simplicity could shroud complexity; serenity concealed danger.

But danger came in many forms, he knew, and instantly he thought of Wallace Clark's daughter. After she'd sashayed out of his office, he'd stood for a long time, watching the door she'd slammed behind her. There was a very real chance he'd never see her again. As soon as the chief met Liam's demands, which he would, his relationship with the enigmatic detective would come slamming to a halt.

Liam had waited for the satisfaction to ease through him, but instead he'd found himself coiled tighter, like a rattler primed and ready to attack. He was in his car and roaring down the street before sanity intervened.

He had no business chasing after Detective Jessica Clark.

Instead he'd come home, where he found Molly pacing the house with a restlessness he understood only too well. Emmie took her dog for a run every day. The big, muscular lab needed to work off tension as much as Liam did.

Over the years, he'd found physical exertion the most powerful form of release. Not even a bottle of whiskey could compare. He enjoyed challenging himself. Testing. Marlena called it punishing, but she didn't understand the needs that drove him. When he pushed himself, sprinted block after block, slammed his fists against the hard punching bag, he felt alive. Sharply, painfully, gloriously alive.

He needed that feeling now. He needed to feel alive and vital, capable. He could not allow himself to feel beaten.

"Kick it in, girl," he called to Molly, then ratcheted up his pace for the home stretch. He swiped the dripping sweat from his eyes and rounded the corner at a full run.

The sight awaiting him almost stopped him dead in his tracks.

He felt his heart stagger, his throat tighten. But he kept on running, straight toward the dark gray sports coupe parked in front of his house. Detective Jessica Clark stood by its side, decked out in that damnably sexy long leather coat. The wind blew her auburn hair about her face, but she didn't try to hold it back. In fact, she didn't move at all, just stood there like a vibrant swatch of life against a pale gray sky and watched him running toward her.

Running toward her?

The thought scraped at him. That's why she was so damn dangerous to him. That's why he was carving her out of his life. Didn't the inquisitive detective realize he meant what he said? There wasn't a damn thing Wallace Clark's daughter could say or do to make him change his mind about having her removed from the case.

She wouldn't persuade him, couldn't touch him.

Awareness of the coming confrontation spurred him on. He kept up his sprint, but as he pounded the pavement and grew close enough to see her expression, his heart almost stopped.

Detective Jessica Clark wasn't there to change his mind.

She knew something. He saw it in the way she held that distracting body of hers so tense, the hard line of the bruised mouth he'd wiped blood from only the night before, the worry in her expressive eyes.

"Come on, Moll," he urged the dog. Through the roar in his head, his voice sounded distorted, almost warped. He commanded his body to run as fast he could, but his senses slowed to a crawl. He wasn't sure how he kept moving. Wasn't sure he did. The street seemed to elongate. Every stride felt like a wobbly baby step.

Oh, God, Oh, God, was all he could think. *Emily.*

Jessica started toward him, that slow, measured walk he'd seen too many times before. The one that held apprehension. The one that never preceded good news. Molly barked an enthusiastic greeting and launched herself against the woman who held his fate in her hands. Her eyes.

Jessica raised a hand to pat the dog's head, but her gaze never left Liam. And in those somber, bottomless pools of rich brown, he read a litany of possibilities that instantly turned his pounding pulse into a river of dread.

"Liam."

He stopped inches from her and tried to breathe. "What? What's happened?"

"I need you to come with me."

"Is it Emily? Have they found her?"

"It's about your daughter, but no, they haven't found her."

The exertion of his run caught up with him, and he felt the sweat pouring from his body. Impatience and frustration cut him to the quick. "What then?"

"Her car."

He staggered. "Christ."

Jessica's gloved hand was on his arm in a heartbeat. "I'm sorry, Liam. It looks like you might be right about foul play. Evidence at the scene suggests Emily wasn't alone."

He wasn't sure how he remained standing. Liam felt as though she'd hit him with vicious blows rather than simple words. He wanted to grab Jessica's shoulders and force her to take back the punishing revelation. Worse, the compassion glowing in her eyes made him want to crush her in his arms and absorb her, pretend they were two very different people, in a far different situation.

His whole life had been an uphill battle, always trying to prove he was right and everyone else was mistaken. But now, for the first time he could recall, Liam wished to hell and back he was the one who'd been wrong.

"No sign of her so far, Jessie, but it's a big field. It's just too early to tell."

"I'll be there in five."

"Keep Armstrong out of the way. We can't have him tampering with a crime scene."

"I know the drill." She clicked off the phone before Kirby could drag the conversation down a pointless path. They were near the airport, the sound of jets roaring into the late afternoon sky growing louder with each mile they drove.

Liam sat by her side. He didn't speak, didn't move, barely breathed. He hardly looked alive. He still wore his running clothes, had refused to take the time to change. The car heater had dried the fine sheen of perspiration on his arms and legs, leaving Jess acutely aware of the half-naked male animal seated next to her. Every nerve ending in her body hummed with the awareness of something primal and disturbing.

She didn't want William Armstrong to affect her like this, make her ache to reach out to him, to lay a hand on his thigh and assure him everything would be okay. To feel the power simmering beneath the flesh. She didn't want to think of him as a half-naked, fully consuming man, knew she was safer regarding him as just another of the victims her job routinely tossed her way.

But victim was one word that did not apply to William Armstrong, and there was nothing routine about him.

Or his unnerving eyes.

Or the precarious way he made her feel. The ache. The longing she didn't understand, didn't trust, knew she couldn't indulge. He was right. Assigning a new team of detectives to the case was safer for them all.

Refusing to look at him, Jess turned onto a dirt road. A circle of black-and-whites about a hundred yards away denoted their destination but obscured the view of Emily's car. A line of officers threaded their way through the tall brown grass. Kirby led the charge.

Her blood ran cold at the thought of what they might find.

"I don't suppose there's any point in asking you to wait in the car while I go find Detective Long?"

"None."

She glanced at Liam, saw his gaze riveted on the line of men searching the field. "I don't suppose you care that you'll freeze to death?"

His steely blue eyes slanted toward her. "What do you think?"

"I'm not sure you feel anything right now," she said honestly.

A dangerous combination of mistrust and hope glittered in his eyes. "I feel something. Trust me on that one."

The need to touch him had never been so strong, but Jess kept her hands curled around the steering wheel. She knew William Armstrong spoke the truth. What he felt was obvious in the hard lines of a face many called forbidding, but she was coming to realize that face masked a surprising vulnerability.

Tension riddled his features. Worry. The kind of agony that ate someone alive, bit by excruciating bit. She felt it, too, radiating from him, suffocating her.

"Holy God," Liam rasped. "No." He threw open the door and took off running between the official vehicles toward his daughter's car. Or rather, what remained of it.

Jess swore softly as she rammed the car into Park, wrenched open her door and raced after him. Kirby hadn't warned her about this. Hadn't given her a chance to prepare Liam for the kind of scene that could easily send a strong man to his knees.

"Hold it," one of the two officers milling about the car said. Jess recognized him as Juan Vasquez. "This is a crime scene."

"This is my daughter's car." Liam ground the words out.

Vasquez moved to block his path. "I'm sorry, sir, but right now it's evidence, and I can't risk you tampering with anything."

Liam kept right on going. "I don't give a damn—"

"Liam!" Jess saw him lift his arm and lunged for him before he could do something stupid. She grabbed his wrist and pulled him toward her. His skin was hot, his pulse hammering.

"Don't make this more difficult than it needs to be," she said as gently as she could.

"More difficult?" The fevered light of disbelief flashed in his eyes. "This is the car my daughter washed by hand every weekend, the car she kept in immaculate condition, and now here it is burned out, and no one's seen or heard from her in over forty-eight hours. How the hell do you want me to act?"

Her heart hammered mercilessly. Her stomach churned. "We need to follow procedure."

"Screw procedure."

She looked into his hard, challenging eyes, then down to where her fingers wrapped around his wrist. She couldn't bring herself to let go. "I didn't have to bring you here," she reminded gently. "I could have waited until we wrapped up our initial investigation. Is that what you would have wanted?"

His gaze crystallized, but he said nothing. Nor did he move. Nor did he pull away.

She looked at Vasquez. "What do we have?"

The rookie looked like he'd just witnessed a magic trick. He glanced at an unmoving but still forbidding Armstrong, then at her. A hint of disbelief flickered in his dark eyes.

"Looks like the car's been here since at least yesterday," he began. "No sign of occupancy when the fire broke out. Two sets of tracks lead away." He glanced to the right. "Looks like another car was waiting."

The brisk north wind whipped hair about Jess's face, but she didn't want to release Armstrong to brush it back. "Do both sets of tracks lead to the second car?"

"Hard to tell," Vasquez said. "Looks like only one."

A chill shot through her. "Anything else?"

"Not yet."

Moments later Jess watched the young officer stride toward his black-and-white, where voices squawked from his radio.

The evidence was inconclusive, but Jess couldn't shake the bad feeling weaving its way through her like a rusty needle. Despite Liam's assertions, she'd been leaning toward labeling the girl a runaway. Now she wasn't so sure. The presence of a second car nagged at her. It could be a setup, sure, the teenage girl's way of throwing them off track. Her father, after all, was a master strategist.

Why shouldn't the daughter be the same?

She felt Liam pull away from her and this time let him go. She didn't look at him, though. Didn't follow. Not yet. Instead she drew a deep breath, enjoying the feel of the cold air stinging her lungs.

A jet roared into the pale gray sky. No more than a

hundred yards away, nine officers combed the tall grass, looking for any sign of William Armstrong's daughter.

Jess turned toward Liam, found him standing before the remains of his daughter's car. If she'd seen only the man and not the surroundings, just the pain in his eyes, she would have sworn she was seeing a man standing before a grave in a cemetery, the last mourner, unable to say good-bye. That's how isolated he looked, how alone.

The ache in her heart changed, deepened. And she couldn't keep up the shield of protocol and indifference. She was a cop by vocation but a woman by birth. A human being. She couldn't just stand there and watch this strong man suffer, despite what her father had thought about the man. She could no more refuse to reach out to him than she could spin time backward and undo the events that had brought them together in the first place.

Her throat tightened. She felt herself move toward him, knew her booted feet crunched down on dried grass, knew the wind whipped at her, but the sensations faded to the background. When she stood mere inches from Liam, she lifted a hand and laid it against his back.

His muscles tensed beneath her fingertips, but he didn't move away, didn't break the connection between them. And for a transient moment, he didn't speak. He just stood there.

Instinct took over, and she lightly rubbed her hand along his upper back, where the loose tank top he'd worn bared his shoulder blades. His skin was hot despite the steadily dropping temperature.

"Oh, God," he rasped, resting his head against the palm of his hand. "Emmie loved this car."

Jess braced herself, alarmed by the sudden, powerful desire to throw her arms around this tall man and hold on tight. Objectivity, she reminded herself. The cloud of emotion, the blur of desire, would only destroy her ability to give William Armstrong the one thing he wanted from her.

His daughter.

Ignoring the ache, she focused on the burned-out car. The fire had destroyed much of it, but she could tell it had been a sports coupe, and not a new one, either. Hardly the flashy convertible she would have expected William Armstrong's daughter to drive. "Did you give it to her?" she asked softly.

He lifted his head and looked at Jess. His expression held equal parts joy and sorrow. "Emmie is a remarkable girl. I could give her the world, but she wants to earn it herself."

Jess felt a smile touch her still-sore mouth.

"We struck a bargain," he continued. "She'd let me pay for half of a car if she could come up with the remainder. She went on a baby-sitting crusade to earn enough money for a red convertible, but after a year of dirty diapers and fussy two-year-olds, she decided a pre-owned sports coupe wasn't so bad."

Something deep inside Jess shifted, and emotion bled through. William Armstrong hadn't been much more than a child himself when he became a father, but he'd done well by his daughter, teaching her responsibility and a work ethic, despite the fact he'd built an Internet-based software development empire profitable enough to set her up for life.

It was getting harder and harder to imagine the girl running away.

Jess looked into his fierce blue eyes, and the cop in her wondered if he was coloring the past his way, leaving out the dark spots a growing number of acquaintances had warned her about. Emily's grandfather. Adam Braxton. Marlena Dane.

Or had they been the ones coloring?

For everyone's sake, Jess found herself hoping Liam was the one with a selective memory, that the girl really had taken off for a breather. Liam would be shattered, but in all likelihood, he'd have the chance to hold his daughter again. To tell her he loved her. To make up for past mistakes.

But if his memory was right, if their relationship ran as true and deep as he said, then his vindication would be as dark and dangerous, as empty as an old abandoned well.

"Well, well, isn't this a cozy little scene?"

The mocking voice shattered the tenuous intimacy and had Jess glancing over her shoulder. Kirby strode toward them, a scowl on his face, a question in his eyes. His gaze was riveted on Liam's back, where her hand still rested against his bare shoulder.

"Decided to take up social services in addition to detective work, Jessie?"

She glared at her partner, wondering why she suddenly felt like she had the night her father found her an hour after curfew, necking with the school bad boy in an out-of-the-way warehouse parking lot. She lifted her chin but didn't sever the tenuous contact between her and Liam. "Find anything?"

Kirby cocked a brow. "That's what I'm trying to figure out."

"Damn it—"

"Quit the games," Liam growled. "Did you find my daughter, or not?"

Kirby's gaze hardened. "I'm the one asking the questions," he reminded, then raised his arm to dangle a plastic bag in front of Liam. "This mean anything to you?"

The blood drained from Liam's face. He snatched the bag and fumbled with its opening.

"You can't do that, slick," Kirby said, reaching for it. "It's evidence."

Liam looked up. "It's my mother's wedding ring," he

corrected. "A gift to Emily for her sixteenth birthday. She never takes it off."

Jess felt her heart clench. The two men held the plastic bag stretched between them, illuminating the intricately carved gold band inside. "Where did you get this?" she asked Kirby.

"Found it a few feet from the car."

Liam winced. "My God." The words were barely a whisper. "Someone's got her."

Kirby started to say something, but Jess rolled right over him. She looked into Liam's eyes and touched his forearm. "What does the ring say to you?"

A shadow crossed his face. "That my little girl is in trouble. She loves this ring, admired it from the time she was just three years old. My mother gave it to her before she died, and Emmie has never taken it off since. She'd never just leave it here on the ground, discarded."

Jess tried to strip the emotion from her voice, but it tightened her throat, leaving her words raspier than she liked. "We'll check it for prints, see if they tell us anything."

"You won't find any but hers. She took it off. She was trying to tell me she's in trouble."

"Or maybe she was trying to tell you she was making a clean break," Kirby said.

Liam went deadly still, all but his eyes, which took on an ominous glitter. "If anything happens to my daughter because of your inability to forget the past and be objective, you will find yourself missing more than just your badge, Detective."

Jess hated standing between these two men. Kirby had a hard edge, but he'd watched her back for over three years. "I'll take it from here, Kirb."

He eyed her a moment before letting go. "Be careful, Jessie."

She let his comment slide, switching her attention to Liam. "You, too. Let go."

His gaze met hers. He looked deeply into her eyes, prodding, touching, then the tension eased, and his fingers released the plastic.

She let out a tense breath, not sure why the fact he'd entrusted her with the bag felt like he'd granted her the keys to a previously forbidden world. She didn't want to slide backward now, but she needed to talk to Kirby. "Give me a minute," she said, motioning for her partner to join her by his car.

"Give me my daughter back, and I'll give you anything you want."

The softly spoken words did cruel things to her heart. Jess ignored the impossible thoughts they conjured and joined her partner at the little black convertible he had dubbed the babe mobile.

"What was that all about?" she asked.

Kirby closed the distance between them. "You tell me."

She frowned. She was tired of everyone treating Liam like he was a monster. "You have no business taunting him like that."

"And you have no business touching him. Which is worse, Jessie? Which is less objective?"

The need to defend welled within her, but she refrained. "You don't know what you're talking about."

"I sure as hell hope not," he growled. "But you're Wallace Clark's daughter, Jessie. What better revenge for Armstrong than to sway you to his side? To make you believe and trust *him,* not your father."

"The man's daughter is missing. This has nothing to do with the past."

"Everything has to do with the past, honey. Everything. It makes us who we are." He paused. "Just know that I'll be watching."

His continued animosity toward Liam disturbed Jess. His resentment belied objectivity. He almost seemed jealous of the man. "This isn't a show," she told him. "It isn't just a case. A young girl's life is on the line, and it's our job to help her, no matter who her father is."

"No matter who the father is? Can you really say that? We've worked a lot of cases together. This isn't our first missing child. But it is the first time I've seen that look in your eyes."

"What look?"

He frowned. "Like you're reaching, lying bleeding on the ground, searching for someone to find you but scared they won't."

The absolute candor of his words hit Jess harder than Braxton's fist. "Trying out for the annual melodrama award?" she asked with a strained little laugh.

He looked her dead in the eye. "No—I'm trying to keep my partner in one piece."

"I know what I'm doing."

"Could have fooled me."

"Apparently, I did."

Kirby's mouth tightened into a hard line. "We'll see," he said, then turned and strode away.

Jess stood there for a moment, breathing deeply of the bitterly cold, late afternoon air, trying to process what had just gone down. She wanted to be angry with her partner but couldn't. She wanted to blame Liam for twisting her inside out but couldn't do that, either.

All the responsibility, all the blame, sat squarely on her shoulders.

She was a seasoned detective. She knew how to walk the line without crossing it. Kirby was right. She just hadn't done a very good job of it. Because she was also a woman.

Whenever she saw William Armstrong, training shattered, everything her father had told her fled, and feminine

instinct took over. She looked at him now, found him staring out over the field of tall brown grass where the line of
officials continued to look for his daughter. Afternoon gray-
ness was turning steadily darker.

Jess walked over to him. "I'm surprised you're not out
there with them."

He glanced at her. "She's not there."

Jess frowned. He sounded so damn certain. "Liam—"

"Don't say it. Don't feel like you have to warn me not
to get my hopes up." He took her hand and drew it to his
chest, where he pressed her palm to warm flesh. The tank
top was loose, leaving part of a mauve nipple exposed to
her touch. "She's here, Detective. I feel her here. My
daughter is not in that field."

Jess's heart staggered under the strain of his words. She
snatched her hand from the moist heat of his skin and gazed
over the field. Had her father felt the same way? Had he
been so certain? So consumed?

Guilt pierced anew, and she quickly looked away. Emily
might not have had a choice in the matter, but she, Jessica,
had. She'd put her father through this, made him wonder
if his little girl had been abducted or just ran away. Neither
possibility boded well for the chief of police.

"Thinking about your own father?" Liam asked quietly.
"Wondering if he felt the same way when you ran away?"

The silky question stripped Jess of all those barriers she
worked so hard to erect, leaving her feeling like she stood
before William Armstrong stark naked. Slowly she turned
toward him, found him watching her with unnerving intensity. It was as though he could see straight through her.

She pulled the sash of her leather coat a little tighter. "It
was a long time ago."

"You think our fates were sealed the moment Heather
ran away? You think our paths have been running parallel

ever since, waiting for the inevitable moment when they would tangle?''

Almost an hour had passed since they arrived at the field, and during that time the temperature had steadily dropped. But Jess hadn't felt cold, not until this very moment. ''What do you mean?''

Liam's eyes took on a glitter, but his voice remained whisper soft. ''I mean the reason your father quit coming home at night, why he became so distracted, so consumed, why he stopped being a father to the daughter who needed him so much. I'm talking about you and the reason you ran away.''

He lifted a hand to streak a finger down the side of her face. ''I'm talking about me.''

Chapter 8

Jess reeled from the impact of Liam's words. "I didn't run away because of you. I didn't even know you."

His expression gentled. "But you saw the differences in your father, didn't you? You knew his temper was short, his patience shorter. You knew he rarely came home anymore. He didn't even notice when his little girl got involved with the school bad boy again, did he?"

God help her, it was as though Liam had found a nonexistent diary and read it—page by painful page. "You make me sound like a spoiled brat. I wasn't a child. I was sixteen."

"But there's no age limit for craving a father's love," he said in that dangerously soft voice of his.

The field around them faded, the buzz of police radios, the officers still combing through the tall grass. Memories took over. She hated thinking about that dark time, how alone she'd felt, the risks she'd taken, but standing alone with the man who occupied entirely too many of her thoughts, his penetrating eyes focused on her, the past came crashing to the forefront. The fear and defiance, the regret.

She didn't know why William Armstrong of all people would coerce those memories out of hiding, but they refused to stay in that dark corner any longer. Perhaps it was because he needed to know what had gone through her mind, what she'd been thinking. Because of Emily.

The last crack in the dam gave way, and the words poured free. "I never thought about it from his point of view. I never thought about what I might be doing to him. I just wanted to be away. To breathe. I wanted to spread my wings and fly without wondering what Dad would think, if he would think, if he would even notice."

Liam stepped closer. "He noticed."

The certainty in his voice made her wonder if he spoke on behalf of all fathers, hers or himself.

"Cold?"

She looked down and realized she'd wrapped her arms around her waist. The fading light left the temperature frigid, but with William Armstrong standing so close she felt the heat radiating from his sparsely clothed body, she wasn't the least bit cold. At least not on the outside.

She hugged herself because of the memories. The strong drive to keep herself together, to not let too much slip beyond her reach. Jess refused to let herself wonder how much Liam could hold, the magnitude of secrets and memories he housed behind his granite expression.

"I'd offer you my coat, but I don't have one."

She glanced at him, tried to determine if his words were sarcastic or sincere.

Uncomfortable with the intimacy of eye contact, she looked instead to the field, where flashlights were being used. "I'll never forget the look on Dad's face when he found me in that old warehouse."

Liam tilted her chin toward him. "Tell me."

"It was the same look you had on your face when you saw me at the house earlier. Hope and horror, love." And she could still feel it, all of it, when she closed her eyes.

He slid his hand to cup her cheek. "Anger?"

Jess went very still. She wanted to back away, but curiosity held her in place. The warmth of his palm against her face tempted her to think he was offering a white flag, but she was painfully aware the chill would return soon enough.

With William Armstrong, it always did.

He looked strong and solid standing in the fading light of early evening, utterly male. Dressed in his ratty running clothes, the man had to be freezing, but Jess could find no trace of it on the outside. He kept what he felt on the inside. He'd hardened the side of him that he showed to the world into such an impenetrable wall she doubted a drill could get through.

"That bad?" he asked, and she realized he'd misinterpreted her silence. Or had he?

"Just the opposite," she said. "Dad never got angry, not with us, not in the loud, ranting sense of the word. The more we pushed him, the quieter he became. He'd go to work a little earlier, stay a little later."

"And did running away change anything?"

"Not with him."

"But you?"

Jess let out a slow breath. This man her father had so despised seemed to see what others couldn't, understand her in ways no one ever had. If she were cautious, she'd turn and walk away. She didn't. She wasn't one to run, even though she knew the ripple effect one little pebble lobbed into a still pond could have.

"I spent three months on the streets," she told him,

"then came home to our cushy North Dallas home. Nothing had changed, and yet everything was different. *I* was different. The way I viewed life was different. It's one of those paradoxes that makes your head spin. Running didn't change the world around me, but realizing that, realizing hiding from problems doesn't make them go away, changed *me*."

Liam held her gaze. "That's a powerful lesson for a sixteen-year-old girl."

She told herself not to read too much into the compassion in his voice. "I regret the grief I caused my family, but I'll go to my grave believing the time on the streets made me a better person. A better daughter, a better cop. Odd, isn't it?"

What little sun there'd been was just about gone now, casting Liam's face in shadow. "No more odd than the crossroads we're standing at," he said in an oddly quiet voice. "I bet your old man is really getting a kick out of this one."

"What?"

He stepped closer. "Seventeen years ago his quest to nail me to the wall drove his daughter out of his home. Now the tables have turned. I'm the one with a missing child, and Wallace's little girl is my best chance of getting Emily back. If ever you wanted revenge, payback, now's your chance."

Jess tried not to wince, but his words couldn't have hit harder if they'd been stones. For a tenuous moment, they'd been communicating. Sharing. Or so she'd thought. He must have realized it, too, because the walls were going back up. She felt them as powerfully as if she'd slammed into a slab of granite. She saw them in the hardening of his eyes. Even his voice was different, harder, more remote.

She'd crossed the line.

William Armstrong was on the offensive. The man who always came out on top was pushing aside the father who stood dangerously close to losing everything. The need, the understanding he'd started to exhibit was wholly unacceptable.

If you get too close…he simply cuts you out, no questions asked.

"I thought you wanted me off the case," she reminded blandly, though there was nothing bland about the way this man unraveled her like a spool of thread.

He again touched a hand to her face, not in compassion as before, but in provocation. His fingertips skimmed her cheekbones, the pad of his thumb her mouth. "Wanting is dangerous, Detective. I learned that a long time ago. I want my daughter back. That doesn't mean she's standing here. A smart man deals in reality."

She started to swat his hand away but realized she didn't want to give him the satisfaction. He was the one who didn't believe in getting too close, and even though he clearly intended to throw her off balance, very few things in life were more silkenly intimate than a man and woman standing in the muted shades of twilight, touching, speaking in hushed tones.

She could withstand the intimacy longer than he could.

"Reality?" she asked in the gentle voice Kirby called the calm before the storm. "I didn't think that word was in your vocabulary. Aren't you the man who doesn't take no for an answer? Who finds a way to have what he wants, no matter what? Who twists and turns every situation to his own liking?"

He laughed. "Ah, Jessica. You really are your father's daughter, aren't you?" He stroked his thumb along the corner of her mouth, still swollen from Braxton's fist. "Just because I face reality doesn't mean I accept it. All I'm saying is you have to know where you are before you map out where you're going. What's so manipulative about that?''

Jess just stared at him. She searched for a flippant comeback, but instead found an understanding she didn't want to have. She opened her mouth anyway, clamped it shut when the tip of his thumb slipped inside.

"Careful," he said in a dangerously soft voice. "Don't want to hurt yourself again."

She grabbed his wrist and pulled his hand away from her face. "Play your games with someone else. They won't work with me."

"I'm not playing. This is as real as it gets." Shadows flickered against the hard planes of his face. "I was wrong to want you off the case. I thought the lines between us were too tangled, too blurred. I didn't think you could be objective."

"I'm a trained professional," she reminded. Him? Her?

"You're also your father's daughter."

"And you're talking in circles."

"No, I'm not. I'm simply saying you've got as much on the line as I do. You can't afford to take the easy way out, to scribble runaway across Emily's file and be done with it, because if it turns out she's in trouble and you didn't help, you'll never be able to live with yourself. You'll realize you let personal distractions blur your judgment. You'll realize you're just like your father."

She winced, realizing the truth of his words.

"The lines *are* blurred, but because of that you might be the only cop in this narrow-minded town willing to turn over every stone to find the truth about Emily's disappearance."

Inevitability wove its way through Jess, the tie that bound her to William Armstrong, even when they'd both just as soon turn their backs on each other and walk in opposite directions.

She couldn't carve him from her life any more than he could her. For now, for reasons pertaining to past and present, they needed each other too badly. And he knew it.

So did she. "I don't need to be bullied by you to do my job," she said, looking at Armstrong. "I promised you I'd bring your daughter back, and I will. We both want the same thing."

A faint light glimmered in his eyes. "Then let's quit wanting and make it happen."

His choice of words, the low tone in which he uttered them, sent an unwanted sizzle through her. He'd done it on purpose, she knew. He always did.

"By all means," she said in a clipped, professional voice, unwilling to let him get to her. To care any more than she already did. The price was too high. She'd grown up with a man like William Armstrong, after all. Loved him. Learned from him. Lost him.

"Let's head on out," she said, gesturing toward her car. "There's nothing else for us here."

The light in his eyes darkened. "Quite the opposite, Detective. I think we're finally making progress."

"This evening a new development in the case of missing heiress Emily Armstrong. Her car was found abandoned in a field near D/FW Airport…"

The television screen cut to an image of William Armstrong standing in front of his daughter's burned-out car. The man looked like he was standing before an open casket.

Everything was unfolding according to plan.

The cops didn't have a clue. Armstrong didn't, either. Taking the man's daughter had been as easy as giving candy to a kid. She'd had no reason not to trust. At first. She'd listened, then all but run out the door. Piece of cake.

"Are you watching? Can you hear me?"

A quick glance at the closed-circuit monitor across the room revealed a glaring Emily Armstrong. She stood in the corner of the Spartan room she'd been provided, staring at the camera mounted far out of her reach. With her long dark hair tangled around her face, those expressive Armstrong eyes flashing and her hands clenched into combative fists, she looked ready to audition for an episode of *Xena, Warrior Princess*. Whereas most teenage girls would be terrified, Emily seemed more furious than anything else.

She really was her father's daughter.

She'd been treated with nothing but kindness, assured over and over she wouldn't be hurt. But she refused to believe. She didn't understand that hurting innocents was her father's style. She didn't understand that she was far more valuable alive than dead.

"You won't get away with this," she warned. "My father will hunt you down and make you pay."

For a seventeen-year-old, she was amusingly ferocious. She really did think her dad could conquer the world.

If only she knew how wrong she was.

Liam slammed his fist against the hard leather bag. It careened back, and he went after it, hitting, punishing. Again. And again. Harder each time. He absolutely refused to grant any mercy.

Aren't you the man who doesn't take no for an answer? Who finds a way to have what he wants, no matter what? Who twists and turns every situation to his own liking?

With an animalistic roar, Liam kicked his leg and sent the punching bag swinging wildly. Damn her. Damn Detective Jessica Clark for throwing his life, his choices, in his face and trying to make him feel shame. To make him feel like he was the one in the wrong, when all he was doing was everything humanly possible to find his daughter.

Where was the crime in that?

Play your games with someone else. They won't work on me.

No matter how hard he hit the bag, her words stayed with him like a warped soundtrack. She was an enigma he couldn't afford. He didn't know how she did it, how she stripped away the layers and bared the raw core he was trying so hard to destroy. Then, rather than attacking, she changed, softened. She applied a balm or a bandage rather than taking the kill when she had it.

The survivor in him warned that he should erase the provocative detective from his life, but every time he saw her, that rare mixture of intelligence and compassion swirling in her amber eyes, he found himself torn between pushing her away and crushing her in his arms.

Liam swore again. The only person he needed to hold was his daughter.

His punishment of the bag grew more frenzied, more violent. That he should feel drawn to anyone at a time like this appalled him. But there it was, and the inappropriateness of it was eating him alive. He couldn't let Detective Jessica Clark get any closer. He couldn't let her keep peeling away layer after layer. He couldn't let her see inside.

He couldn't let her offer her own blend of healing balm.

But he couldn't ban her from the case, either. She really was his best chance.

He knew what he had to do.

Breathing hard, he went to pummel the training device that had become his best friend but found himself grabbing it instead. The tough facade crumbled, the fight drained. He was so damn tired of standing alone.

Exhausted, Liam pulled the thick bag to him and slumped against leather. Wrapped his arms around it. Dropped his head. He absolutely refused to let himself imagine holding anything or anyone other than his daughter, certainly not the svelte body of the lady detective charged with bringing her home.

No good could come from Detective Jessica Clark's arms. Only damnation, a shame greater than any she'd accused him of. There sure as hell wouldn't be strength or comfort. No ridiculous saving graces.

He wouldn't let there be. Couldn't.

Jess paced the length of her small condo. The night was still and quiet, suffocatingly dark. No moon, no stars, only heavy clouds rolling in from the north. From her aquarium glowed the only light, a bluish hue illuminating an underwater world she found fascinating. Angelfish glided through the fronds of the plants she provided while neon fish milled about a submerged statue that had caught her fancy. No Fishing Allowed.

Jess drew in a deep breath and tried to let the serenity soothe her. She'd tried reading, meditation, but too much energy zinged around inside her. Moving closer to the fifty-gallon tank, she concentrated on the aquatic life, but found not even the graceful movements could supercede thoughts of William Armstrong. She closed her eyes, but the images loomed stronger. Liam and Molly running toward her, those long, powerful strides, man and dog at full throttle. Pushing. Maybe even punishing. The memory pulled at her heart, made her feel things, want things she knew better than to think about.

The sound of shattering glass broke the silence, and Jess

immediately dropped to the floor. Instinct kicked into high gear. She rolled across the rug to the coffee table, where she quickly retrieved her .38. She never left it far out of reach.

Through the bluish glow of the aquarium, she surveyed her condo. The door was still secure. She heard no sounds of footsteps or anything other than an old regulator clock. No shadows moved beyond the broken window. She inched toward it, careful to avoid shards of glass, and eased into a standing position with her back against the wall. Her heart pounded so hard she thought if anyone stood on the other side, they would hear. Gun in hand, she peered into the night, standing still until she was sure no danger lurked beyond.

Only then did she turn her attention to the gaping hole in the window. Too big for a bullet. She surveyed the surrounding area, found the culprit. There on the carpet, amidst the broken glass, sat some kind of cloth bundle. Jess knew better than to touch it with her bare hands.

Seconds later, gloves on, she carefully untied the fabric. A rock awaited inside, but a careful inspection turned up nothing significant. Then she glanced at the cloth, and her heart went into her throat. Not a cloth, but a bandanna, aqua in color with a school of colorful fish milling about what looked to be a coral reef. Jess glanced across her room at her aquarium, then had a flash of the comforter she'd seen on Emily Armstrong's bed. And the bandanna she'd seen on the dog Molly.

Her throat tightened. She looked at the fabric open against her carpet and saw the words written in black.

Ticktock goes the clock.

Ticktock. Ticktock.

Liam stepped from the shower and grabbed a towel. A few vicious swipes had his body dry enough. In the foggy bathroom mirror he caught sight of the grim lines of his unshaven face, the uncivilized glint to his eyes. He'd never been a soft man, but the hard man staring at him seemed more stranger than ally.

He was going back out there. Tonight. Questions and worry sloshed around inside him, slivers of the dreams he'd had for his daughter. He didn't care that the hour was past midnight. No way could he just crawl into bed and go to sleep.

Liam lifted the towel and rubbed it over his hair, stilled when he thought he heard something. Lowering the dark terry cloth, he went on full alert. The faint noise grew louder. An engine, he realized. Only someone passing by.

Until the hum stopped just outside.

Emily.

Liam bolted from the bathroom and ran toward the bedroom door. If he hadn't almost tripped over the jeans he'd left in a heap on the floor, he probably wouldn't have remembered he was naked. He grabbed them and fought to pull them on as he ran through the darkened house. He took the stairs two at a time.

His bare feet hit the cold marble of the foyer at a full run. He reached the front door and pulled it open, charged out into the frigid night.

She stopped dead in her tracks. Surprise flooded her eyes. Uncertainty. She almost looked frightened.

His heart kicked harder. His pulse.

The moment of indecision passed, and she rallied. The caution drained from her features, replaced by determination. An uncharacteristic ferocity. And she started up the walk once again.

The sight of Detective Jessica Clark striding toward him hit like a swift punch to the gut. She didn't look upset or concerned as she had that afternoon, but furious, like an avenging angel swooping down to exact punishment for some heinous grievance. The wind blowing through the cedar elms whipped loose auburn hair about her face. Moonlight glittered in her eyes.

Liam wanted to charge down the three steps and take her shoulders in his hands. To demand she—

He didn't know what he wanted to demand, only that he didn't trust himself to move. Didn't want to think about what could happen if he touched her. Obviously he hadn't succeeded this afternoon in warning her away from him.

The clearly agitated detective marched up the steps and got right up in his face. Then she lifted some sort of bag and dangled it before him. "Recognize this?"

He took the plastic from her hands and used the light spilling from the foyer to inspect the contents.

Everything inside Liam went deadly still. He refused to let his hands shake. "Where did you get this?"

Jessica's eyes narrowed as she flipped over the bag, revealing dark handwriting scrawled against the cheerful fabric.

Horror numbed Liam to the darkened world around him. The cold wind was nothing compared to the chill freezing his lungs, his heart.

"Where the hell did this come from?" He barely recognized the raw sounds tearing from his throat as his own voice.

Jessica met his gaze head-on. There was no sympathy in her expression, no trace of the compassionate woman who'd laid a hand against his back earlier that afternoon, somehow realizing how badly he'd needed the warmth of human touch. She was all cop now, more reminiscent of her father or partner.

"That's what I'd like to know," she said firmly. "Notes

like this are typically delivered to the family, not the investigating officer.''

"What are you talking about?"

"For some odd reason, what appears to be the first communication from your daughter's alleged kidnapper found its way into my condo.''

Shock galvanized him, and he knew his mistake. Beneath the woman's body that lulled a man into lowering his defense resided a detective's mind always on the hunt. She was not his ally, not his friend. She was Wallace Clark's daughter.

"You think I'm responsible?"

"Are you?"

The urge to grab her shoulders was strong, but somehow, he resisted. "Are you trying to push me to the edge?" he asked in a deceptively quiet voice. "Or do you just enjoy acting in the same heartless fashion as your father?"

She glared at him. "Answer my question."

"You really think I'd do something this passive?"

"Don't you get it?" She erupted, for the first time showing a flicker of emotion. Except it was more like a bonfire. She snatched the bag from his hands and shoved it into her satchel. "I'm trying to do you a favor. I'm trying to keep you from digging yourself a hole you really don't want to dig. Don't you know what Detective Long will think when I show him this?"

"I don't care about your partner," he growled, "I care about—" He bit back the dangerous word that almost slipped free and stepped closer. *You.* "Tell me what *you* think."

Her eyes widened. A soft sound of surprise preceded the hoarse sound of her voice. "You've been drinking."

Liam tried not to let the breathy disappointment in her

voice sway him. He'd only taken one measly gulp before he dumped the glass of bourbon into a nearby potted palm.

"Can I guess from your attempt to change the subject," he asked very softly, "that you have no opinion of your own about whether I'm manipulative and underhanded enough to send that note?" The question scraped on the way out. "That you just adopt what other people think and go along with it? Your father, your partner—"

"You want to know what I think?" Her voice was hot and challenging, her eyes full of fire. "Fine. I'll tell you," she said, stepping closer. "I think you're a man who won't stop until he gets what he wants. I'm not sure there's a limit to what you would or wouldn't do, not if you thought it would bring Emily home faster. You've made it perfectly clear you're not a man to play by the rules."

"Rules?" The word left a bitter taste in his mouth, and he found himself strangely disappointed. He didn't know why he kept expecting—wanting—her to believe in him. Understand him. Stand by him. But he did.

"My child is missing and you're talking to me about rules?"

"Someone needs to. Every time I turn around, there's another William Armstrong stunt I have to deal with—you digging into my past, going after Braxton yourself. You're working against me more than you're working with me."

"You'd rather me sit at home and wait for Lady Justice to save the day?"

She lifted her chin. "Attacking me won't change anything."

"Neither will following the rules," he bit out. "Don't you think I know that by now? Me, of all people? I followed them before, when Heather left, and look where that got me." He searched her face, looking for a glimmer of retreat. Instead, the porch light cast shadows across her cheekbones, her parted lips, making her look provocatively soft when she wanted him to believe she was every bit as hard as her father.

"Half this damn town thinks I got away with murder," he told her, clenching his hands into tight fists. He didn't trust himself not to touch her, to see if her skin would be as hot as her eyes. "Not again. Not anymore. Not with Emmie's life on the line."

"You're distorting the issue," she said, and her voice softened. "This isn't about before. It's about now, your daughter, bringing her home. How many times do I have to tell you?" She paused, stepped closer. The fervor in her eyes outshone the stars in the night sky. "We want the same thing, Liam."

Once, he'd insisted she use the casual version of his name. Now, the sound of it on her smoky voice struck him as entirely too intimate. "You want rules," he corrected, trying to erect the walls he'd let fall into disrepair. "Procedure. You want to make your daddy proud. But you know what? It's too late for that. What you do doesn't matter to your father. He's gone."

"This has nothing to do with my father."

"Doesn't it?"

She shook her head, sending her loose hair swirling. "Not even close. You're lashing out at me because I'm here, and there's no one else."

He winced, hating the hurt in her voice. That wasn't what he wanted, just distance. Space. Objectivity. "I've got a punching bag inside if I just want to lash out blindly. That's not what this is about. This is about the fact those rules you cling to aren't going to bring my daughter home."

She frowned. "Neither will carelessness."

Frustration tightened through him. She didn't understand,

and he didn't know how to make her. Didn't know why it mattered so much that she did.

Silence stretched between them, accentuating the warm air rushing against his back from the open front door, the frigid night air cutting into his chest. He knew what happened when temperature extremes collided.

"There's a difference between carelessness and calculated risk," he said as levelly as he could. You think your father didn't know that? You think he always followed the rules?"

Jessica eased the flyaway hair from her face. "Everything I know about right and wrong, about rules, I learned from him. The structure and procedure, the safety net. Without them, we'd have nothing but chaos, and you'd never get your daughter back."

"You're a smart woman—don't tell me you really believe that."

"I said it, didn't I?"

"You said it, but you're also standing on my front porch in the middle of the night with a piece of evidence in your purse. What do the rules say about that?"

Her mouth tumbled open. "Don't—"

"I think you know as well as I do that rules are for the weak, and that's what you're fighting. Because you're not weak. You're strong. You were taught one thing, but instinct, your heart, tells you something altogether different. You realize rules hold us back, put parameters and restraints on desire like a wet straitjacket."

A strangled noise tore from her throat.

"You're actually going to stand here and tell me you reject rules because they're like a strait-jacket to *desire?*" She looked like she wanted to press her hands to his chest and shove him backward, but she didn't. She just glared at him with those magnificent, expressive eyes of hers, her chest rising and falling with each jerky breath. "You? The one who calls himself entrepreneur and father, but not man? The one who keeps every crumb of desire locked so firmly away you might as well be a eunuch?"

Everything inside him went very still. "A eunuch?"

"A man who can't—"

Instinct took over. Need. Without thinking, he took her shoulders in his hands and pulled her against him. Her eyes flared wide. Her breathing caught. She stared at him, lips parted, as though he held a switchblade in his hands, not the soft wool of her sweater.

Primitive satisfaction at finally rattling the unflappable detective spurred him on. Blood roared through his ears like a battle cry. His vision blurred.

"Let there be no mistake, Detective. I can. And I do." His mouth came down on hers then. Hard.

Chapter 9

Shock streaked through Jess. Hot. Swirling. She lifted her arms to push Liam away, found her hands curling around his biceps instead. The heat of his flesh seared into her, and the night no longer seemed quite so cold.

She'd been rash to come here and push a man like William Armstrong so hard. She'd been reckless to let emotion override logic. And now, she would have called the crush of his mouth to hers punishing if it hadn't been so desperate. The man kissed like he ran. Full throttle. She tasted the need. Even more, she tasted the desire, the barely concealed restraint, and something deep inside reached for him.

A raw cry tore from her throat, and she opened to the demands of his mouth, sliding a hand along the warm flesh of his shoulder and into the thick strands of his hair.

She refused to think that she was holding him as close to her as possible.

What was it Kirby had said that afternoon? That she looked like she was lying on the ground, bleeding, searching for someone to find her, but scared they wouldn't?

He'd been wrong, she realized as Liam mirrored her movements and slid a hand along her neck. She felt his fingers weave into her tangled hair, felt his palm cup her head. She wasn't the one bleeding; Liam was. From his heart, his soul. But it wasn't blood he was losing, it was hope, the indefinable part of him that made him appear bigger than life. She was the one reaching out to him, stanching the flow.

His kiss was hot and hard, deep, almost desperate. He kissed her as though his life depended on it. On her. The cop in her struggled to refute the ridiculous notion, but the woman at her core refused to let thinking dismiss feeling.

And she felt so damn much. Not just the physical promise of his lips, the strength of his body pressed to hers, but the emotional thread between the two of them, the one that pulled her to his house in the middle of the night even when caution warned her to stay away. The one that strengthened with every moment in his presence. His arms.

His mouth ground against hers; his whiskers scraped the sensitive skin of her jaw. She reveled in it, found power in the raw noises tearing from his throat, the fact that he needed her. A woman could lose herself in the promise of his lips, she realized in some barely functioning corner of her mind. A woman could fall into believing she was vital. That she mattered.

God help her, she wanted to matter to this man.

The rush of awareness pummeled her like an avalanche, deceptively beautiful, seductively dangerous. She knew she should run before the sensation smothered her, but there in Liam's arms, she realized there was nowhere else she wanted to be. She would make it better—

He tore his mouth away and swore softly. The fierce blue of his eyes glittered at her. "Still think I'm a eunuch?"

The hurt was instantaneous. A lesson, she realized

numbly. That's all his kiss had been. His way of proving a point. "You bastard!" she cried, and slapped him hard.

His hand caught hers and held it to his cheek. "A man, Jessica, that's what I am. I'm well aware of that fact, just like I know damn good and well you're a woman." His gaze dipped over her furiously rigid body, then lifted to her eyes. "No man alive could spend one second with you and not see what a beautiful, smart, sexy woman you are. But you're also the cop who's supposed to find my daughter." He paused, injected something uncomfortably intimate into his gaze. "The man knows, Jessica, but so does the father. How can I let the man see you as a woman when the father sees you as his only hope?"

His only hope. The detective in her knew good and well how he meant the words, but the woman caught fire. "Liam—"

"My daughter is missing," he said point-blank. "She could be hurt, in trouble, scared. I don't have time for desire right now. I don't have time to hold hands and whisper secrets. What kind of man would that make me? What kind of father?"

"Human, I'd say." She pulled her hand from under his and pressed it against the corner of her mouth, still bruised from Braxton's punch, bruised again by this man's shattering kiss. "There's nothing wrong or shameful about accepting comfort and help, about needing other people."

His eyes went wild. He took her arms in his hands and pulled her close. "I need you, all right. I need you so damn much it scares the hell out of me." He paused, sucked in a breath so roughly his nostrils flared. "Is that what you wanted to hear? Does that make you happy?"

Her heart thrummed hard and deep. Caution flowed thick. The simple word *happy* didn't come close to describing the maelstrom of emotion barreling down on her. Nonsensical ideals like right and wrong crashed down like broken branches. The force buried logic like a dead weight.

Need drove her forward. She pushed up on her toes and brushed her lips across his. "Let me help, Liam...."

"Don't." He stepped back as though she'd tried to slip a knife through his heart. He didn't let go of her, though. He held her arms in his hands, keeping her at a distance. "On the streets. That's where I need you. Looking for my daughter. Not in my bed."

Hurt stripped away the haze. Alarm bled through. For ten years she'd trained herself to feel nothing. Need nothing, no one. To be strong and independent, to wall herself off from those around her, particularly the cases on which she worked. But as she looked into Liam's ravaged eyes, she felt the punch of his words clear down to the core of who she was.

He was right. She wanted to reach out to this man every way she could, professionally, personally, physically, emotionally. She wanted to do whatever she could to ease his pain, and for a blind moment, the desire to do so had obliterated her deepest, most finely honed survival instincts.

Never need a man who believed himself an island.

Standing there in the dead of night, the frigid wind blowing against them, Jess realized the truth. The man let himself feel nothing, need nothing, give nothing. Only a granite man could stand in subfreezing temperatures in nothing but faded blue jeans and not even shake. Even if Liam's daughter was safe and sound and sleeping upstairs, nothing would be different. The man had nothing but stolen moments to parcel out, and she'd long promised herself to never settle for crumbs.

Emotion scratched at her throat. "I'm here to find your daughter, Liam, not for stolen kisses or to save your soul. I'm on your side. I'm not the enemy."

With a lost laugh, he lifted his hands and turned them

palm down. "Are you done lecturing me, Detective, or would you like to take a ruler to my knuckles, too?"

Jess pulled the sash of her coat tighter. "God only knows why I thought I could help, why I even wanted to. You can throw up shields of duty and fatherhood all you want, but they don't change the truth."

"And just what truth is that?"

She took his hand and led him toward the light spilling out the open front door. He didn't resist her, but nor did his fingers curl around hers.

Inside, the heater's warmth washed over her like a lover's caress, but Jess knew it would take more than processed air to thaw her out. She led Liam to the marble-top console table she'd seen on her first visit and glanced at the ornately framed mirror hanging just above.

In the reflective surface, Liam's blue-hot gaze met hers. She tried to hold on to her objectivity, the message she wanted to convey, but it was hard to look at a man like William Armstrong and breathe, much less think rationally.

"Did you bring me inside for a reason, or are we back to playing games?"

She tried to summon the anger, the cop's objectivity, but the woman drank in the sight of their faces side by side in the mirror. She saw her expression, the determination in her eyes, her flushed cheeks, her tangled hair. He looked equally on edge, his expression uncompromising, his dark hair rumpled, his jaw unshaven. His chest was bare, his jeans unfastened.

"Look in the mirror, Liam. Take a long, hard look." She paused, trying to concentrate on the hard lines of his face, not the blue of his eyes. They reminded her of an ocean with a storm gathering on the horizon, deep and turbulent, restless, dangerous, and with them, he watched her as steadily as she watched him. The air around them seemed to thicken. The heater's warmth turned punishing, and the hand in which she still held his grew hot and damp.

Or at least, that's what she told herself.

The manufactured heat was far less dangerous than the physical kind. The heater could be turned off.

"You just told me why you reject rules," she said softly. "You said they limit possibilities, that they stagnate us. Hold us back. But you're living by your own set of rules—about fatherhood, involvement, need, proper and productive uses of time—and they're destroying you."

Deep inside, something started to tear. She felt herself reaching for him, more emotionally than physically, and knew she was in way over her head. "You're so lost in your rules, you can't see the fabric of your life, the threads that tie everything together, that make us human." She let go of his hand and stepped away, too aware of the desire to touch him with more than her gaze, her words.

Oddly, he said nothing.

"Fatherhood, involvement, time, they're all related," she continued. "The more you have, the stronger the fabric. But if you keep them separate, your life becomes as sparse and threadbare as a wool blanket left in a closet full of moths."

In the mirror, Liam's gaze darkened. She waited for him to say something, to tell her to mind her own business, that she had no idea what she was talking about, that she was wrong. But he didn't. He just stared at her, his eyes curiously unreadable.

Jess swallowed against the tightness in her throat and tore her gaze away from their reflections. Looking at the cold white marble at her feet, she realized how close to the edge she'd stepped. How steep the fall.

Stolen moments, she reminded herself. Stolen moments were not worth the pain of the fall.

She glanced one last time at Liam's gaze—he hadn't

spoken one word since she'd led him inside—then lifted her chin and pivoted toward the door. Part of her wanted to feel his big hand on her shoulder, to hear his raspy voice tell her to stay. But with each step she took away from him, she knew they were better off if she left.

"Jessica—"

The sound of her name pierced like an arrow to the back. Her knees went weak. More than anything she longed to turn toward him, but she kept right on walking toward the frigid night air awaiting outside.

He caught her at the door. His hand curled around her arm in a grip that was shockingly gentle, considering the strength she knew he possessed. "Jessica—"

"Don't." She ignored the impact of his tired, hoarse voice, the note of pleading she wanted to believe she heard. She didn't trust herself to look at him.

"I'm sorry."

She stiffened. Emotion bled through her crumbling defenses. She wanted to ask him what he was sorry for—for kissing her like he meant it, for pushing her away, for being cold, for not letting her reach out to him—but she didn't want to hear him say any of that. She wasn't a woman for punishment. She didn't need the words when she already felt the truth deep in her heart.

"So am I," she said. For everything. But most especially, for the man who wouldn't let himself feel. Need. She swallowed, spoke before he could say anything else. "Let me go, Liam. Let me do my job."

A tense moment spun out between them, and the world around them slowed—the wind blowing through the naked branches of the cedar elms, the cloud of vapor left by her breathing. Even the silence. It deepened and intensified, making Jess acutely conscious of the pounding of her heart.

She drew in a deep breath, felt the sting of the cold deep inside. She waited for him to say something, to turn her toward him, touch a hand to her face, pull her inside and close out the cold night air.

His fingers slowly uncurled from around her arm.

He said nothing.

Moisture flooded her eyes, as though his hand had been pressed against cracks in a dam, rather than the wool of her sweater. She refused to turn around, though. Refused to say anything further. She'd already said too much.

Head high, shoulders straight, Jess walked into the night. She waited to hear the door close behind her, wanted the knell of finality. Instead she felt the heat of William Armstrong's gaze track her down the walkway to her car. Only when she slipped inside and slammed the door shut, cranked up the engine and put the car into gear, drove down the street and far, far out of his sight, was she able to breathe.

And then she did something she hadn't done since the night she'd held her father's hand as he drew his last breath.

She cried.

She pulled the sedan to the side of the road and left the engine idling, rested her head against the steering wheel and let the pent-up emotion come pouring out.

She didn't know why.

She didn't want to, either.

"Mind telling me what went down between you and William Armstrong yesterday?"

The booming request snapped Jess to attention. She lowered the report she'd been reading and pushed at her glasses, then glanced up to find Commander Ben McKnight towering over her. His question had been hard, but his eyes twinkled. She still wasn't used to thinking of the man who'd once bounced a young Jess on his knee as her commanding officer. He'd been her father's best friend, but his style was as different from her father's style as day was different from night.

"Morning, commander," she said, using his formal title instead of Uncle Ben, as she'd done for as long as she remembered. "What's up?"

He propped a hip against her cluttered desk. "I just hung up the phone with William Armstrong."

Her heart started to pound a little harder, and a strange roar rose inside her. All she'd wanted to do was help the man, and now he was going to hang her out to dry. "He's worried sick about his daughter," she said by way of explanation. "I'm not sure he's thinking clearly."

"Apparently not."

"Whatever he said—"

"I don't know what you did or said to that man, but he wants you something fierce, Jessie girl."

Jess went very still. Deep inside she started to shake, but she kept her expression noncommittal. "Excuse me?" she asked, pushing to her feet.

This was not news a girl could take sitting down.

Uncle Ben shook his head. "I've known that man for over fifteen years, and never once do I remember him changing his mind. About anything."

Uncompromising, she remembered thinking. A man of singular focus. An island unto himself. And that's the way he wanted it.

"Yesterday he insisted that I remove you from the case, but this morning, he's threatening to scream bloody murder if I take you away from him."

Jess braced her hand against the side of her desk before her legs went out from under her. Surely Uncle Ben had no idea of the impact of his words, but they pummeled like shards of granite. She'd sat on her sofa the remainder of the night, staring at her aquarium, trying to forget the need she'd tasted in Liam's kiss, seen in his eyes. They were bad for each other. An accident waiting to happen. "I don't think that's a good idea."

Uncle Ben looked at her queerly. She'd never once turned down an assignment. "Something going on I don't know about? Is Armstrong back to playing games?"

Jess almost laughed. "I wouldn't call them games—they're just part of who he is. I'm not sure he can see me as anyone other than Wallace Clark's daughter."

"And that makes you uniquely qualified to work with him on this case. You've been where his daughter is. You know what it's like to grow up with a powerful father. You know how her mind—"

"Emily Armstrong didn't run away," Jess said abruptly.

"Detective Long thinks she did."

"Because he wants to," she countered. "Because when he looks at William Armstrong, he sees only the man he thinks got away with murder. He can't see the father, the man who loves his only child so much he's built his entire life around making her as happy as possible."

"And who do you see?" Uncle Ben asked gently.

A lump of emotion lodged in her throat. "I see them all." And it was tearing her apart.

"That's what makes you such a good cop, Jessie. You see both sides of the coin. You don't let yourself get blinded by preconceived notions."

She sighed. "Sometimes it's hard."

"Of course it's hard, especially when the man I'm asking you to help is one you grew up hearing your father malign. But there was no evidence against him seventeen years ago, and there still isn't. Too many people, your father included, let emotion cloud objectivity. We may never know what happened to Heather Manning, but with you on the case, I have every confidence we'll find out what's happened to her daughter."

Jess winced. Moisture rushed to the backs of her eyes,

but she refused to let it seep forward. "I want her to be okay so damn badly."

Uncle Ben put a hand to her shoulder. "You can't control that. You can only control the effort you put into the case, how hard you try." His eyes gentled, and his smile turned sage. "It's time to lay the past to rest. It's time to come full circle. You can do it, too. I know you can. Find that man's daughter. End the hostility."

Jess forced a smile, but deep inside, she wept. The tension would never ease, not even if she found Emily Armstrong alive and well. The last time a Clark crossed paths with William Armstrong, the repercussions had lasted over fifteen years, beyond even the grave.

Instinct warned this time the fallout would last even longer, extend far deeper.

"Of course," she said with a brittle smile. "I'll give him my all."

The house was dark. Only one light shone from an upstairs window. The skeletal branches of an old post oak extended across the golden glow, swaying with the wind, but they didn't obscure Liam's view. He sat in his car, waiting. Watching.

For what, he wasn't sure.

He should leave. Liam knew that. Voyeurism wasn't his style, but that awareness hadn't made him crank up the engine thirty minutes before, and it didn't now. Just a few more minutes, he told himself. Then he would drive away.

In the back seat, Molly whimpered. She was a good dog, loyal and patient, but she clearly knew something was not right. She missed Emily, and Liam knew he wasn't helping matters. The tension radiating from him was enough to choke a horse, much less a dog. He probably shouldn't have dragged her out on this late-night crusade, but she'd looked at him with those soulful chocolate eyes of hers, and he'd been unable to turn his back on her and just walk away. So here he was, sitting in a darkened car, an antsy Labrador retriever in the back seat, staking out the condo of the lead detective assigned to his daughter's case.

He really had lost his mind.

"It's okay, girl," he told her. "Daddy's going to make everything better, you'll see."

Focused on his daughter's dog, he almost missed the shadow move across the glow of the window. The slender silhouette was fleeting, graceful and one hell of a call to arms.

Detective Jessica Clark was home, and she was awake.

Leave, he told himself again, but instead opened the door and stepped into the cold night. "Come on, girl," he said, taking Molly's leash and leading her onto the concrete. She'd been alone enough recently. He couldn't leave her in the car while he had a word or two with the enigmatic detective.

He hadn't heard from Jessica all day. Not even a phone call. He had a right to know what was going on, he thought, as he led the dog to the door. He had a right to updates.

And if Detective Jessica Clark wouldn't give him one on her own, then by God, he'd get one his way.

He raised a fist to knock on the solid wood door, found himself pounding instead. Loudly. Forcefully. The words *open up* almost tore from his throat, but he wasn't a cop, and this wasn't a raid.

Through a nearby window he saw a light come on downstairs, then another. He resisted the urge to step aside and look inside. He didn't want her to have advance warning of his identity. He wanted to see her expression when she opened the door. Or if she demanded to know who was there first, he wanted to hear her voice when he announced himself. There was truth in initial reactions, and even a trained detective couldn't completely hide the slight flaring of her eyes, the catch to her voice.

The door swung open, and Detective Jessica Clark greeted him with her arms crossed over her chest. "Good evening, Liam."

Something inside him lightened at the simple sight of her, and he realized he suddenly felt more okay than he had all day.

She didn't look the least bit surprised to see him. Nor did she look suitable for visitors. Nor did she look like a cop. Her hair was twisted off her face, her cheeks flushed. She wore only a leopard-print silk robe that revealed the arch of her collarbone and the indentation of her waist. The swell of breasts beneath silky fabric invited a man to wonder if anything else lay beneath. Even her feet were bare. A light musky fragrance clung to her scantily clad body like a cloud of temptation.

Liam bit back a strangled groan of surprise.

And that's when it hit him. Detective Jessica Clark was a beautiful, desirable, passionate woman. She was dressed for bed.

She might not be alone.

Chapter 10

"Are you standing on my doorstep in the middle of the night for a reason?" Jessica asked, much as he had the night before when she led him to the mirror in the foyer. "Or are you in the mood for another game? I've always favored chess myself, but you strike me more as a poker man."

Just like that, the weight on his heart lightened. He looked at her standing there in that skimpy robe and wondered how she did it. She looked as soft as a dewy rose petal on a spring morning, but instinct warned that if he didn't tread carefully, he'd find thorns beneath the beauty.

He hadn't come here to bleed.

"I didn't hear from you today," he said gruffly.

She met his gaze. "I told you I'd call if anything changed. Nothing has."

But something had. And like last night when he'd shattered the line between them, Liam stood between two temperature extremes. The coldness at his back, the warmth inside Jessica's condo.

His gaze dipped over the body she usually hid behind boxy suits, then returned to her face. "Do you always answer the door half-naked?"

She lifted her chin. A slight smile played at her lips. "Does it matter?"

"Just doesn't seem very smart to me."

"I'm a detective, Liam. I knew who was standing on the other side, and I knew you were here for the cop, not the woman. I figured how I'm dressed didn't matter."

Her voice was low and throaty, infuriatingly indifferent. It was the *woman's* voice, he realized. Coming from the *woman's* body, in the *woman's* home.

Just like a cop to vanish when you needed one the most.

"Does it matter, Liam?"

He looked into her eyes, knew he was safer concentrating on her face, not her body. "Not in the least bit."

Something shockingly close to disappointment flickered in the amber depths of her gaze. She glanced at Molly, sitting patiently at his heels. "Out for a late-night walk? Aren't you a bit far from home?"

Again, he bit back the urge to laugh, not sure how the hell she kept diffusing him. "She misses Emily," he said, rubbing a hand along the dog's head. "I didn't think it was fair to leave her home alone."

Jessica went down on a knee to cup the dog's face. She rubbed her thumbs along Molly's snout, then stroked her silky ears. "You changed her bandanna," she murmured, fingering the burgundy fabric covered with gold angels.

Liam frowned. Detective Jessica Clark was entirely too observant. She was also entirely too distracting down on the floor with Molly, giving him a glimpse of her cleavage. "I found one Emily had laid out, figured it was what she'd want."

Jessica pushed to her feet. She looked him in the eye,

her expression suddenly fierce. "She's coming home, Liam. I promise you. We're going to find your daughter."

He bit back a blast of emotion. "She's all I have."

"I know," she said softly, holding his gaze. "I know."

The compassion in her eyes sent a surprising shot of warmth cascading through him. He wanted her to touch him in other ways, he realized grimly. Deeper. Longer lasting.

"You must be freezing," he said. She wore only the skimpy robe, and here he was, standing in her doorway while the night air hovered in the low thirties.

Jessica's expression turned somber. "Not with you standing there." She glanced beyond him, then over her shoulder into the condo. "Would you like to come in for a few minutes? I could make some hot cocoa."

The offer surprised him. She was always doing that, showing him consideration when he deserved contempt. "I'd like that very much."

She stepped back and ushered man and dog inside. "You can wait in there," she said, gesturing to the living room. "I just need a few minutes."

Liam glanced at the inviting cream-colored sofa, the glass table in front of it, the large aquarium across the room. It was all very feminine, very cozy; there was nothing coplike about the room lit only by the light of a single Tiffany lamp. "Nice place," he commented.

"Thanks."

He looked toward Jessica, found her watching him with curiously speculative eyes. Decked out in that silken robe with her hair pulled from her face, a few strands scraggling against her cheeks, she looked dangerously tempting in this feminine sanctuary. "Aren't you going to get dressed?"

She glanced at her robe, at him. "What's the matter, granite man?" she asked with a wry smile. "Don't know how to handle yourself around a half-dressed woman?"

The taunt brought a slow smile to Liam's lips. Not one

to be cornered, he let his gaze dip over the curves of her body, all the way to her burgundy-painted toenails. Heat flashed through him, and he realized how much time had passed since he'd savored the sight of a woman's body. She looked soft, smelled inviting. He felt himself stiffen and quickly raised his gaze, only to stall on her breasts. They were larger than he'd realized, the swell of creamy flesh just visible above the silk of her robe.

Liam bit back a groan and abruptly found her face. She looked flushed, startled, as though he'd been skimming her flesh with his hands, not his gaze.

The pleasure he found in her reaction pushed him closer to the edge. "Challenging me again, Detective?"

Her eyes sparked. "And if I am?"

If she was, he was in big trouble. "Go get dressed. I don't need to be charged with harassing an officer."

A smile broke on her lips, and she laughed. It was a rich, provocative sound, that of a lover, not a cop. "No," she said, "that you don't." With that, she turned and vanished up the stairs, leaving Liam staring after her, wondering what the hell had just gone down between them.

Leave, he again told himself. *Just walk out the door before she comes back downstairs.* Instead, he led Molly into the kitchen and pulled open the refrigerator.

By the time Jessica came downstairs wearing an oversize SMU sweatshirt and faded jeans, he was sitting on her sofa with two steaming cups of hot cocoa waiting on the glass table. Molly lay on her side by the aquarium.

The unflappable detective stopped dead in her tracks. Surprise flooded her eyes, and her mouth fell open.

And Liam wanted to smile. Once, he'd enjoyed stripping away her cool, calm, collected facade through taunts, but now he found greater pleasure in doing so by extending a morsel of goodwill rather than the antagonism she expected.

"I couldn't find an olive branch," he explained. "I'm afraid hot chocolate will have to do."

"An olive branch?"

"You were right last night." He found he needed to tell her. "We're on the same side. It's time I start treating you that way, giving you the respect you deserve."

Her eyes narrowed, and he realized she was too smart, too thorough, to take his words at face value.

"No games." He extended a cup of steaming cocoa to her. "Just an honest peace offering."

She stepped closer, eyed the mug. "You're a brave man."

"Oh?"

"After last night, you're handing me hot liquid? Some would consider that a weapon."

"Some would," he agreed.

"And you?"

"I'll take my chances, see if Lady Justice believes in innocent until proven guilty, after all."

A soft laugh broke from her throat. "Ah, there he is."

"There's who?"

She crossed to him and sat by his side, took the hot chocolate from his hands. Her amber eyes were alive, vibrant.

"Innocent until proven guilty? Honest motives may have led you to make this," she said as she took a slow sip, "but you didn't hesitate to resort to tactics when I didn't immediately accept your offer." She lowered the mug to her lap and wrapped her hands around it. "You can try on a sheep's clothing all you like, Liam, but we both know the wolf will always be inside."

His admiration for her ratcheted up another few notches. Not only was she beautiful, but smart and gutsy, determined. Challenges didn't deter her; they spurred her on.

"I was going over my notes today," she said after taking

another sip. This time she put the mug on the coffee table. "Do you know how to contact Emily's mother?"

The deceptively casual question pierced the cozy intimacy, and too late, Liam realized his error. He'd let the lateness of the hour, the intimacy of his surroundings, seduce him into relaxing. Jessica Clark may have been all woman when she answered the door, but with a simple change of clothes, the detective was back.

How like a cop to show up when they were least wanted.

"If you're interested in Heather, you'll have to ask her parents."

"They think she's dead."

"And you?"

"No body was ever found. I can't help but wonder if Emily's disappearance is connected to the past. Could Heather have resurfaced, curious about her daughter? Could Emily be with her?"

"Emmie's not with her mother," he said point-blank.

"How do you know? By your own testimony, Emily's mother walked out on you and her infant daughter, leaving everything in her possession behind, never to be seen from again. She could be anywhere. How do you know she hasn't resurfaced?"

Liam went on red alert. Less than five minutes before he'd been admiring this woman's intelligence. Now her clever line of questioning made his blood run cold. He didn't like to talk about that long-ago time, nor did he like to be backed into a corner.

So much for the olive branch.

Very deliberately, he placed his mug on the coffee table, when in truth he wanted to hurl it against the wall.

Then he looked Detective Jessica Clark dead in the eye. "We were just kids having fun. We weren't in love. We weren't ready for commitment or parenthood, especially

Heather." He spoke slowly, clearly, deliberately. "She wanted to give my child away. To strangers. Forever."

The memory, the knowledge of how close he'd come to losing Emily, sent a chill through him. "I offered to give her the world. I offered to make her my wife. Instead, she had adoption papers drawn up without my consent."

Jessica drew a pale hand to the lips he'd kissed the night before. "Oh, Liam," she said softly.

"She was a lost soul," he went on, reliving the darkest time of his life. He'd never talked about it before. "She was desperate. She didn't want a child. She wasn't ready. She didn't want to lose her freedom." The old rage boiled within him, stronger than ever. "She'd had a bad childhood—her father was a powerful man, tried to plan her life for her, even picked out a boy to marry. She rebelled. That's what I was to her. A way of defying her father. But then all the fun and games ended when she found out she was pregnant—she was terrified about her father's reaction. I practically had to lock her away to make sure she didn't do anything rash."

Frowning, Jessica lowered her hand from her mouth and placed it over his. "I'm sorry. I had no idea."

Her hand was soft yet cold, and Liam found himself resisting the urge to turn his palm toward hers, to lace their fingers. He'd never been a man for touching, didn't understand this sudden compulsion to do so.

"You mean that little tidbit wasn't in your father's files?" he asked, fighting himself as much as her.

"I knew you had a volatile relationship, that the cops had been called a few times for loud arguments—"

Temper flared. "Go ahead and ask me, Detective."

"Ask you what?"

"How I killed her. If she struggled. How a no-account nineteen-year-old outsmarted the entire department. Where I hid the body."

Jessica sighed. "Liam, don't."

He slid his hand from beneath hers and lifted it to her face, held her so she couldn't look away. "I did not kill that woman."

"I didn't say you did."

"But you wondered."

"Liam—"

"How do you think I felt, Detective? I was nineteen years old. I had an infant daughter to care for and a lynch mob breathing down my neck. No one wanted to believe the perfect Carson Manning's daughter would abandon her own child, her own life, so let's just blame it on the no-account who knocked her up. And while we're at it, let's take his kid from him, too. Did you know about that? Did you know that the esteemed congressman tried to take Emily from me? After screwing up his own daughter, he tried to take mine?"

Jessica's eyes darkened. Her hand against his thigh tightened. But she said nothing. She just looked at him, studied him, as though she could see beyond his words to some deeper truth inside.

Liam was not a patient man. He was not used to standing on the sidelines, watching the world go by. He was used to calling his own plays, executing them, ensuring the appropriate follow-through. But there was nothing he could do to make Detective Jessica Clark believe him.

And for some reason, her belief, her faith, mattered.

"I've hurt you," she whispered.

He didn't want her words to be true but realized they were. "This isn't about me."

She lifted a hand to remove his from her face. "I make my own judgments," she said, curving her palm around his knuckles. "I study the evidence, draw my own conclusions."

"And what does the evidence say, Lady Justice?"

"That you love your daughter with your whole heart. That even though you were no more than a child yourself when she came into your life, you've put your needs, your desires, aside in favor of hers."

"And what about her mother?"

Jessica's fingers tightened against the back of his hand. "She was a fool to turn her back on such an honorable man, an adorable daughter."

The conviction behind the words punched him in the heart. "You don't think I killed her?"

"You've done everything in your power to give your daughter a full life. It doesn't add up that you would have robbed her of a mother, no matter how undeserving the woman was."

Liam stared. Since the brutal night seventeen years before when he'd returned to find Heather gone, his daughter hungry and cold and crying, he'd faced down an entire police force, endured a town's scorn, clawed his way to the top, moved heaven and earth to make sure Emily never suffered. Never once had anyone, anything, undone him as powerfully as Jessica's belief in his innocence.

"Your daughter is a very lucky girl," she added.

He heard the bittersweet edge to her comment, the longing he knew could never be fulfilled. Animosity had always sparked between him and Wallace Clark, but now a deeper anger surfaced.

"And you?" He found himself asking. Worse, he found himself caring. "Did Wallace Clark's daughter consider herself a lucky girl, too?"

The light in her eyes dimmed. Her voice softened. "Dad was…complicated."

Liam turned his hand over so their hands were palm to palm and wove his fingers between hers. "Yes, he was."

"He was bigger than life to me," she added with a sad smile, "more like an action hero than a flesh-and-blood man. He loved me, he loved all of us, but you were right, what you said yesterday. That love didn't bring him home for dinner, or to my softball games. Not even to my high school graduation.''

For the second time in just a few days, Liam wished he'd been wrong. Work was important, but family was sacrosanct. ''The man was a fool.''

A sudden rush of moisture glistened in Jessica eyes. She blinked furiously, turned away from Liam and toward the aquarium. ''He did the best he could. That's all you can ask of anyone.''

He followed her gaze to the watery world across the room, illuminated only by a soft blue light. Several angelfish hovered around a wispy green plant, while a school of neon fish darted from side to side.

''Spend a lot of evenings like this, do you, Jessica? Alone in the dark, watching your fish?''

He heard her sharp intake of breath. ''They help me relax. They're a good distraction.''

''From what?''

''The world, I suppose.'' She glanced at Liam and smiled. A single strand of hair had slipped from the twist, drawing his attention to her mouth as she talked. ''They're innocent, you know? Graceful. Hypnotic. It's hard to think about greed and murder, abuse and neglect, when I'm watching them.''

Liam still held her hand in his and couldn't resist the urge to stroke his thumb against her palm. She seemed to need the human touch every bit as much as he did.

''Why do you do it?'' he asked, and again realized he cared.

''Watch the fish? I just told you.''

''No,'' he said, extending his stroking beyond her hand and to her wrist. ''Police work. Why do you do something that tears you apart on a daily basis? Why do you expose yourself to so much ugliness?''

She paled, as though he'd just peeled away a bandage, exposing the tender flesh beneath. ''It's who I am.''

''No, it's not, Jessica. It's who your father was. You're an intelligent, compassionate woman who deserves to see more than the dark side of human nature.''

He caught the telltale flare of her amber eyes a second before she glanced toward the aquarium.

Liam wasn't about to let her get away quite so easily. With his index finger he turned her face toward his, and their eyes met. The punch of need caught him by surprise. He felt like a parched man, she a glistening spring. But she wasn't innocent or fresh, wasn't water. She was amber whiskey, drugging, addictive, dangerous to a man on the edge. The compassion in her husky voice, the intelligence and vulnerability in her healing eyes, they called to him on a primal level he had a hard time resisting.

''I was out of line last night,'' he told her. Regret rubbed at him. ''I know you're just trying to help.''

She blinked, looked more unsure than he'd ever imagined possible. ''You're not yourself right now. I understand that.''

Liam couldn't help it. He laughed. ''But that's just it. I *am* myself right now. Hard, driven and like you said, manipulative.'' He'd looked in the mirror every day of his life, but it hadn't been until she forced him to do so and he saw their faces side by side that he felt shame at the man he'd let himself become. ''I am a bastard, Jessica, and I've never once wished I was any other way.''

Her eyes filled, but she said nothing.

Liam fought the dangerous urge to pull her into his arms and hold on tight. ''I never wished I was any other way,'' he said again, ''until I met you. When I see myself through your eyes, suddenly I don't like who I see very much at all.''

"Liam—"

He pressed two fingers to her mouth, the lips he'd kissed last night and wanted to taste again now. "Don't say anything. Just know that I'm sorry for the way I've treated you. Every time I see you, I think to myself, there she is. Wallace Clark's daughter. But every time you walk away, I realize that you're your own woman, one hell of a woman at that.''

She looked at her arm where his hand continued to stroke the inside of her wrist.

He wanted to tilt her face toward his but knew he was dangerously close to drowning in her eyes. "You're sitting there wondering how much of what I'm saying you can believe. You're wondering if I'm being sincere or manipulating you in some way.''

She looked up abruptly. "Can you blame me?"

"Not at all. It's one of the traits I admire most about you. You take nothing at face value.''

"A cop who wants to stay alive can't afford to.''

"Neither can a woman who doesn't want her heart broken.'' The words freed themselves before he could stop them.

Alarm flashed in her gaze. "Liam—"

"Has anyone other than your father ever broken it, Jessica? Have you ever let anyone that close?"

She pulled her arm away from his hand and offered a quirky smile. "I'm the cop here, Armstrong. I ask the questions.''

She also erected walls as fast as he could chip away at them. "I didn't think so.''

The light drained from her eyes. "It's late," she said, standing. "Perhaps you should get Molly home."

He looked at his daughter's dog, sleeping across the

room. She lay on her stomach with her back paws stretched out behind her, her front paws crossed in front of her, her head resting on them. She looked shockingly peaceful.

"Come on, girl," he called. Molly slowly opened her chocolate eyes, and with great protest, rolled to her paws and stretched.

Jessica crossed to her, stooped and ran her hands over the dog's head, her soft floppy ears. "You're a good girl," she cooed. "Take care of your daddy for me."

The sight of Jessica with his dog, the longing in Molly's liquid eyes, made Liam's chest tighten. It really was time to go.

"Come on," he said, heading for the door. After another leisurely stretch, the dog ambled over.

Jessica joined them, wasting no time opening the front door and letting in a blast of cold.

Liam knew she wanted him to leave but lifted a hand to her soft face instead. He loved the feel of her skin, the way her eyes went wide at his touch.

"I've never missed one of Emily's track meets," he murmured, because somehow it seemed important. He knew she saw the similarities between himself and her father. He wanted her to see the differences, too. "Not a single one."

Her expression softened, turned bittersweet. The light in her eyes became more of a glisten. "We'll get her back," she said, pushing up on her toes and brushing her lips along his. "I promise you that."

Liam went very still. Last night their mouths had met in anger, maybe even challenge. But nothing hard underscored this slide of lips. Only compassion and promise, honesty.

God help him, he wanted to drink in more. He wanted to fold his arms around this special woman, immerse himself in her, take all she had to offer, give back even more.

She was an amazing woman, Jessica Clark was. He wanted to press her to his heart and hold on tight. He wanted to put his mouth to hers and absorb all she had to give. He kept coming back to the dangerous thought that she would miraculously make everything better.

Everything.

The thought ground through him. He hated hanging his future, his daughter's well-being, on someone else. Especially a cop. Especially Wallace Clark's daughter.

He wasn't a man who relied on others.

There was the danger. In Jessica's fathomless whiskey eyes, he found a glowing promise that lit the darkest corners of his heart. If he stayed in her cozy condo any longer, if the conversation deepened any further, he risked crossing a dangerous line and ending up in a place that would crater them both. Her bed.

He'd always prided himself on being a good father, but the ridiculous thoughts needling through him made him wonder. What the hell kind of man was he?

He knew the answer. He just didn't like it.

Pulling back abruptly, he stepped deeper into the night. "I've got to go."

"Yes," she said with a punishing punch of acceptance. "I know you do."

But still…he hesitated.

"It's for the best," she added. "We both know that."

The urge to crush her in his arms almost toppled him. Instead, he took her fine-boned hand in his and squeezed. "I was wrong last night. You *are* a smart woman."

Her eyes widened, revealing something dangerously close to yearning. Then she blinked and lifted her chin. "I'm a cop, Liam. And I'm going to give you back your daughter."

Because he wanted to lift her in his arms and carry her upstairs, he barked out something gruff, then released her hand and walked into the cold of night. He'd said all along the only thing he wanted from Detective Jessica Clark was the one thing she'd promised to give him. His daughter.

And yet, as he slid into his car and sped into the night, he couldn't destroy the feeling of hollowness deep inside, the one that spread like an oil spill in a marine preserve, the one he found relief from only in the presence of Wallace Clark's daughter and those amazing, assuring eyes of hers.

The old man had to be laughing in his grave.

Liam was a firm believer in life coming full circle, but never in a million years could he have imagined such a cruel, cruel twist.

Payback really was hell.

Jess closed the door against the cold night and hugged her arms around her midsection. Emotion surged through her, making her body feel alive, on fire. Humming with desire. She'd never wanted to kiss a man so damn badly. Never wanted to feel his mouth come down hard on hers. Never wanted to press her body to his and lose herself in his touch. Never feared she was about to explode like a Roman candle against a night sky.

God help her, she was in too deep.

William Armstrong wasn't just intricately linked to one of her cases and he wasn't just the man her father would have given anything to lock away. He was a man who'd built his whole life by keeping the world at arm's distance, a man who'd trained himself to never let anyone too close, never give more of himself than meager crumbs he could live without.

He was the kind of man who broke a girl's heart without even trying.

She crossed to the sofa and sat, picked up the cocoa Liam had made for her. Her first sip had been steaming hot, but now it was cold, much like she was. She drew it to her lips anyway and sipped deeply. Even cool, the flavor was dark and sumptuous, enticing, much like the man who'd stood at her stove warming milk, then adding just the right amount of chocolate.

Her throat tightened, and moisture rushed to her eyes. She wasn't a woman to cry, couldn't believe she'd almost done so in front of William Armstrong. *Be strong,* she told herself. *Focus on the case, not the father.*

She didn't have room in her life for a man who guarded his time like a prison warden. She wouldn't go down that road again. She wouldn't subject herself to that cutting disappointment, the waiting, the stolen moments, the awareness that she was never a priority, that something else always came first.

She shook herself. The man had dedicated his life to his daughter. He was worried sick about her disappearance. How could Jessica fault him for that? How could she condemn a father willing to move mountains to find his baby girl?

She couldn't. But she couldn't afford to step any farther over the line, either. She couldn't get involved on a personal level, let herself want anything from him. She could only do her job, and that meant exploring the past, whether Liam wanted her to or not.

After yet another sleepless night, Jess stepped out of the shower and ran a thick Egyptian cotton towel along her shivering body. She absolutely refused to imagine Liam's hands instead, what they might feel like skimming down her belly and along her inner thighs—

Stop it, she admonished herself, then caught sight of her face in the foggy bathroom mirror. She leaned closer and wiped away the condensation, stared at her pale cheeks, the dark smudges beneath her eyes. She'd worked around the clock before. She'd gone without sleep more times than she cared to remember. But she couldn't remember a time she'd looked so haggard, not even during the final days at the academy.

Frowning, she slipped into her silk robe and raised a comb to her damp, tangled hair. She was still fighting with it when the phone rang.

Adrenaline rushed. The sun had yet to come up. The hour was well before six.

This was not a social call.

Emily.

She ran into her bedroom and grabbed the handset from the nightstand. "Clark here."

"Mornin, Jess." The words came in an easy drawl. "Didn't wake you, did I?"

The room started to spin, and her heart flat-out stopped. She knew that slow voice, always wondered how its owner could sound so unaffected in light of the grimness he faced on a daily basis. "Phil? That you?"

"'Fraid so, hon. McKnight wanted me to give you a call. We just had a body brought into the morgue, found down near the Trinity River."

Jess sank onto her unmade bed. Dread turned her blood to ice. "And?"

"She was a pretty thing, looks to be a young white female, probably in her late teens. Brunette. Blue eyes. Died hard. McKnight thought she might be yours."

Chapter 11

Jess splashed cold water against her face and tried to breathe. Her throat burned; her stomach churned.

Emily.

Dread lanced through her. She glanced up and caught her reflection in the mirror, tried not to cringe. She couldn't go to Liam like this, couldn't let him see her pale skin and bloodshot eyes. Couldn't let him see the nasty fear lurking in her gaze. She had to pull herself together and be strong for him, had to be rock steady. Even if her heart was breaking.

"Please, God," she said aloud. "Please don't let it be her."

She had to reach Liam before someone else did. She needed to be the one to tell him. She didn't want him hearing it from Kirby, or God forbid a reporter. She didn't want to call him, either, not when she knew what the news would do to him. No matter how much she hated the thought of doing so, she needed to tell him in person.

Her heart raced as she hurriedly dressed and ran out the door. She forced herself to breathe deeply as she drove, searched for the right words, just how to tell a father his daughter might be in the morgue.

They wouldn't form.

How could they? How could words exist to tell a man the light of his life might be permanently extinguished?

By the time Jess stopped her car in front of Liam's house, the first rays of the morning sun streaked across the eastern sky. Splashes of yellow and peach promised a new day, a new beginning. The nasty irony made her blood run even colder.

She glanced at the imposing stone fortress Liam had built for his daughter and braced herself. He was in there. Maybe sleeping, maybe just waking up, maybe preparing to take Molly for a run. The man who'd looked so tenderly into her eyes last night had no idea of the grim news awaiting him.

A fleeting thought of the night before flashed through her, of the fragile bond they'd forged. My God, she thought. If things had gone a little differently, if she and Liam weren't such cautious people, he could well have ended up spending the night in her bed. Which meant he would have been there when the call came. Maybe even making love with her.

The thought unsettled her.

She pushed open the car door and started up the walkway. The insistent northern wind cut through her, making her realize she'd forgotten her coat.

The cobblestone seemed to elongate with each step she took. Her breathing turned choppy. Dead man walking, she thought grimly, but knew *she* was the executioner, the man strapped in the electric chair someone she couldn't bear hurting. He'd suffered enough.

Finally, she reached the door and rapped her numb fist

against the hard wood. Nothing. An interminable second dragged by before she knocked harder, louder. Then she reached for the bell, heard its deep chime echo through the house.

She hated the thought that he might still be sleeping.

At last footsteps sounded on the marble inside, and she braced herself. God help her, she'd never dreaded anything more. She took a deep breath as the door opened, knowing what the next few minutes would hold.

Marlena Dane stared wildly at her. "Detective Clark, thank God you're here."

Jess went very still. Her heart staggered. She took in Liam's former lover standing there, wearing red silk pajamas and an open black robe, and feared she might be ill. Of all the possibilities she'd imagined, finding Marlena here was not one of them. It simply hadn't occurred to her that Liam would leave her last night with the taste of her lips on his and turn to Marlena.

But it should have. She was the detective assigned to find William Armstrong's daughter, nothing more.

The bitter splash of reality burned and scraped, shredded.

"Marlena." She managed to speak. "I need to see Liam."

"He'll be out in a minute."

"It's important," Jess added.

"Let me go see what's keeping him," the flushed woman said, then turned and vanished down the hall.

Emotion crammed its way into Jess's throat, her heart, making breathing difficult. She couldn't believe what a fool she'd been, what a dangerous path she'd let her thoughts race down.

Numbly, she looked around the foyer. The mirror she'd forced Liam to look into no longer hung above the marble-top table. A stack of flyers sat on the shiny black surface,

Emily's picture smiling up at her. The word *reward* stood out.

"You had no right to answer the door." Jessica heard Liam's harsh voice from the back of the house. "You shouldn't even be here, damn it."

"I was worried," Jess heard Marlena say. "Mr. St. Clair said he needed to talk to you but couldn't find you. I couldn't imagine where you could be, thought maybe—"

"That I'd fallen apart?" Liam growled. "So you rushed over to save the day? I was in the shower, damn it. St. Clair had no right to call you. I've already told him that."

Relief pulsed through Jess, so pure and profound, for a gossamer moment, she forgot why she stood in Liam's foyer in the first place. He hadn't invited Marlena over. He didn't want her here. He hadn't shared his bed with her, his body, while Jess lay alone in the darkness, longing for something that could never be.

"It's not her, damn it."

Liam's low growl stabbed through her, and she blinked to see him striding toward her, all tall and forbidding. His eyes were wild, the planes of his face harsh. His dark hair was damp, his jaw unshaven. He looked capable of tearing someone apart with his bare hands. And the truth cut her to the quick.

He already knew.

She swallowed, hard. "Liam—"

"My private detective already told me about the girl by the Trinity River, and I'm afraid you're wasting your time every bit as much as Marlena wasted hers rushing over here to check on me. That girl is not my daughter."

Her heart beat harder, faster. "Have you heard from her?" she asked, hopeful. "Did she call? Is she home?"

Liam stopped mere inches from where she stood. "She's not here, but she's not there, either."

Jess braced herself, realizing Liam's words were rooted

in faith and hope, a parent's undying love for a child. Not fact. She looked at the granite man standing so close, at the harsh set to his jaw and the severe lines at the corners of his eyes, and realized how close to the edge he was teetering. He knew about the girl found overnight. He knew she was dead. He knew she could be his daughter, even if he refused to voice the possibility.

Never in her life had Jess wanted to touch someone more, to fold her arms around another human being and hold on tight. But she also knew Liam wouldn't accept sympathy from her. He didn't want her compassion, didn't know what to do with it.

He only wanted her to do her job, even if doing so ripped her heart into shreds.

"Liam," she said as levelly as she could, "I know this is hard for you, but we need you to come downtown, to look—"

"No. There's no reason for me to go to the morgue. My daughter is alive."

"I want to believe that, too, but until we go—"

He took her hand and drew it to his chest, splaying her open palm against the gray cotton of his Henley shirt. "She's here, damn it, I can feel her. She's not on some cold slab."

Jess bit back a sob but could do nothing about the tearing deep inside. Beneath her fingertips she felt Liam's heart beating hard and true, so unlike the frenetic pounding of her own. It was breaking in two, and there was nothing she could do to stop it. "We have to be sure."

"I am sure."

"Liam—"

"Why are you doing this?" he rasped. All tall like that, with whiskers darkening his jaw and those midnight-blue eyes glittering, he looked like he stood face-to-face with his own personal Judas. "I didn't take you for the kind of woman to enjoy turning a grown man inside out. Are you trying to see how much I can take without snapping in two?''

The words were harsh, the pain behind them unbearable. It slammed into Jess, knocked the breath from her lungs. She knew he was lashing out but also knew nothing she could say, nothing she could do, would ease his anguish. The depth of his torment was too great, the strands of the bond they'd forged the night before too tenuous.

''This isn't about you and me, Liam. It's about your daughter. Coming here this morning is the hardest thing I've ever done,'' she told him honestly. Emotion scratched at her. Only a few hours before she and this man had shared tender moments—stolen moments—but the memory of them prompted her to speak honestly, as a woman to a man, not a cop to a—

She could think of no word to describe her relationship with William Armstrong.

''Standing here, seeing the pain in your eyes…'' She swallowed against the thickening of her throat and resisted the urge to push up on her toes and lay her hand against his face. ''I want to help you, damn it! I want Emily alive. But what I want doesn't change the fact there's a young girl down at the morgue, and she could be—''

''She's not.''

Frustration tore through Jess. He was a strong man, the kind who shoved everything deep inside. The possibility Emily could be dead was too awful to consider, so he simply wasn't.

She glanced at Marlena standing quietly in the doorway to the dining room, then she laid a hand against Liam's arm. ''I'll go with you,'' she said gently but firmly. ''I'll be with you every step of the way.''

He stared at her fingers against his flesh. ''No.''

''Liam, *please*.''

He pulled away and grabbed the stack of Emily's pictures from the console table. "We're wasting time," he said flatly as he turned and strode away. "I've got flyers to post, and you've got my daughter to find."

She followed him down the hall and grabbed his arm as he entered the darkened kitchen. "Ignoring the situation won't change anything. I know you're hurting—"

He swung toward her. "I'm not ignoring anything."

"I hope to hell and back you're right," she said, alarmed by his refusal to consider the possibility. This was one situation he couldn't change through sheer force of will. "Come with me. That's the only way we can make this awful cloud go away."

He tore away from her. "Go if you want to, Detective, but leave me out of it." He grabbed a set of keys from the counter, hesitated. "Last night was a mistake. I should never have gone to you. I don't know why I did. The lines are too tangled as it is. You shouldn't come here again, not unless you've found my daughter and are bringing her with you."

Jess watched the door slam behind him, and the tears broke free. She didn't try to stop them. She'd never seen a human in so much pain, and having it be Liam only made it worse. She didn't understand the draw she felt toward him, the compulsion to reach out. The man was used to willing things into being, but he couldn't will his daughter into coming home and he couldn't will that body into not being Emily's.

"He's not worth your tears, Detective."

She glanced back to find Marlena in the doorway. "He's hurting."

"If he is, it's the first time in his life, which probably only makes him more dangerous. What is it they say about a wild animal in pain?" Sadness tinged Marlena's voice. Moisture glazed her eyes. "I was scared half out of my mind when that private detective called, unable to reach Liam. But did you hear how that man talked to me? He couldn't have cared less that I raced over here to check on him.''

Jess realized Marlena still had feelings for Liam, feelings he didn't return. She hated to think how badly that must sting. She and Liam had only shared a few embraces and a couple of kisses, and already she'd lain restless in her bed last night. She couldn't imagine being his lover, having him in her bed, in her body, then having nothing at all.

Stolen moments, she thought again. That's all he had to give. "I'm sorry."

The other woman pulled her robe tighter and withdrew a set of keys from her leather purse. "Now he's turned his back on you, too. I'd warn you again not to fall in his trap, but I can see you're already there. I'm real sorry, too. I know how it feels to be cast aside by William Armstrong, to be discarded like nothing more significant than an old beer can. Keep your eyes open, Detective, or you run the risk of slipping and falling even further. Trust me, it's a long, hard climb out.''

"Cause of death appears to be strangulation. The girl put up a fight, though. We've got skin under her nails.''

Jess looked away from Kirby to the overflowing file sitting atop her cluttered desk. A picture of Emily and Liam awaited her there, father and daughter in hiking gear somewhere in the Rocky Mountains. They looked so happy. So alive.

"I'm going to send a car to pick up Armstrong," Kirby said. They stood in the belly of the detective bullpen, already humming with activity despite the fact the clock had yet to reach nine. "We need him to make an ID. There was nothing on or with the body.''

Jess fought the emotion tightening her chest. She had a

job to do. She had to remain objective. But the thought of a squad car picking up Liam and driving him to the morgue, of an unknown, uncaring person forcing him to look at that body, ripped her up inside. Among those on the force, too many still believed he'd gotten away with murder. Too many would enjoy watching him fall apart.

Kirby among them. "If Armstrong needs to be picked up, I'll get him."

"You already tried." For a change, Kirby looked compassionate. Child murders had a way of rattling even the most seasoned cop. "This time, more than your magic touch is needed, Jessie."

"What about the girl's clothes? A purse?" *Anything.* Anything that would spare Liam the gruesome task of seeing that body laid out on a sterile metal table.

"Nothing."

"It's not supposed to be like this," she said more to herself than Kirby. This part of the job never got any easier, the grim fact that sometimes good didn't always win. "She was so young, had such a bright future ahead of her."

Kirby rested a hand on her shoulder. "It might not be the Armstrong girl."

She glanced back. "But she was someone."

Kirby frowned. "I'm worried about you, Jessie. We've worked cases like this before, but I've never seen you this close to the edge. You need to pull back."

She didn't know how to tell him that was impossible. She didn't know how to tell him this case was different than any other. She didn't know how to tell him she'd fallen in love with the missing girl's father.

"I can't."

Kirby removed his hand, but the concern in his eyes sharpened. "It's Armstrong, isn't it? He's gotten to you."

"He's not the monster you think he is," Jess said simply. "He didn't kill Emily's mother."

"If he didn't kill her, then he ran her off. Because of him, her family, her friends never saw her again. How's that so different from murder? A life was lost all the same."

She gave him a brittle smile. It was the only kind she had left. "Broken relationships aren't a crime."

"Tell that to the people left to pick up the pieces."

Instinct warned Jess that Kirby's bitterness toward Armstrong had little to do with the case. It was a manifestation of his disappointments. His hurts.

"He loves his daughter, Kirb. She's his whole world." And though Jess had never met the vivacious Emily Armstrong, she felt a bond with the girl, an alliance that could only form between two females who'd grown up with strong fathers.

But whereas Wallace Clark's focus had been singular, Liam's included his daughter.

"Hey, Jess, K.L.!" Lieutenant Jason Ander ambled over, bagel in hand. "Phil just called. Said he should have a positive ID on that girl pretty quick."

Jess went very still. "Did they find something else?"

"Nah," the rookie said. "The dad just got there."

Somehow Liam made it through the door leading from the room where the body lay on a cold metal table. So beautiful, she was, even in death. Young, innocent, but she would never smile again. Never laugh.

Bile backed up in his throat. His legs shook. His heart barely beat. He glanced down the long corridor, saw the men's room and staggered toward it.

White floors, white walls. White door. Everything was so white. Shocking white. Sterile. Dead. The smell of disinfectant permeated every inch of the place, burning so deeply into Liam's senses he wasn't sure he'd ever smell again.

He pushed open the door and found another sea of endless white. The urinal, the sinks. Inside him. He'd never felt so cold in his entire life. Cold like death.

The room started to spin. A merry-go-round, like Emily had loved as a child. But this one was out of control. Faster. Faster. Off its axis. Sending everyone flying. Crashing.

A raw sound of anguish ripped from his throat as he made his way to the sink. He turned the water on full blast, cold, and slapped it against his face. Over. And over. Breathing hard, he glanced up and caught sight of himself in the mirror, realized he was sheet-white, too. All but his eyes. They were dark and decimated, indicative of some-place deep inside.

The pain cut sharper, deeper. He squeezed his eyes shut, not wanting to see, and hung his head. He'd never felt so gutted in his entire life.

"Liam."

He thought he heard his name, but the voice that carried it was soft and warm, and there was nothing soft or warm in this place.

"Liam."

He looked up and saw her reflected in the mirror like a vision. Pale, trembling, her beautiful amber eyes wide. A beacon through the fog. Her life, her energy stronger than the brightest star in the night sky.

Liam had never needed the light more.

Something ragged tore from his throat as he turned to her. He wasn't sure who moved first, only knew she was across the room, then she was in his arms. *Hold her,* that's all he could think. *Hold her tight. Absorb her. Never let her go.*

"Oh, Liam," she cried, running her healing hands up his back and down his arms.

He buried his face in her hair and breathed in the clean scent of apples. On a groan, he held her tighter, drowning in the feel of her arms wrapped around him, the sounds of her soft, soothing words.

God help him, he'd never needed anyone more. Not just anyone, though. *Her.* Jessica. The woman with courage and fire, conviction, the woman who kept after him no matter how hard he pushed her away.

"Liam?"

He wanted to keep holding her, but something about her voice, the apprehension in it, made him pull back to see the question burning hot in her eyes.

"She was so beautiful." Somehow he got the words out. "Young. Innocent. All gone. *Gone.* Just like that."

"No." Her voice was barely more than a whisper. "No."

He lifted his hands to her pale face and cupped, smoothed the hair from her cheeks. Her eyes were wide and damp, devoid of pretense or defense, and in their amber depths, he found the lifeline he needed.

"I wanted to be here for you," she whispered. "I didn't want you to do this alone. I'm so sorry—"

He pressed his thumb to her lips. "That beautiful girl in there is some man's daughter, Jessie, and he'll never see her smile again, never hear her laugh."

A spark of hope flared in her gaze. "What are you saying?"

"Not Emily. Not my little girl."

For a heartbeat, he thought she hadn't heard him. She stood there staring at him. Then the purest smile he'd ever seen lit her face like a bright sunrise.

"Thank God," she whispered, then pushed up and wrapped her arms around his neck. She felt so right, pressed against his body. Somehow she made him feel like he wasn't alone.

Relief finally began to override the horror of seeing a young girl lying lifeless on the table. "I was so sure it wouldn't be her." He ground the words out, running his hands along her slender back. "I came here to get everyone off my case. But when I saw that table, the sheet lying over a body, it all became so real." He'd never felt more alone.

And his first thought had been of Jessica. He needed Jessica.

She pulled back and gazed at him. "It wasn't her, Liam. It wasn't her."

He'd held steadfast to the belief Emily was okay, that she would burst through the front door, smiling and laughing, and life would go on. "But it could have been her. I might never see my little girl again."

"She's still out there, and we're going to find her."

But for the first time in his life, Liam realized he couldn't make this better by sheer force of will. All the demands and threats, all the money in the world, wouldn't necessarily bring his daughter home. And all he could think of was Jessica. He needed Jessica. Not the detective, but the woman with the compassionate eyes and gentle touch. She spoke to him like no other, knew how to reach him when no one else did, made him want to believe. Made him want to be alive.

Made him want to make her his in every way imaginable, never let her go.

And that rocked him beyond imagining. What kind of man longed for a woman's smile, her touch, her embrace, when his daughter was missing?

The haze shattered, and Liam realized how far he'd let himself go. Appalled, he pulled back. "I have to go."

"I'll go with you. We can go back to your place—"

"No. Alone."

She went very still, almost as still as the body on that table. "It's okay to reach out. You don't have to climb every mountain by yourself."

But he did. He always had. It was the only way he knew.

"I appreciate your concern, but I meant what I said this morning. This thing between us can't go any further. I have to focus on Emily."

"Don't do this, Liam. Don't shut yourself away from the world."

Not the world. Just her. Because if he looked at her one second longer, at the entreaty in her gaze, he knew he'd pull her into his arms. And then he'd never be able to let her go.

"I have to," he said, then turned and strode from the bathroom.

She didn't follow.

Armstrong Worldwide IPO Soars Past Expectations.

Armstrong Secures New Licensing Agreement.

William Armstrong—The Toast Of The E-World.

The articles sent the blood pressure soaring, just like always. Didn't those journalists know what the man had done? Couldn't they see behind that king-of-the-world smile to the black heart inside? The heart of a man who ruined lives at will and never looked back to see, much less help restore, the debris?

Obviously not.

But that didn't matter. Those who needed to know the truth knew. Too well. For all of Armstrong's accomplishments, there were three things he'd yet to experience.

He hadn't suffered.

He hadn't paid.

He hadn't atoned for his sins.

But he would. Oh, yes. He would.

Across the room, the monitor revealed Emily Armstrong pacing the length of the Spartan room. She was an amazing girl. Her loyalty was almost admirable. How in the world had she sprung from Armstrong's seed? Maybe she had more of her mother in her then anyone realized.

"Emily." A quick press of the intercom button brought them into contact. "You really should get some rest."

She stopped and glared at the camera. "I want to talk to my father."

"You know that's against the rules."

"I don't care about your stupid rules. I care about my father. Just let me call him. Just for a minute."

That was impossible. Great lengths had been taken to make sure the girl felt as comfortable as possible, to make sure she wasn't afraid, but a phone call was out of the question. It would bring Armstrong too much relief. The man needed to suffer. He needed to know how it felt to be out of control. To be in the dark. He needed to know how it felt to hurt, to bleed. To lose.

And he would. But Emily didn't have to.

It was time to give the girl some company.

Five angelfish swam through the fronds of an underwater fern. Their movements were graceful, like an underwater ballet. Jess sat on her sofa, watching. She wasn't sure what time it was, only that the sun no longer shone. The bluish glow of the aquarium was the only light in her condo.

Deep inside, she hurt. She'd come home, showered and changed into her favorite flannel pajamas, but couldn't make the cold, sick feeling go away. No matter what she did, she couldn't destroy the image of Liam standing by himself in that sterile men's room, hands braced against the counter, head hung. The second she'd see him, her heart had stopped.

She'd thought the worst had come to pass.

Even now, the memory left her cold and shaky.

The investigation would go on. One note had already been sent, making it likely another would follow. Notes usually meant someone wanted something. The trick was finding out what.

William Armstrong was a powerful, enigmatic man. Many believed he'd gotten away with murder, but Jess knew he no more deserved that dark cloud than he deserved to lose his daughter. He'd pushed forward in the face of great adversity and given Emily the best childhood he could.

But a man didn't achieve what he had without making enemies. Her investigation proved that to be true, but she hadn't found anyone who really seemed to wish him ill. Taking a child was personal. What could that person want from Liam?

The question pierced deep. She knew the most likely answers. Money and revenge, but when she thought about wanting something from Liam, another answer kept nagging at her. Because deep in her heart, she knew what she wanted. Him. There with her. Holding her. Letting her hold him.

She'd been attracted before. She'd been in relationships. But never had a look into someone's eyes felt like fitting two pieces of a puzzle together. Never had a simple touch electrified every nerve ending. Never had the mere act of embracing someone stopped the breath in her throat.

Jess tried to concentrate on the fish but saw only the truth. It was the worst possible time for her heart to take an active role in her life. He was an anguished father. He could think of nothing but getting his daughter back, and here she was, practically daydreaming about walks down the beach, Sundays spent in bed, laughter.

Stolen moments, she knew. Dangerous thoughts for a woman responsible for finding William Armstrong's daughter. She should be more objective. She should be doing more, be on the streets, poring over case files, *making* something happen. The last thing she had any business doing was the only thing she couldn't seem to stop.

Loving Liam.

If she really wanted to help him, she needed to quit long-ing for the feel of his arms around her, the warmth of his body pressed to hers. She needed to realize she wasn't the magic potion he needed, a match to his darkness.

She needed to quit all that silly female stuff and do what she'd promised him she would. Find his daughter. Instinct warned that the past had finally caught up with them all. Tomorrow she would ask Carson Manning for a list of Heather's friends, find her father's old files.

Jess stood abruptly and strode to her kitchen, where she made a cup of hot cocoa. They were overlooking some-thing, she couldn't help but think, a key piece to the riddle. It was a damn good thing she'd never encountered a puzzle she couldn't solve, not even the new ones where she didn't know what picture she was trying to create until she created it.

A noise jarred her out of deep concentration. She jumped, realized someone was knocking on her door. Pounding.

"It's me, Jessica. Open the damn door."

Chapter 12

He stood on her doorstep, a man in a pair of jeans and a worn leather jacket, all tall and strong and alone. The sight of him hit Jess like a shot of whiskey straight up. Her body surged to life. Thoughts jumbled.

After the way they'd parted that afternoon, he was the last person she'd expected to see. With her heart raw and exposed, he was the last person she *should* see. But with need tearing through her, he was the only person she *wanted* to see.

She couldn't shut him out.

Standing in a pool of porch light, he looked tired, lost. The pain in his eyes knocked the breath from her lungs. It blazed and burned and beseeched, and Jess knew a fire could not rage so fiercely unless it came straight from the heart. The soul. He reminded her of a magnificent sequoia tree, but with the bark stripped away one painful ribbon at a time. Still standing, but depleted. Tortured.

If the wind blew hard enough, he might just topple.

Caution crashed up against longing. Instinct told her to open her arms and let him in, give him the embrace he so clearly needed. Prudence kept her standing on the inside of her condo, where it was warm, staring at him on the other side of the partially open door, where it was cold.

"Liam?"

A moment passed before he answered. A moment when he simply stared at her as though searching for the answer to some riddle on her face. Then he released a ragged breath.

"Am I still welcome?"

She heard the raw need in his voice, felt a like need tear through her. Everything inside her that was female reached for him, for this man who didn't know how to accept comfort. Her heart strained against better judgment.

Judgment lost. "Always," she said, opening the door wider and stepping into the cold night. "Always."

He reached for her. She reached for him.

They met somewhere in the middle.

His arms crushed her against his body. Strength was the first sensation, heat the next. The rich smell of sandalwood mixing with the leather of his jacket washed through her in a dizzying wave. She was acutely conscious of the feel of her face against the softness of his bomber jacket, her legs against his. She wanted to hold him like that but needed to see him even more.

Tilting her head to look, she barely had time to brace herself. The kiss was hot, all-consuming. His mouth took hers in a heady swirl of need and desire. A river could only be contained for so long, she realized in some hazy corner of her mind. Man-made constraints could only withstand so much pressure.

Nature always won.

For too long the force had been crashing against restraints, steadily chipping away. The intensity built. The urgency. The need. Now it broke through the barrier, everything else crumbled away, and the surge of inevitability overrode all else.

Jess knew no emergency patch job could tame this river. She didn't want it to.

His need cratered her. She was a strong woman. She'd faced down angry gang members and cold-blooded killers; she hadn't thought twice about storming a crack house. But Liam's need penetrated her defenses like nothing she'd ever experienced. His big body she could handle. His shield of anger didn't faze her. But his need…the depth of it, the rawness, made her feel like a rookie inching along a slender ledge at the top of a skyscraper, trying to talk a lost soul into not jumping. Drawn yet terrified at the same time.

"I thought you said no more late-night visits." She managed to speak against his demanding mouth. Part of her mourned saying the words, certain they would jar Liam to reality and end the passion between them. But no matter how easy it would be to lose herself in his kiss, she couldn't let desire override the obvious.

A man like William Armstrong wouldn't just break through her barriers, he would break her heart.

He pulled back and took her face between his big hands. "This isn't a visit."

"What is it then?"

"The hell if I know." He almost looked angry. "I tried to stay away from you, damn it. But I was home…and it was too damn quiet. Dark. I kept wondering where you were."

She swallowed. "You told me to stay away."

His eyes took on a feverish glow. "I've done a lot of stupid things in my life, and knowing they're wrong has never stopped me. This time I tried. So damn hard. But—"

"It's okay," she said, raising her hands to cup the back of his. "It's okay to reach out, to need someone."

He winced. "I've never wanted to."

"Then it's high time you start."

That seemed to startle him. He was quiet for a moment, almost looking more inside himself then at her. Then those piercing eyes of his returned to hers, and his hands slid from her face, taking her hair with them. His thumbs stroked along her cheekbones.

"What do *you* need?" he asked.

Somehow she stayed standing, even though the question made her knees go weak. She thought about lying but realized now was no time to start being a coward. "The same thing I want."

"That's not an answer."

"No, it's not, is it?" The truth stunned her. She wanted to give this man all she had. Once, the thought of doing so would have made her cringe, feel depleted. But in Liam's arms, she found that in giving of herself, he gave her even more.

"Then maybe this is." She returned her mouth to his for a kiss that was more hers than his. A heady sense of power and inevitability rushed through her as she slid her hands along the roughness of his jaw and into his thick hair. She loved the feel of him, the taste, the texture. He held her to his body with a seductive combination of strength and gentleness, as though she were both vital and priceless.

As though he never wanted to let her go.

She pulled back and tried to catch her breath, found she couldn't.

Confusion hardened his gaze. "Jess—"

"This, Liam. This." She took his hand and urged him into the warmth of her condo, then kicked the door shut behind him.

''It's cold out there,'' she whispered. The husky clip to her voice spurred her on. ''You need some heat.''

Awareness flashed in his eyes, sending a ribbon of female satisfaction unfurling through her. ''It's even warmer upstairs.''

Liam stood in the semidarkness. Across the room, the dim light of the moon filtered through gauzy, feminine curtains, providing enough illumination to see Jessica opening a drawer by the big bed. A second later he heard a faint scratching noise, then saw a flame flare against the darkness.

Candles, he realized. She was lighting candles. For him. *Get the hell out of here,* he told himself, but before he could, she turned to him and smiled. Her pajamas were old and obviously well-worn, some kind of green-and-blue tartan. The poets talked about a woman in silk, but nothing compared to Jessica in flannel. The V neckline bared her throat and collarbone, made him long to touch the creamy flesh there. Her thick, unruly hair tangled around her face. The light of the candle flickered in her bottomless eyes.

The sight stripped him bare.

She was so brave, so elemental. Like air and water. He found himself craving her smile, her touch, needing her like a tonic he could no longer go without.

He knew he should leave. Warning signs flashed everywhere. He should get the hell out of there while he still could.

''Liam,'' she said, and extended her hand, just like she'd done when leading him up the darkened staircase.

His body tightened. He wanted to destroy the distance between them and take what she was offering, but didn't. He wasn't sure she'd still be there if he did. Too easily, she could be a trick of the shadows. A smart man, a safe man, would turn and walk away before he got burned yet again.

But Liam couldn't do that, either.

He was so damn tired of standing on the outside looking in. He'd spent his whole life there, where it was dark. Cold. He'd seen the light inside, the warmth, but he'd never wanted to step over the threshold. Never known how. Until Jessica.

For the first time, he found himself wanting in.

He could still see her that moonless night not so long ago, facing him down at Braxton's house. There'd been no fear in her beautiful eyes, only a steely determination and ageless awareness he'd responded to instinctively.

"Why are you doing this, Jessica? You're a smart woman. You know you deserve better."

She lifted her chin, inviting the hair to fall from her face. "Better than what? A man capable of deep emotions and fierce loyalty? One who tries to do the right thing, even when that means denying himself what he wants most?"

She wore only flannel pajamas, but in the flickering light of the candle, she looked every bit as sure of herself as if she held a gun outstretched in her hands, as she had that first night. She might as well have, too. Her words pierced as deeply as a bullet.

He hated to be the one to shatter her illusions. "That man only lives in fairy tales, sweetheart."

"That's not true. He's standing right in front of me. He's the only one who could make me do this." Defiance flashed in her eyes as she raised her hands to her pajama top and slipped the top button through the fabric. Then the next. The next.

"Damn it, Jessica," he snarled, storming toward her.

She looked up and smiled. "What's the matter, granite man? Scared?"

He stopped dead in his tracks. For the first time in his

life, he knew how a rock must feel when someone took a jackhammer to it. Shards, debris, dust flew everywhere. Jessica just kept right on looking at him with those defiant eyes of her, her fingers working on the gold-covered buttons.

And then she flicked the fabric off her shoulders and let it slide down her body to pool at her feet.

Liam felt his knees go weak, his body stiffen.

That night in the bar, when she'd taken a fist meant for him and lay sprawled in his lap, dazed and unguarded, he'd realized she hid more under her boxy jackets than he'd thought. But even that insight hadn't prepared him for the sight of her standing in the flickering light of a candle, nude from the waist up.

Her beautiful shoulders gave way to her collarbone, inviting him to look lower. Her breasts…took his breath away. They were full and heavy with large dusky nipples. Nipples that were hard and puckered. Nipples he wanted to taste.

On a muffled oath he looked lower, down her beautifully flat stomach to where the pajama bottoms hung on her hips, just below the indentation of her waist. In one flick of his wrist he could have them down her long legs, see all of her at last.

He knew Jessica Clark in the nude would be a sight like none other.

And he wanted none other. Just her.

Jessica.

The woman with the tough talk but big heart.

She crossed to him, the moonlight streaming in behind her and making her look ethereal, every bit a goddess straight out of his most erotic fantasies. Her chin was lifted, her hair flowing over her body, her movements sure.

She stopped before him, close enough to touch, to feel

each breath she expelled, to smell the scent of baby powder and apple that was all Jessica.

He held her gaze a moment, then when she let hers dip, he did the same, to where her breasts almost brushed against his jacket. He wanted to skim his fingers across them. Close his mouth around them. He wanted to suckle, to lave his tongue round and round, to feel her writhe in pleasure. To hear raw moans tear from her throat. He wanted to taste her until neither of them could stand another second without falling over the edge.

The thought made him go even more rigid.

She fingered the leather of his bomber jacket, then slipped her hand inside to the T-shirt beneath. Her touch seared through the cotton, fueled the fire burning lower.

Point of no return took on a whole new meaning.

"Damn it, Jessica," he said almost angrily. He didn't know where this burst of honor came from. He'd never been plagued by it before. "You don't have to do this. You don't need to forfeit yourself like some damn virgin sacrifice at a volcano."

A strange light glinted in her eyes. "A virgin sacrifice? Is that what you think I'm doing?"

"Isn't it?"

She held his gaze just a heartbeat before a slow, provocative smile curved her lips. "Who are you trying to stop, Liam? Who are you trying to protect? Me? Or yourself?"

He looked at her standing there and knew he'd never seen a more beautiful sight. "You're one of the most innately good people I've ever known."

"And you think good girls don't do what you want to do right now?"

He almost laughed. "I've never known one to."

"Then you've never been with the right woman, or I'm not so good after all." She pressed closer to him, slid her hand down to where his erection strained against his jeans.

A lesser man would have lost it right then and there.

"I want, Liam," she said huskily, still looking directly at him. His fearless Jessica backed down from nothing, even when she should. "I want you to keep that promise I see in your eyes."

He was tempted to grab those shapely shoulders of hers and give her a good shake. He was trying to be serious, and here she was, rubbing her body all over him, teasing him with bold words. "Don't," he growled, then stroked the hair from her face, giving himself an unencumbered view of the glow in her eyes. "You're the only one who's ever made it better." He wasn't sure where the words came from, only knew he had to say them.

She had to know he wasn't here for sex.

He was here for her.

"Your courage and conviction," he added, watching her eyes flare wide, moisture flood in. "Your compassion. Your loyalty. You're the only one who makes me feel not so alone, and I don't want to fight it anymore."

A single tear spilled over her lashes. "Then don't."

"I don't have protection," he growled.

"It's okay. I'm on the Pill."

On a low oath, he crushed her to him, took her mouth with his. She opened to him, let him in, made him feel like he belonged. Like he was home. He held her tighter, kissed her more deeply. He loved the way her arms twined around his back, her breasts pressed into him. He splayed his hands against her back, then let one trail forward to cup the weight of her breasts.

Honor be damned. He'd never had a heroic bone in his body. Didn't know why he'd tried to find one now.

Sensation sizzled through her. Heat. Need. And for the first time in her life, Jess knew what it was to be possessed. Liam's mouth expertly claimed hers, his tongue making promises she wanted him to fulfill with his body. One of his hands tangled with her hair; the other flirted with her breast. Down lower, she felt the ridge of his erection pressing into her abdomen. She'd never felt more alive in her entire life.

Instinct took over. She tore her mouth from his and stepped back, needing to see him, to convince herself this wasn't a dream. That this was reality. This was Liam.

Through the flickering light of the candle, she glanced up and caught the play of shadows against his face. The sheer male beauty of him made her want to weep. Need glittered in his eyes, but not aggression. She saw restraint there, maybe even confusion. Strength. And isolation.

Always isolation.

And that's what she longed to change.

The man had survived more storms than an army of men should ever have to face. He'd weathered them all, but they'd taken their toll on him, chipping away at him until he'd learned to protect himself. To feel nothing. To want nothing.

But he felt now. And he wanted.

She saw it in his eyes, felt it in his body.

She felt, too.

"Liam," she whispered, then reached out, hating the way he winced, as though bracing himself for a blow. With a soft smile she took the flaps of his bomber jacket in her hands, eased the worn leather over his shoulders and down his arms. She loved the thick but soft feel, the rich smell of man and sandalwood.

And then he stood there in a pool of moonlight, a man in a black T-shirt and black jeans.

She wanted him naked.

He seemed to want the same thing. Something resembling a growl tore from his throat as he reached for his T-shirt, yanked it from the waistband of his jeans.

"Let me," she said, then took over, pulling the cotton over his head. His shoulders were broad, his pecs well defined. Dark hair covered the expanse of his chest, whirled around his dark mauve nipples. She wanted to take one in her mouth, tease it with her tongue, see if she could make him groan.

But even more, she wanted the rest of him.

"Like to be in charge?" he asked darkly.

She glanced up and tossed him her most wicked smile. "Of you, yes. But you can have free rein with me." She saw the shock flare in his eyes, the pleasure, and immediately went for the fly of his jeans.

She barely got the zipper down before his hands joined hers in shoving the worn fabric down his legs. A primal rush streamed through her when she realized he'd taken off his underwear, too, and stood before her naked. And beautiful.

In one graceful move he kicked free of his jeans and pulled her against the warmth of his body. His mouth reclaimed hers, and he skillfully backed her toward the bed. It was a good thing he was holding her, because her bones went so liquid she could hardly move.

When the backs of her legs bumped against the mattress, he eased her down, following her on one knee. He braced himself with his arms, his big body hovering over hers. They were separated only by her pajama bottoms.

She knew what came next, had never wanted anything as badly as she wanted Liam inside of her, making love to her. Making her his.

"Liam," she whispered, loving the sight of him above her. She feathered her fingertips against the rough surface of his jaw, then slid her hand to the back of his head and pulled him down.

He went willingly. As he did, he grabbed a pillow and positioned it under her head so that they lay horizontally across the bed. Her legs fell open; her whole being almost cried out when he positioned himself between her thighs.

The kiss started out gentle but quickly raced beyond flash point. She mourned when he left her mouth but thrilled when his lips trailed down her throat to her aching breasts. The pinpricks of sensation were almost unbearable. He twirled his tongue around her nipple, steady strokes that only increased her need for him, made the emptiness inside seem all the more severe.

"Please," she said, arching into his mouth. She could have sworn she heard a growl of satisfaction as the suction began. But she didn't know from which of them the raw noise came. Didn't care.

His body was big and strong and powerful, and Jess knew what it was to be worshiped. His mouth took care of her breasts while he slid a hand down her stomach and into her pajama bottoms, where he quickly discovered how badly she wanted him. She was wet; she was ready. Again, she heard a ragged sound of satisfaction, and this time she knew it came from him. He slipped a large finger inside, withdrew it slowly.

And this time, the cry came from her.

She grabbed his hair in her fists and pulled his head from her breasts. A wicked light gleamed in his eyes.

"You're a cruel man, William Armstrong," she rasped, then tilted her hips as he slid a second finger inside.

"Is that a complaint?"

"Not yet," she said weakly, trying not to give over to the demands of his talented fingers, "but if you don't hurry, I might just have to take control, after all."

His smile heated. "That sounds suspiciously like a dare."

An odd sense of wonder heightened her desire. She'd never seen Liam like this, darkly seductive, almost playful. She'd never known him to lower his guard so completely.

She'd never wanted so badly to stretch a single moment into an entire lifetime.

"Don't test me." She reached down and curled her fingers around the length of him. "I'm not above taking hostages."

Surprise registered in his gaze only a heartbeat before he groaned at her brand of torture. She squeezed him, let her thumb skim along the part of him she wanted to feel inside her.

"You're a brave woman," he said in return, increasing the pace and pressure of his fingers, "but I'm not sure you realize what waits on the other side."

"Then show me."

Something unintelligible tore from his throat as he grabbed at her pajama bottoms. Together, they clumsily discarded the last restraint between them. Her whole body was alive and on fire, poised on the brink of something powerful. Their eyes met, and her breath caught.

"Jessica," he said in a strangely hoarse voice, then raised a hand to cup her cheek.

In return, she slid her hands down the warm flesh of his back to curl around his firm buttocks. "Now."

For the first time since she'd known him, Liam obeyed. He pushed inside her, slowly, achingly, letting her adjust to the sheer size of him. She wrapped her arms around him and cried out, felt her head loll back. She'd never been promiscuous, had only had intercourse twice before.

But she'd never made love.

And now she knew the difference.

Liam's loving brought far more than her body to life. The feel of his body joined intimately with hers touched her emotionally, spiritually. The connection tapped into a primal place she'd never known existed, a place of vulnerability she'd innately protected. Never before had the physical infiltrated the emotional.

But she knew no fear in Liam's arms, only a sense of rightness far more profound than she'd ever imagined possible.

"Liam." She tried to whisper, but a soft moan tore from her throat instead. Only then did she realize moisture had flooded her eyes, emotion her body. He started moving within her, steady strokes in a rhythm she eagerly matched. The need was unbearable. She wanted all of him. She wanted him deep. She never wanted the dream to end.

But she had to open her eyes. She wanted to see him, to experience every exquisite detail as fully as possible. The candle cast shadows across the hard planes of his face, providing just the right play of light and darkness. His jaw was set, his mouth partly open, his eyes glazed in passion.

Strength and pleasure in its most elemental form.

"You like?" he asked wickedly, and only then did she realize he'd caught her staring.

"Very much."

His eyes gleamed. "It gets even better," he promised, returning his mouth to hers for a deeper kiss. At the same time, he hooked an arm behind one of her knees and brought her leg up against her stomach, giving him a more intimate angle. She arched into him, wrapping herself around him as fully as possible.

She never wanted to let go.

With each thrust the gathering storm intensified. Lightning prickled through her nerve endings; thunder rumbled through her blood. She held off letting go as long as possible, savoring the gathering intensity, but the sensations grew stronger, more demanding.

"*Liam,*" she cried, feeling his body tense, as well. "Please."

And that was all it took. With one final deep thrust, Liam cried out as they came together. Thoughts and feelings and dreams fragmented into slivers of exquisite sensation. But

Jess didn't fight it. She let go, completely, irrevocably, giving herself to Liam in the most intimate, unguarded way imaginable.

Stolen moments, she thought in some hazy corner of her mind, but for the first time in her life, she didn't care.

The chill woke her. Early morning sun streamed in through her window, and a thick down comforter still encased her, but neither delivered warmth to her naked body. She curled her knees to her chest and squeezed her eyes shut, but reality slid through anyway. She didn't need to go downstairs to know the truth. Liam was gone.

Disappointment pushed aside the lingering glow of their loving, and the rose-colored glasses shattered. She'd taken William Armstrong in her arms, her bed, then her body, telling herself the moments were nothing but stolen, but in her heart hoping she could show him another way, offer him a gift he'd never had. Show him the beauty of sharing.

Jess opened her eyes and looked at the bright wash of sun against the destroyed bed. The sheets were tangled, the pillow indented from where his head had rested. Gingerly, she ran her fingers along the cotton, imagining she still felt the warmth of his body.

She blinked back tears, refusing to cry.

God help her, she'd crossed the line. Cops belonged on the street, not in bed. But when he'd shown up on her doorstep in the middle of the night, he'd been at an emotional low, out of his mind with worry. And rather than let Jessica Clark the street-smart cop handle him, she'd been Jess the woman, a woman so deeply in love with the wrong man she'd given him free use of her body for hour after hour, letting him have her and use her, while all the while, she'd spun silly dreams and fantasies about making love and rainbows and white picket fences, forgetting one fundamental truth.

The granite man always walked away.

Chapter 13

"Drop it, girl. Drop it." Molly obediently released the Frisbee and let it fall to the brown grass, then gazed at Liam with adoration and excitement dancing in her big chocolate eyes.

"Good girl," he said, then picked up the bright red disk and flung it toward the back of the yard. The dog took off after it, then caught her trophy midair.

"Good girl!" Liam praised. "Now bring it back to Daddy."

Jess stood at the wrought-iron gate separating Liam's back yard from his driveway. She breathed deeply of the crisp morning air, savored the feel of the sun against her face. She knew she should announce her presence but needed a moment to make sure the walls she'd slapped up around her emotions, still raw from the night before's loving, would withstand what she had to say.

The sight of man and dog wasn't helping matters. The unconditional love shining in Molly's eyes tugged at her heart, made her long for a simplicity that could never be. During the long, dark hours of the night, she'd thought they were carving out a near painful intimacy. A bond to make them stronger. But with his departure and the stark light of day, Jess faced reality. What for her had been powerful and meaningful had likely been little more than sexual gratification for him. A release.

Too bad her body didn't care, still hummed deep inside.

He looked completely at home in the dormant back yard, his dark jeans and sweatshirt as devoid of vibrancy as the brown grass and naked oaks, the threadbare shrubbery. A gorgeous lagoon-shaped pool glistened beneath the morning sun, but standing deserted, it looked as lonely as the man. Even the trickle of an impressive rock waterfall evoked solitude.

"Drop it," he said when Molly raced up with the Frisbee. She obeyed, prompting him to pick up the disk and launch it again. As before, the dog raced toward the back of the yard.

A stab of empathy cut through Jess, forcing her to look away, toward a barren post oak beyond the pool, its branches scraggling toward the bright blue sky. She didn't want to see Liam like this. Didn't want to see him alone. Didn't want to see him playing with his daughter's dog.

"My, God, Jessica."

She glanced toward the cabana to find him striding toward her. Molly raced after him. His expression was fierce, alarmed. His long legs made quick work of the pebbled concrete separating them.

"What is it?" he barked, fumbling with the padlock on the gate. He yanked it off, swung open the wrought iron and took her shoulders in his hands. "Tell me."

His touch seared through her. There was no gentleness from the night before, no sensuality. Just desperation. "Tell you what?"

"I can see it in your eyes. Something has happened. Emily—"

She realized it then, and her heart sank. Something had happened, all right, something dangerous and irrevocable. "No, not Emily," she said softly but firmly. "Us."

Disappointment hollowed his gaze. "Damn it," he growled, then released her shoulders as though he'd been holding hot coals, not the body he'd thoroughly explored the night before. "I asked you not to come here again unless you had news about my daughter."

Jess refused to wince, refused to let him see how deeply his words cut. "I'm not a coward, Liam. I don't run anymore."

"Be that as it may, I'm not into S&M."

"What is that supposed to mean?"

His eyes went wild. "You, damn it! *You.* I'm talking about you." He lifted a hand toward her face, let it drop. For the first time since she'd met him, he looked at a complete loss. "Every time I see you...my heart just stops."

The words, the tortured tone, did cruel, cruel things to her heart. Fantasies, dreams, reality...they crashed and merged, fought for domination. She wanted to interpret his words in an intimate sense, one that had to do with their lovemaking the night before.

The cop in her, the realist, knew the truth. It lodged in her throat, scratched and burned. "Because you think I have news about your daughter."

He looked at her. Through her. "Only a fool continuously sets himself up for disappointment."

Disappointment. The word landed like a fist to the gut.

"Last night should never have happened," he said in a voice devoid of emotion. "I was tired, not thinking clearly—"

"Don't." She stepped closer, lifted her chin. "Don't you dare stand here and tell me you didn't want last night every bit as much as I did. Don't make excuses.'' Hurt and anger pushed her on, and she found her lips curving into a bitter smile. ''You just can't stand it, can you? You can't stand that for once in your life, you let yourself need someone. You lowered your guard. You let someone in. And you liked it.''

His expression darkened. ''You don't know what you're talking about.''

''Yes, I do,'' she said, and realized that she did. Somehow that gave her strength. ''You're so used to being alone, being on the outside looking in. You're used to fighting, to keeping an iron-clad control on everything.'' Much like the massive gate surrounding his home. ''But last night the control wavered, and for a few unforgettable hours you were free. Really free. Free to be the warm, compassionate man you really are, not the granite man you hide behind. And that rattled you. Rattled you as deeply as it did me, and so now you're just going to pretend it didn't happen.''

He stiffened, looked like she'd slapped him. ''Leave it alone, Jessica.''

There was no way she could. She was a cop. A trained professional. She knew how to sniff out a lead, how to interrogate, when she was onto the truth. Standing there in his back yard, with the midmorning sun shining down and a cool breeze pressing against them, Liam looked like a man facing his own mortality. His expression was harsh, his shockingly blue eyes dark.

''You just can't admit it, can you?'' The draw she'd felt to him since the beginning pulled her closer. ''Can't admit you're scared—''

''Like hell.''

''Scared of taking a chance again, scared of not always being rock solid, scared of—''

He took her shoulders in his hands and pulled her toward him, silenced her words with his mouth. The kiss was hard and heart-stopping. Frustrated. *Lost.* His lips moved possessively against hers, strong, yet gentle, as well. Just like the man himself. Releasing her arms, he slid one hand to cup her neck, the other to press against her lower back.

Shock streamed through Jess, followed closely by hope. She twined her arms around him, welcoming the warm, solid feel of man, the soft cotton of his shirt. She returned his kiss with a fervor that sprung from deep inside, the need to beat down the obstacles between them and become just man and woman again, to show Liam how good it could be, that he didn't have to be afraid. That love made him stronger, not weaker.

Abruptly, he pulled back. A peculiar light glinted in his hard blue eyes. His jaw was set, the dark stubble there making him look shockingly dangerous.

"Does that feel like fear?" he asked.

Jess blinked at him, scarcely able to breathe. The truth shimmied around and through her, made her want to weep. "Sheer terror."

The planes of his face hardened, and for a moment, she thought he meant to tell her she was crazy, to demand she leave him alone, then turn and storm away. Instead he swore softly and pulled her to him, returned his mouth to hers. This time he drank even more deeply of her, almost greedily.

She did the same of him.

She didn't know what it was about this man that made her forget common sense, fling everything she knew about survival into the cool morning breeze, but standing in his back yard, with his arms holding her to his big body, she didn't care, either. She knew he was fighting the need between them. She knew that for some insane reason, to him, reaching out to her was tantamount to failure.

She had to show him that wasn't true.

His hands were all over her, big and strong and capable,

the rough feel of his fingertips skimming along the smooth skin of her face. Somehow the gesture made her feel special, precious. Important. And she felt the meltdown deep inside.

"Liam," she murmured against his mind-numbing mouth. "It's okay."

His hands abandoned her face, and for a moment she thought he meant to pull away, but instead he wrapped his arms around her waist and lifted her off the ground. A thrill speared through her as he strode toward the cabana, over the deck, toward the house. Wrapping her legs around his waist, she savored the feel of his body moving against hers.

His mouth never left hers.

They barely made it inside before desire boiled over. He made quick work of her sweater and slacks, she of his shirt and jeans. She was aware of him tearing away her panties, releasing her breasts. The sensation of his big hands claiming her body blotted out all else. They weren't going to make it to his bed.

"Jessica," he murmured, easing her down on the wide sofa. She opened to him body and soul, invited him back to that special, rare place where the darkness dimmed, and the light of the future shone. There were no preliminaries. They weren't needed. Her body still burned from the night before, a hunger intensified by the gulf between them. There was only one way to fill that gulf, she thought as she let her legs fall open and felt him slide inside.

Only one.

Only Liam.

She lay in his arms, all warm and silken and flushed. Her cheek rested against his chest. Her beautiful auburn hair fell across his abdomen. Their legs tangled intimately. Liam would have thought she slept were it not for the way her long fingers played with the hair surrounding his nipples. Slowly. Reverently. Tenderly.

A damning sense of contentment welled within him. He loved the feel of her silken skin, the steady thrumming of her heart. He loved the purely feminine smell of her, the drugging taste. He loved the way she never backed down, the way she lifted her chin and challenged him with those intelligent, defiant eyes of hers.

His need for her went against everything he'd ever taught himself about survival. She was the most amazing woman he'd ever met. And that made her dangerous. Distracting. She made him forget what he needed to remember, made him want a future on which he'd long since turned his back.

But she also made him feel alive.

Guilt pierced anew. He should have never gone to her condo the night before. He should have never indulged the need to see the light in her eyes, feel the warmth in her touch. He should have remained alone, as he'd done for so long. But he hadn't, and now he had to deal with the fallout.

Sex had never been complicated before. Sex had been two consenting adults enjoying each other's bodies. Sex had been a release. Sex had been easy to walk away from.

But this wasn't sex, and he damn well knew it.

That was the problem.

This morning he'd awoken in Jessica's arms feeling more complete than he had a right to. And that was why he'd left. The mindless release of sex, he rationalized on the drive home, but then he'd seen her standing on the other side of the wrought-iron gate, a brave woman with the sun glinting off the copper highlights in her hair, and had wanted nothing more than to eliminate the bars separating them, let her in. Even when she'd revealed she had no news about Emily, he'd wanted her in his arms. He'd wanted to feel her heart thudding against his chest. To smell the clean scent of apples and baby powder.

He never wanted to let her go.

"You should probably get that," Jessica murmured, shifting so he could reach the ringing phone on the table by the sofa.

Reluctantly, he slid from beneath her arms and grabbed the receiver. "Armstrong here."

"When are you going to learn?" taunted a distorted voice.

Liam surged to his feet. "Who is this?" Jessica stood, as well, pressing against him and resting a hand against his arm.

"Do I have your attention now?" the sexless voice mocked. "Doesn't feel so good to lose, does it?"

He knew. God help him, he knew.

"What do you want from me? Where the hell's my daughter?"

"I think a better question is where's her dog?"

The line went dead.

Liam stood stock-still for an excruciating second. He tried to breathe, found he couldn't. His heart beat mercilessly in his chest. Blood roared through his veins.

"Christ," he swore, then yanked on his jeans and headed for the back door. "Molly!"

Horrible thoughts and possibilities chased him across the cabana, deep into the yard. The brown grass crunched beneath his bare feet. "Molly? Where are you, girl?"

Nothing. No barking. No eager dog bounding to him. He'd been playing with her when Jessica arrived. The dog had followed him to the gate. He'd opened it…

He turned toward the side of the house but found the gate closed.

He didn't remember securing it.

Jessica caught up with him. She'd thrown on her slacks and sweater, but her hair was tangled, her eyes fevered.

"I wasn't paying attention," he said, then pivoted toward the back of the yard. "Molly!"

"She's got to be here somewhere," Jessica said.

But Liam knew his daughter's dog. She *always* came when called. He ran past a cluster of old post oaks, toward the gazebo he'd built for Emily. Sometimes she and Molly would sit in the morning sun—

He saw it then, the black heap on the wooden floor, and his heart stopped. He didn't know how his legs kept moving. *"Molly!"*

"Oh, God," Jessica cried behind him.

"Molly!" He ran toward the lifeless form. He could see paws, a tail. No movement. Through his blurred vision he saw a flash of red—the bandanna he'd secured that morning.

He stopped dead in his tracks, and his blood ran cold. He couldn't bear it. Couldn't. Emily loved that dog... "Molly."

Jessica took over, mounting the steps when he couldn't. She slowed, went down on one knee, lowered her hand. Let out a low, keening sound.

Liam blinked several times, trying to convince himself he saw what he thought he did—Jessica lifting a huge stuffed animal in the shape of a black lab.

She swung toward Liam. Horror and hope collided in her gaze. "It's not her."

He staggered forward, sick inside. Molly wasn't there on the gazebo floor, but someone had clearly designed the scene to make him think what he had. "The bandanna?"

Jessica pulled the sleeves of her sweater over her hands before untying the bandanna. She slowly unrolled the fabric, revealing that, like on the one hurled through her window, someone had scrawled a warning.

First the mother, Then the daughter, Now the dog. Who's next?

* * *

"I'm going to kill him," Liam swore. "So help me God, I'll kill the bastard who thinks he can turn my life into a game."

Jess pushed to her feet, torn between comforting the man and cataloging the evidence. Liam's face was hard and pale, making the glitter in his eyes all the more threatening. Almost unearthly.

The cop in her took over. Someone was playing games with this man. Kidnappings by nature were personal, but her gut screamed this extended beyond the typical motivations of money and greed to the dangerous realm of punishment. Torture.

Training overrode emotion, and objectivity pushed aside the sickness in her stomach. "Liam, I need you to think back on—"

"He was here, damn it!" Liam slammed a fist through the latticework of the gazebo. "The bastard who took Emily was close enough to take Molly, too, and I didn't know. If I'd been out here... If I'd been paying attention—"

"Liam, don't do this to yourself." She crossed to him and took his arm in her hands. "You're bleeding."

He snatched his wrist out of her grip and turned on her. "I was wrong to leave you on this case," he said with pinpoint precision. "I was wrong to think this thing between us wouldn't blow up in our faces."

Jess winced. He was retreating from her, a powerful wave churning back to the cold and dark depths of the ocean. "You weren't wrong," she said, reaching for him.

He caught her wrist. "I knew from the start you were dangerous, that this attraction between us was an accident waiting to happen, but for some insane reason, I talked myself into letting you stay on the case. I made excuses. I told myself you could make it better. But that's not true, and we both know it."

"Liam—"

"We were having sex, damn it!" The words were dark and tortured, appalled. He released his hold on her and shoved a hand through his hair. "We were having sex when we should have been paying attention. What else have we overlooked? Isn't that cop rule number one? Never get involved?"

She cringed. Because he was right. But the word *sex* made what they'd shared during the long hours of the night sound so crude and common.

"Sometimes we can't control what happens," she said softly, as much to him as herself. "Sometimes the best plans, the best intentions in the world aren't strong enough to stop fate." She hugged her arms around her rib cage, suddenly cold. The sun still shone from high against the bright blue sky, but the breeze seemed more biting, almost vicious. "This is hardly what I had in mind, either, but it's too late now to go back and change things. All we can do is move forward. Together, we can—"

"Not together." He bit the words out. "This thing between us is like poison, a distraction no good can come from. I'm calling McKnight. I was right in the first place, should have had him remove you from the case after that night in Deep Ellum."

His words sliced and serrated, left her raw and bleeding. But she refused to run and take cover. Not when so much lay on the line. "Don't insult us both with excuses, Liam. Not now."

His eyes hardened. "What are you talking about?"

"You're right. I crossed the line. Making love with you while we're involved on a case was wrong." She lifted her chin, looked him dead in the eye. "But we both know that's not why you're pushing me away. You yourself told me you've never been one to shy away from breaking the rules."

He stood stiff and unmoving. "This is my daughter's life—"

"It's your life, too." She wanted to go to him, put her arms around his big body and hold him tight. But the time for comforting embraces had come and gone, flashed out of control.

William Armstrong wasn't a man who let himself need anyone. She couldn't change that any more than waves could knock over an ancient sea cliff.

"Sex isn't why you're shutting me out," she told him, wanting—needing—the truth on the table. "You let me in last night, you let me close, and it scared the hell out of you. You've dedicated your life to Emily, as though by sacrificing everything, you can make up for what happened with her mother, but one day she's not going to be your little girl anymore. One day she's going to ask you to give her to another man." A stab of guilt pierced through her as the words fell out, but she refused to tiptoe around the truth. For all Liam's strength, he hid behind his daughter. "What happens then? What will your excuse be then?"

He winced as though she'd slapped him. "This isn't about me. This is about an innocent girl whose life is on the line."

"Yes, it is. But it's also about her father, a man who shuts himself off from the world, a man who refuses to let himself feel. Want. Need. Even if Emily was upstairs right now, happy and safe, we'd still be having this conversation."

Jess had come here angry and hurt, believing she'd been wrong about last night, but now she knew the truth. By some miracle, she'd chipped through Liam's defenses to the core of who and what he was. Not the father, not the protector, not the survivor. Not the tycoon, the suspect, nor the pariah. Just the man and his need. No barriers, no pretenses, no defense mechanisms. Just Liam.

And for William Armstrong, that was the most heinous crime imaginable.

"We made love, Liam." Saying the words sent warmth surging through her, but sadness, as well. The intimacy had been too great for Liam, the sharing too acute. "You need me, and you can't stand it, and that's why you're pushing me away."

He stepped toward her. "Damn it, Jessica—"

She held up an arm to stop his progress. "You say you don't have time for love because your daughter is missing, but even before, you never let yourself have a life." He'd spent too long learning to be numb, to hold feelings at bay, to not need anything. One night of loving, no matter how mind-numbing, couldn't erase a lifetime of deeply engrained survival tactics.

"You never let yourself need. Love. In all your attempts to save time and make time, to protect time, all you've done is waste time, and now it's too late."

"You don't know what you're talking about, Detective."

She recognized the acid tone, knew she'd hit pay dirt. She also knew there was nothing she could say or do to change the truth. No matter how long and hard those waves battered the cliff, they always crashed, then fell back to the sea.

"I'm not talking to you as a detective. I'm talking as a woman who knows how destructive stolen moments can be." Her heart broke on the words, but she refused to let him know that. "You're right. They aren't enough to find your daughter, and they're not enough for me."

She turned and strode across the gazebo before he could see the sadness flooding her eyes. She wasn't doing any of them any good trying to tear down a wall with a toothpick.

"Jessica."

Just that, the sound of her name on his voice, and her

heart staggered. She squeezed her eyes shut but kept right on going.

"Don't walk away from me, damn it!"

The pained words stopped her more effectively than one of those sea cliffs. She paused, straightened her shoulders, turned toward him. To hell with him, if he saw the tears in her eyes. He was a grown man. It was high time he faced the consequences of his actions.

"Where are you going?" he demanded.

She looked at him standing there in the bright morning sunshine, all tall and dark-haired, wearing just his jeans, the man who'd made love to her less than thirty minutes before. Somehow, the small, faded gazebo made him look even bigger, more isolated. Emotion sparked in his volatile cobalt eyes, a need that ripped at her. Again, she wanted to go to him, touch him, love him, but she refused to torture herself any further. She'd been careless to lose her heart to this man, but she wouldn't make that mistake again.

A granite man, she reminded herself. Hard and enduring. Alone.

"I'm doing the only thing I can do, Liam. I'm going to forget how it felt to make love with you. I'm going to pretend I never thought we could have a future. I'm one of two detectives assigned to find your daughter, and that's what I'm going to do." Starting with her father's files. "I won't come back until I do, and after that, I'll walk away, and we'll both go on with our lives. Case closed."

And then, though it killed her to do so, she turned and headed for the gate.

Liam watched her walk away. Her back was stiff, her movements determined yet graceful. The breeze lifted the ends of her tangled auburn hair, the apple-scented strands he'd buried his face against less than half an hour before.

The memory sent a blade of panic slicing through him.

He wanted to charge across the yard and stop her. He wanted to pull her into his arms and destroy the hurt he'd seen glistening in her eyes. The hurt he'd put there. He wanted to tell her she was wrong, that he did need her.

But he didn't. Couldn't. Instead, he stood in the cool breeze and watched her stride through the iron gate.

She was a strong woman. She was a survivor. She was hurt and angry right now, but that would pass, and she would be all right. Better than all right, she would thrive, like she had before their paths crossed.

It was better that way, he knew. There was no room in his life for the kind of love a woman like Jessica Clark inspired. She deserved an uncomplicated love, a man who could make her smile, not rile her temper every time their paths crossed. She deserved a man without a tarnished past, a man she could walk beside and not feel the bitter sting of scorn and shame. A man she could be proud of.

Liam was not that man. He had a past that would never leave him. There would always be people who wanted to hurt him, those who believed he'd gotten away with murder, who sought to punish him by hurting those he loved most.

Like Emily.

He couldn't let Jessica suffer the same fate. Wouldn't.

Jess threw several coins into the tollbooth basket, then pressed her foot against the accelerator. She gunned the engine and zipped ahead of a rusty pickup that was ambling along. Too much adrenaline raced through her for her to tolerate a slow speed. Her heart beat as though she'd just finished a set of grueling wind sprints.

But she wasn't tired, didn't want to rest.

She wanted to drive and drive, faster, faster. She wanted to get away from Liam. Even more, she wanted to find his daughter. The truth hovered just out of reach, much like the way her father had taught her to swim by holding out his arms to her, then backing away when she got close.

Tears spilled over her lashes. She swiped angrily at them, letting out a keening sound of frustration as she did so. Now was not the time to mourn foolish dreams. She had a job to do. Liam's daughter was the only gift she could give him that mattered. Her body, her heart, her soul…they were for the man. And so long as the father ached, the man didn't exist.

The man didn't exist, period, she corrected. Liam wouldn't let him.

She pushed the morose thoughts aside and focused on the newest puzzle pieces.

Do I have your attention now? She'd heard the distorted voice on the phone. *Doesn't feel so good to lose, does it?*

No mentions of money, only of suffering. The kidnapper had made demands for nothing other than Liam's attention…

First the mother, then the daughter, now the dog.

Who's next?

Her heart beat a little faster, and a cold sweat broke out on her body. The nasty suspicion she'd been harboring needled deeper. She needed her father's files, damn it.

Everything has to do with the past, Kirby had commented, but in focusing on one battered tree, she'd neglected to see the forest. *Everything. It makes us who we are.*

She inhaled sharply. She'd worked countless cases over the years, yet it never ceased to amaze her how obvious the answer usually was. How personal.

To this day, Carson Manning held Liam responsible for his daughter's disappearance. The man still wanted to make him suffer.

"My God," she rasped. Adrenaline zinged through her as she sped past her exit with a new destination in mind.

Her heart hammered hard. They'd been looking in the wrong place. In focusing on the here and now, they'd overlooked the events of seventeen years before.

The sound of the doorbell pierced like a bullet. He hurriedly locked the thick door and rushed to the front of the house, where the peephole revealed his visitor. The early afternoon sun glinted off the copper highlights in her hair, making her look like a warrior goddess.

Damn it. He almost swore aloud. *What was she doing here?*

He thought about not answering the door, but the ferocity glittering in her eyes warned him she'd be back. Detective Jessica Clark was nothing if not tenacious. Better to deal with her now, before she came back.

The next time she might not be alone.

With a pasted-on smile, he swung open the door. "This is a surprise. I didn't expect—"

"I know, I should have called, but thought I'd stop by instead. We need to talk."

"You sound upset—has something happened?" Inspiration struck, and he manufactured some horror for his next question. "Is it Emily?"

She frowned. "In a way." She glanced behind him, into the darkness of the house he'd turned into a prison. "Can I come in? There are a few things I'd like to run by you. About the past. About Heather's disappearance."

A jolt of unease cut through him. "Now's not a good time. I've got some appointments downtown."

"Please," she said, pushing past him. "It's important."

He sighed. "Five minutes."

She stopped by the leather sofa and turned to him, her eyes on fire. "My father's files from Heather's disappearance are missing."

His heart started to pound so hard it hurt. She couldn't

know. Nobody was that smart. Except maybe Armstrong.
"What?"

"Missing. Gone. As in someone has taken them."

He swore hotly. Convincingly. Precaution always paid off "Are you sure?"

"Positive." Suddenly, she smiled. "Which makes me think I'm on the right track by looking for answers in the past—who were Heather's friends, what was her state of mind, when was the last time she called home, that kind of thing."

"What's going on? Has something happened?"

She shoved a hand through her hair, clearly agitated. "What's the shortest distance between two points?"

The question made no sense. "A straight line."

"Bingo," she said with a sly smile.

A cold frost settled in his gut. "I'm sorry, I'm not following you, and I really need to get downtown." He glanced down the hall, glad he'd pulled the shades. "Maybe we can take this up later?"

She checked her watch. "How about tonight? I should know by then what's in my father's files."

"I thought you said they were missing."

"His official files, yes. But not his private files. As far as I know, they're still in the attic."

Everything inside him went very still. "Private files?"

"He kept them on the major cases he worked, just in case. If there's something about before that links to now, I'll find—" She stopped abruptly, her eyes narrowing. "Is that a dog?"

His heart slowed to a crawl. He'd heard it, too. "Just a stray," he told her, moving toward the still-open front door. He had to get her out of here. Fast. "Look, I really need to—"

"What kind?"

"What kind what?" He tried to act casual, though there

was nothing casual about the adrenaline zinging around in him.

"The dog," she persisted. "What kind of dog is it?"

He shrugged. "Just a mutt," he said, pulling the door open wider. He didn't like that look in her eye. Didn't trust it. "Come on, Jessie, we can finish up—"

She didn't move. "Can I see it?"

"The dog?"

"I'm thinking about adopting one—"

"Now's not a good time." The barking grew louder, more frenetic. He should have muzzled the damn thing. He'd only wanted to make the girl happy, show her he wasn't a monster. And, of course, make Armstrong think that he was.

"Please," she said. "Just one look."

And in that instant, he knew his goose was cooked. She was too damn smart for her own good. If she saw the dog or her father's files, she would know.

He smiled. "I'm afraid I can't let you do that."

Chapter 14

She knew. He saw it in the shocked gleam in her eyes, the readiness to her stance. Wallace Clark's daughter had connected the dots with damning speed.

"Guess you won't be needing those files, after all." Thank God she'd come to him first. "I'm sorry," he said, and meant it. "This wasn't part of the plan."

The woman who prided herself on control didn't bat an eyelash. "What plan?"

He knew what she was doing, what any good cop would do. Buying time. Trying to get him to talk. Formulating a plan of her own. "What is it they say in the movies? I could tell you, but then I'd have to kill you? Is that what you want?"

She narrowed her eyes. "This isn't the movies."

"No, it's not. It's my life." And thanks to Detective Jessica Clark, despite his efforts to point her elsewhere, his plans to pay William Armstrong back were in serious jeopardy. "You know I can't let you leave now."

She kept her gaze on his, but he saw her reach slowly for her gun. Her courage really was something to admire.

He almost felt sorry for her when she realized her mistake. "Not there, Jessie. You left your purse by the door, remember?"

Like Emily, she'd had no reason not to trust him.

Her gaze hardened. "You'll never get away with this."

"No?" he asked pointedly. "How are you going to stop me?"

In a lightning-quick move, she lunged toward her purse. She never made it.

He was bigger, stronger. He tackled her as she reached for the table. She fought him, but his strength easily overpowered hers. She cursed him, but he took care of that by stripping off his T-shirt and using it to gag her. Her hands and feet would be next.

No matter how much he admired her, he couldn't let her spoil his plan. Not now. Not after waiting so damn long.

But his heart pounded furiously as he realized time had run out. He had to get those files, couldn't toy with Armstrong any longer. Couldn't draw out the agony. When an officer of the law turned up missing, the manhunt was massive.

Damn it, why did she have to be so smart? He'd been damn careful, hadn't wanted to hurt her. Hadn't wanted to hurt anyone. Anyone except William Armstrong.

He wanted that man to suffer. To pay the price. To lose everything. It was the ultimate payback for the life, the future, Armstrong had stolen seventeen years before. Strip the man bare. Take everything.

Leave nothing.

"Jessica? Open up, it's me." Liam pounded on the door, harder than before. Maybe she hadn't heard him the first two times. Maybe she hadn't heard the phone ringing, either. She could be in the shower. Or sleeping.

Or she could be flat-out ignoring him.

It was what he deserved after the way they'd parted. That was why he'd started calling in the first place. Why he'd followed her home. The hurt he'd seen in her fathomless eyes had been too sharp. He needed to make sure she was all right. He couldn't leave things the way they were.

He had to make her understand.

I'm not a coward, Liam. I don't run anymore.

Her words from just that morning taunted him because he knew they were true. Avoidance wasn't Jessica's style. She didn't play games. She wasn't one to hide. She met every challenge head-on.

That was only one of the traits he loved most about her.

Unease settled low in his gut. Paranoia, he told himself. He was letting the past send his imagination sprinting down a ridiculous path. Just because unanswered phone calls were how it started with Heather and Emily didn't mean a damn thing. Millions of phone calls went unanswered every day. She was a cop. She could be anywhere.

But fifteen minutes later, he discovered she wasn't at the station, either. She'd been there earlier, had requested some files, then left. No one had heard from her since.

Liam looked around her cluttered desk, lingering only a moment on a photo of Jessica and her father. They were both in uniform, at what looked to be some type of ceremony. He saw love in the old man's eyes. Pride.

He could relate.

Damn it. Where the hell was she?

Reaching for a pen to leave a note, Liam noticed a file on her desk, several pages of notes and transcriptions scattered about. A picture of Emily.

Curiosity got the better of him, and he quickly devoured

the details. He was on Carson Manning's interview when a note scribbled in the margin snagged his attention.

"Good God," he muttered. The memory hit Liam broadside. Swearing, he saw what he'd been missing all along. Jessica had been right.

"Armstrong. What the hell are you doing here?"

Standing on the front porch of an old rambling house just south of town, Liam looked at Jessica's suavely dressed partner and reminded himself to play it cool. He couldn't let the animosity seething between him and Kirby Long jeopardize Jessica's safety. This was the last step. He'd already made phone calls, lined up the pieces.

Lives depended upon securing Long's cooperation.

"I can't find Detective Clark," Liam said, and the words scraped. The possibility of being too late scraped even harder.

Long frowned. "You came all the way down here to tell me you've lost another female? This is becoming a pattern with you."

Liam glanced beyond Long's shoulder to the darkened living area. "Something's come up—I need to talk to her."

"Well, if she's as smart as I think she is, she's done listening to your lies." The familiar hint of mean shot into Long's gaze. "Anyway, she's not here."

Any hope of this being as simple as finding Jessica at Long's kitchen table, reviewing aspects of the case, faded.

"He's got her," Liam said. Rage slashed inside him. He could hardly believe what he'd discovered. Commander McKnight had been shocked, too. "He's taken her, just like he took Emily."

Long gaped at him. "What the hell are you talking about?"

"He never quit blaming me for Heather's disappearance. That's why he took Emily. She's almost the age Heather was when she disappeared. He wants me to suffer, to know what it feels like to lose.''

Long's normally smug expression contorted into shock. ''Who? Who are you talking about?''

''Carson Manning. Emily's grandfather.''

The revelation flared in Long's cold eyes, then he laughed. ''The former state congressman? Are you out of your mind?''

''You're damn straight I am,'' Liam rasped. Standing in the pleasantly mild late afternoon, playing nicey-nice with Long while the clock ticked, was shredding him. ''The two people who mean the most to me are missing. How do you expect me to feel?''

Long swore under his breath. ''How do you know Jessie is missing?''

''I just do. Now, come on, Detective. We've got to get out of here before it's too late.''

''This is police business, Armstrong. *We* don't need to do anything.''

''The hell we don't. They're in trouble because of me, damn it. I can't just sit in my house and wait while their lives are on the line.'' Liam turned to leave. He wasn't going to negotiate with Long one second longer. He'd already wasted enough time.

''Where the hell are you going?''

''To Manning's.''

''Hold up there,'' Long snarled from behind him. ''You can't just take the law into your own hands.''

Liam continued down the cracked walkway, confident Long was following. ''Watch me.''

''You lousy son of a—''

''Hold it right there, Kirby.''

Liam swung around to see Jessica's partner staring in shock at their commanding officer. Long's eyes were narrow, his mouth twisted. "Commander McKnight, what are you doing here?"

The older man moved cautiously toward his subordinate. "Need to talk to you, son."

Liam's blood pressure soared. Impatience mounted. He wanted to get on with it, but lives depended upon the details.

"Jessie might be in trouble," Long said, glancing from his commanding officer to Liam. His hand hovered in the vicinity of his gun. "Armstrong here thinks she's been taken."

"I'm well aware of what Armstrong thinks," McKnight said. Two other detectives emerged from the side of the house. "Now why don't you and I take a walk for a spell, let these boys have a look around inside."

Long went absolutely still. All save for his eyes. They went hot with betrayal, like a wild animal's just before the net closed around him. "What the hell are you talking about?"

"Five minutes, Kirby. That's all."

"This is bull!" the detective roared, then spun toward Liam. "You son of a bitch! You set me up!"

"Easy there," Commander McKnight said, laying a hand on Long's shoulder. "You and I both know we have to follow up on every lead. Humor us, son. Let us get this over with, then move on." The commander sounded like this was just an exercise, a mere formality, another way of pacifying the big bad wolf.

Long glared at Armstrong. "You won't get away with this, you sorry son of a bitch! First Jessie, now McKnight. I don't know how the hell you convinced them to listen to you."

Long kept ranting, but the second McKnight motioned the two detectives to proceed, Liam broke for the house. He half expected Long to lunge for him, but Jessica's partner stood there watching, hatred glittering in his hard black gaze.

Inside, the abrupt switch from blinding sunlight to the dimly lit house momentarily blinded Liam, but he blinked hard and kept running. "Emily! Jessica!"

The two detectives ran ahead of him toward the darkened hallway. All the doors stood closed.

"Emily! Answer me, sweetheart!"

Nothing.

Liam's heart pounded harder than his feet.

"Jessica!"

The detectives each pushed open a door and charged into the rooms, guns in hands, ready for whatever they might find. Liam ran toward the remaining two closed doors.

Fear almost gutted him.

"Jessica!"

He heard it then. A strange thumping coming from the fourth door. "Emily?"

He tried the knob, found it locked. "I've got something!" he shouted, and the two detectives were behind him in a heartbeat. They turned the knob. Nothing. Left with no choice, they reared back and threw the weight of their bodies against the thick wood. Again. And again.

The thumping grew louder. More insistent.

Liam's heart thudded erratically. They were in there, he knew. He wanted to throw open a door and find them, safe and together, to gather them in his arms and never let go.

The men crashed against the hard wood once more, and this time broke through. Gun in hand, one of the detectives entered first. Froze. Swore viciously.

Liam let out a guttural cry and pushed past him. Saw the bed. Almost went down on his knees.

Jessica.

Rage tore through him. The urge to kill. The need to punish.

Instead he ran toward the woman he'd made love with that morning. She lay on the bed, a T-shirt gagging her mouth, her hands and feet bound by rope and secured to the bedposts. Her beautiful amber eyes were wide with fury and urgency.

"Good God," the second detective exclaimed.

"Get me a knife!" Liam roared. He needed to touch her, free her, hold her. "It's okay," he said, dropping to the side of the bed and running his hands along her body. "You're okay. I've got you now."

She blinked several times, tried to say something.

"Hang on," he said, fumbling with the knotted strip of cotton wedged inside her mouth and tied behind her head. "I've got you," he said over and over. All along, the murderous rage built within him. "I've got you."

He needed to hold her so damn bad but had to free her first. One of the detectives came in with two butcher knives, and the men went to work on her hands and ankles.

The gag fell free first. "Liam!" Her voice was raw, hoarse, barely there.

"You're okay," he repeated, running his hands along her face. The sight of the corners of her mouth, cut and bruised and bleeding, sent rage blasting through him.

The rope fell from her abused wrists, and he was able to scoop her into his arms. He held her close, running his hands gently along her back. She was shaking. So was he.

"You're okay," he said again and again, fearing she was in shock. He wanted to keep holding her, never let go, but he had to know what had happened. What she'd found out.

Why her partner had turned on her.

"Sweetheart," he said, easing her back and framing her face with his hands. Her eyes were wide, her pupils dilated. "What happened?" he asked as gently as he could. "Did you find Emily?"

He'd never feared the answer to a question more.

"Barking," she whispered on what little voice she had left. "Molly. H-heard barking."

Liam glanced sharply at the other detectives. "Where?"

"Other side of house."

The two men ran out of the room.

"G-go," Jessica rasped, lifting a hand to his face. Her wrist was bruised, but an incredible combination of courage and compassion glowed in her eyes. "Find your daughter."

"I—"

The sound of shouting killed his words. "Don't come near me!" He heard Kirby Long yelling. "So help me God, you try it, and I waste the girl."

Liam was on his feet and running out the door before he could breathe. The sight awaiting him stopped him cold.

Emily.

Detective Kirby Long stood in the doorway to the kitchen, Liam's daughter securely in front of his body. Her long, dark hair was tangled and her beautiful blue eyes wide with defiance, but she didn't seem to be hurt. Yet. Long had his gun out, pointed it threateningly. A muzzled Molly jumped against his back. Commander McKnight was nowhere in sight.

"Let her go," Liam said through clenched teeth.

"Long, buddy," one of the detectives said. "Hold up here. This ain't the answer."

"It's too late," Long snarled. He no longer looked suave, as he had only ten minutes before. He was sweating, his hair mussed, his gaze that of a wounded, trapped grizzly. "You and I both know there's no other way out of here."

Liam inched forward. "I'm the one you want," he said, drinking in the sight of his child. "Let Emmie go, and take me."

"Dad!" she cried. "No!"

"Kirby."

The sound of Jessica's hoarse voice jolted through Liam. He slid her a glance as she moved to stand by his side and realized he'd never seen a more courageous sight. The corners of her mouth were still bleeding, her hair was plastered to her pale skin, but the light of a warrior glittered in her amber eyes. He'd never loved her more.

"Don't make this worse than it already is," she said. "Let Emily go."

"Worse than it already is?" Long waved his gun erratically. "This son of a bitch took everything I ever wanted. Took it. Used it. Destroyed it. I'll be damned if I'm going to let him take my freedom, as well."

Liam took another step toward Kirby. "Heather walked out on us both."

Jessica sucked in a sharp breath. "Heather? What are you talking about?"

"I didn't kill her," Liam said. He was vaguely aware of the two detectives flanking him, their guns ready.

McKnight had yet to surface. The older man hadn't believed him, Liam realized. And he'd paid the price, too.

"I would never hurt the mother of my child," Liam added.

Long's mouth twisted into a sneer as he took a step into the kitchen. "I loved her first. I loved her always. But you took her from me, gave her the child I was supposed to. You got everything, and I got nothing."

"My God," Jessica whispered. "All this time, it was her. The woman you loved. The woman you lost."

"And now it's time to pay," he snarled.

Jessica had been right all along—Emily's disappearance was linked to Heather's.

"It's been seventeen years," Liam said. Then, for emphasis, he used the nickname he'd seen in Jessica's notes, the one Carson Manning had used to refer to the boy he'd handpicked for Heather to marry. Seventeen years had passed since he'd thought about the punk Heather had once warned wanted to hurt Liam. Badly. It took seeing the initials to make the connection. "Kale." K. L. Kirby Long.

"Took you long enough, ace. But hey, I'm a patient man. I knew this day would come. I knew if I waited long enough, if I was in the right position, the day would come when I could show you how it feels to lose."

Tears flooded Emily's eyes. There was no way Liam was letting Kirby take her out of the house. He'd lay down his life first.

Jessica took a step forward. She held one hand out, exposing her badly bruised wrist. "Kirby—"

"No!" Everything went down so fast, Kirby lay crumpled in a heap on the floor before Liam knew what was happening.

"Emily!" Liam charged across the room and swooped his daughter into his arms. She collapsed against him, holding him as tightly as he held her. Relief swamped him. The dread he'd been living with since the night he'd come home to find her gone dissolved into a relief so pure, so profound, it swamped him.

But then he looked toward the kitchen where a lone woman stood. The woman who'd slammed the lamp down on Long's head. The woman staring at him in absolute terror.

The woman who'd walked out on him seventeen years before. "My God. Heather."

Chapter 15

The woman with the faded blond hair went sheet-white. "Liam."

Shock drilled through him. Disbelief. For seventeen years he'd tried to find this woman, and now here she stood, staring at him with wide, terrified eyes. Kirby Long lay crumpled at her feet, one of the detectives securing him in cuffs.

"It was you!" he realized, stunned. Sick. Jessica had suggested it, but he'd never thought... "You put Long up to this. You took my daughter—"

"No!" she cried, blinking rapidly. Her voice was barely there, clearly frightened. "No."

His hold on a sobbing Emily tightened. He ran his hands along her back, through her tangled hair, but never took his eyes off her mother. "After all this time. You thought you could waltz back and take my daughter from me? The daughter you left behind?"

"What the hell is going on in here?" Commander

McKnight staggered into the living room. There was blood on his temple.

"Commander!" Jessica and one of the detectives rushed to him. "Are you all right, sir?"

He looked a little dazed, his wound clearly the result of a pistol butt. "What's going on?"

"I'll tell you what's going on," Liam growled, looking at Heather. She remained standing on the dirty linoleum in Long's kitchen, gray sweats hanging on her rail-thin body. "This is the woman who put Long up to everything."

"No," she denied. "That's not how it happened."

"She used her old boyfriend to do her dirty work. She—"

"No!" Emily struggled out of his arms and gazed at him. Her eyes were wide and red-rimmed. "It wasn't like that, Dad. She wasn't part of it. She took care of me."

"Emily, sweetheart, you've been through a terrible ordeal—"

"But so has she!" his daughter cried. "He turned on her—"

"I would never hurt her," Heather cried, wrapping her arms around her waist. "Never."

He looked at her, but rather than seeing the lost soul who'd caught his eye so long ago, he saw a woman whom time had not treated well. She'd never been vibrant, more like a delicate flower than anything else. She looked faded, a daisy at the end of a long drought.

"Then what do you call abandonment?" he asked harshly. "That's not hurt?"

She shook her head. "I did what I thought was best. For everyone, but most especially Emily."

"Best? You call running away best?"

"I was trying to avoid a disaster before it was too late," she said sadly. "We didn't love each other. We could barely tolerate each other. I saw the way you looked at me.

I saw the realization in your eyes that you'd strapped your life to someone you didn't want, didn't need.''

"I'm not talking about me," Liam corrected. "I'm talking about your daughter."

Tears spilled over her lashes. "It broke my heart to leave her, but you know as well as I did that I was in no position to be a mother to her. I didn't know who I was. I...I wasn't ready. There was no way I could be the kind of mother Emily needed." She extended her hands in pleading. "But you...you were born to be a father. I knew you'd move mountains for her. I knew the two of you would be so much better off without me. I knew you'd find someone else, someone able to be the kind of mother Emmie deserved, and live happily ever after."

Incredulity blasted through him. "I could have gone to prison, damn it!"

"I didn't know that! I had no idea they'd think you did something to me."

"You knew your father. You knew how he doted on you, controlled you. You thought he'd just settle for no explanation?"

She pushed the hair from her face. "I...I didn't think he'd turn on you."

"You didn't think, period! You should have called someone, let someone know you were okay."

"Then my father would have brought me back, and everyone's lives would have been worse. He would have tried to force us to marry, and we both know what a disaster that would have been. We would have destroyed each other, and Emily in the process."

"There was a manhunt," Jessica said. She'd returned to stand by Liam's side.

"I didn't know that," Heather told her. "I went to Mexico. Stayed there. News of a missing girl didn't reach the

small village where I was, and I eventually married a local.
I just wanted to start over, start new.''

God help him, he almost believed her. Heather had never
been strong like Jessica. She'd grown up smothered by a
domineering father, had just started to spread her wings
when she and Liam fell into bed and created Emily. ''So
you ran away.''

Regret flooded her eyes. ''I can say I'm sorry a thousand
times, but it won't be enough. I can't undo the past. I know
that. God knows, I've tried to pretend the past didn't exist.
I knew I had no right to come back. I knew I had no right
to intrude upon the life the two of you had built. But deep
in my heart, I could never forget.''

Liam looked at this woman he'd cared for but never
loved. Once, he'd responded to her neediness, as though
playing protector to her had allowed him to pretend his
needs didn't exist. Until Jessica.

''Why now?'' he asked, needing to fit the pieces together. ''Why come back now? Emily is almost all grown
up.''

''I...I almost died. There was a car wreck. Rico, my
husband, he was killed instantly. And I realized how fleeting life is. How precious. And I could no longer live with
the choices I'd made. The mistakes. I had to find out if
there was room in my daughter's life for me. That's why I
called Kale.''

Kale. The name from the distant past burned. K. L. Kirby
Long. ''What the hell does Long have to do with meeting
Emily? I'm her father.''

Heather glanced at the cuffed but still unconscious man
on the hardwood floor. The man who'd taken his daughter,
then bound Jessica's hands and feet.

The urge to inflict bodily harm had never been so strong.

''He loved me,'' Heather said brokenly. ''He loved me
from the time we were children, through high school, even

after I started seeing you, he loved me. He promised to always be there for me.''

"So you convinced him to kidnap my daughter?"

"No!"

"It wasn't like that, Dad!" Emily protested.

Surprised, he looked at the pleading in his daughter's eyes. "He locked her up, too," she said. "Said he couldn't risk her going soft on him. Couldn't risk her calling you."

"I called him more to test the waters than anything else—he was safe," Heather said, before Liam could question Emily. "He was so warm when I called, even paid for me to come to Dallas, told me you'd turned into a dangerous, vindictive man, but that he'd pave the way for a reunion with Emily. That's all he told me. I had no idea exactly what he had in mind until the morning he showed up with Emily. I was shocked. Told him he couldn't do this, that this wasn't what I wanted, but he said it was the only way I'd ever get my daughter away from you."

"My God," Jessica whispered.

"I didn't know, Liam. I swear. I didn't know the hatred ran that deep. I didn't know he'd spent seventeen years believing you killed me. I didn't know he became a cop to make sure he was in a position to make you pay."

"What did he hope to gain by kidnapping Emily?" Jessica asked.

Liam could only imagine the shock and betrayal she must be feeling, as well.

Heather glanced at Kirby, then at Jessica. Sadness swam in her eyes. "Me. He said he was giving me the one thing Liam never would. My daughter."

"And making Liam suffer in the process," Jessica whispered. "Putting him through the same hell he went through when you turned up missing."

The term *full circle* had never carried so much meaning.

"I know what I've done is unforgivable," Heather whispered, "and I'll be sorry every day for the rest of my life. But I was young and confused, lost. Desperate. I thought I was doing the best for everyone."

Emily struggled from Liam's arms. "That's not true."

A stricken look tightened Heather's features. "Emily…"

"It's not unforgivable," the teenager clarified. "Maybe if you'd just shown up one day, I wouldn't have believed you, but…"

"But what, Emmie?" Liam asked.

Wisdom and maturity shone in her eyes. "I was alone at first, but then he threw her in the room with me. I could tell she was scared, but she told me over and over everything would be okay. That you would find us."

"She told you who she was?"

"She didn't have to. She looks just like Grandma." Emily glanced at her mother. "It was hard to be angry at her when I could tell she was more concerned about me than herself."

Heather looked toward Liam. "I'm sorry. I never meant to hurt either of you. That's what I was trying to avoid."

He sucked in a sharp breath. "We were kids," he said, and realized he believed her. He also realized the hatred he'd once felt for this woman was gone. In truth, he felt only relief to have his daughter safe, not what he knew he should be feeling—the sweet taste of vindication.

He knew they couldn't go on as if the past had never happened, but with time, wounds would heal. They'd all suffered enough. "I'm not interested in reliving the past."

"Ma'am," one of the detectives said to Heather. "We need you to come downtown with us. We've got a lot of questions for you."

She smiled through her tears. "Yes, of course."

The detective looked at Liam. "You and your daughter, too, Mr. Armstrong."

"I want her checked out by a doctor."

"Ambulance is on the way."

Liam pulled Emily into his arms, held her against his chest. His little girl. Safe. In his arms. At last.

Shock and disbelief merged with relief to cut straight through Jess. Kirby. No wonder he'd always been vague when she questioned him about the love he'd lost. She'd always known he had an edge to him, a chip on his shoulder, but she'd never realized the hatred that seethed inside him. The hatred her father had inadvertently nurtured.

Jess wrapped her arms around her rib cage and watched Liam hold his daughter. She wouldn't cry. She absolutely would not cry. But, God, how the tears burned the back of her eyes.

Emily was tall, but she looked small in Liam's arms, almost like a little girl. He held her fiercely, his whole body curled to protect hers, like she was the most precious gift in the world. Which, of course, she was. His eyes were clenched shut, his jaw set.

The dog Molly barked and licked frantically. Someone had taken off the muzzle.

Deep inside, Jess started to bleed. She wanted to go to father and daughter, wrap her arms around man and child and join in the reunion, but knew she had no place there. Her role in Liam's life had come to an end.

"Let me look at you," he said in a voice more tender than Jess had ever heard. He pulled back and brushed the long, tangled hair from Emily's cheeks, then gently framed her face in his big hands. "This is a lot to take in. Are you okay?"

Emily's blue eyes filled with another flood of tears. "I didn't know if he'd hurt you, Dad. I was scared that maybe—"

"Shh," he said, pulling her back for another hug. "Everything's okay now."

And it was.

Jess looked away from the painfully tender scene and headed outside. The sun was setting, putting on a spectacular show of pink and red swirls. She dug deep to find the expression of a cop in control, not a woman whose heart was breaking.

"Jessie?" Commander McKnight intercepted her before she made it halfway down the walk. "You okay?"

She forced a smile. "I'm not the one whose temple is bleeding."

McKnight frowned. "He got me good. I only took my eye off him for one second, and he was off."

"I should have figured it out sooner." She ground the words out. "I knew Kirby resented Liam, but I didn't realize it went beyond the bounds of the law."

"How could you have? He was your partner. You trusted him, and he used that against you. He knew how you thought, used that to stay one step ahead. You didn't know there was a connection between Kirby and the past, did you?"

"I was so close," she said. So close to uncovering the truth. Just a few more hours... "If I'd just reviewed Dad's files earlier, I'm willing to bet there's an interview with Kirby, and I would have known there was a link. None of this—"

"Don't beat yourself up over something none of us saw."

"This explains so much, though!" And it did. Long's duplicity explained the oddities that had eaten at her from day one of this case. "Why Emily's disappearance looked like a runaway at first. Why Liam found Adam Braxton before we did. Why that first note went to my house, not Liam's. Kirby set us all up, kept everyone off balance. He threw suspicion in so many directions, no one looked in the right place."

"I have to admit, when Armstrong called, I thought he was out of his mind."

"Liam called?"

"Found the notes from your interview with Carson Manning on your desk, saw a note from Kirby signed with his initials."

"K.L.," Jess repeated, stunned. She remembered Carson Manning using the name. "Kale."

"Exactly. Armstrong was looking for you when he saw your notes, and everything clicked. He'd never met Heather's ex but remembered her saying she hoped they never met. That it would be messy if they did. It was a long shot, but he had me call Kirby's mother, ask if he'd ever known Heather Manning. When she said yes—"

Jess shivered. "My God."

McKnight shucked off his jacket and draped it around her shoulders. "We need to get you to a doctor."

"I'm fine."

He took her hands and turned them palm up, revealing her cut and bruised wrists. "Humor an old friend, then. Let me be Uncle Ben for a change, rather than Commander McKnight."

Somehow, she smiled. She looked into his kind eyes, and for a moment, time slipped away. She saw him as he had been some twenty years before and remembered how he used to throw his beefy arms around her and hoist her high above her head. She would laugh and laugh....

Everything had been so simple then. So uncomplicated. So innocent.

"It's a shame your dad isn't around to see this day," he told her, draping an arm around her shoulders and pulling her against his side. "He was wrong about Armstrong, but he would have been proud of how you handled the investigation. You exhibited courage and objectivity in the face of very difficult circumstances."

The emotion her father had trained her to conceal broke free. She looked toward Kirby's old wood-frame house. Liam and his daughter continued their reunion inside.

I'm one of two detectives assigned to find your daughter, she'd told him that morning, when her body still hummed from their loving. *And that's what I'm going to do. After that, I'll walk away, and we'll both go on with our lives. Case closed.*

Her job was done. Liam had what he wanted. Not just his daughter, but a future free of the shadow that had dogged him for years. His life could go on.

Jess straightened her shoulders and looked at Uncle Ben. "Come on then," she said. "Our job here is done."

"Let's get you to the hospital," Liam said, pulling back to look at his daughter one more time.

She rolled her eyes. "I'm fine. Really. He didn't hurt me at all. I think he wanted me to like him—he brought me Molly!" The dog had yet to quit licking their hands. "Heather didn't mean for this to happen," she added.

Liam went very still. "She's been gone a long time."

Emily frowned. "It's kinda weird, you know? I'm not sure I can ever call her Mom, but I kinda hope she stays for a little while. I...always wondered what she was like."

"It's going to take some time."

"I know."

Pride zinged through him. His daughter had always been wise beyond her years. "Now there's someone I'd like you to meet," Liam said, glancing toward the living area behind him.

But no one stood there.

The detectives had taken a sluggish Kirby away. She must be outside.

"Who, Dad?"

He took Emily's hand and led her outside, where the sun

was just about gone. He didn't understand why the hollowness had returned to his gut, why his heart pounded so hard. Several black-and-whites had joined the scene, and a paramedic was tending the wound at Commander McKnight's temple, but Jessica was nowhere in sight.

And then it hit him.

I'm one of two detectives assigned to find your daughter, and that's what I'm going to do. After that, I'll walk away, and we'll both go on with our lives. Case closed.

Detective Jessica Clark was a woman of her word. He could still see her as she'd been that morning, staring at him with defiant eyes, the breeze whipping her auburn hair about cheeks still flushed from their loving.

She'd done exactly what she promised to do, what he'd told her he wanted her to do. She'd given him back his daughter, and then she'd walked away.

Case closed.

Chapter 16

"And this afternoon, an unexpected footnote to a bizarre story of obsession and revenge. Former state congressman Carson Manning and Commander Ben McKnight of the Dallas PD held a news conference to address the appearance of Manning's daughter, Heather."

The name grabbed Jess's attention from the two wrestling puppies she'd brought home from the animal shelter earlier that day. Heart pounding, she reached for her remote and zipped up the volume on the television.

"You'll recall," the stern-faced anchorwoman said, "Heather Manning vanished some seventeen years before, leaving a cloud of suspicion hovering over her boyfriend, Internet mogul William Armstrong. Today, the elder Manning and Commander McKnight addressed reporters to set the record straight."

Three days had passed since the ugly showdown at Kirby's house. The press had jumped on the story of a cop gone bad, turning tragedy into melodrama. Jess was surprised Manning and McKnight would join the frenzy, but curiosity got the better of her. She watched the picture on the television switch to the steps of the courthouse. Carson Manning and Ben McKnight stood side by side.

"Very few things in life are as abiding as a parent's love for their child," Manning began. "When my daughter, Heather, vanished seventeen years ago, the shock and grief ripped me apart. I wanted her back. And when that didn't happen, the need to place blame overrode all else."

One of the puppies, a fourteen-pound shepherd mix named Bonnie, nudged Jess's hand. She obediently scratched behind the pup's floppy ears, but her gaze remained on the television set.

Manning cleared his throat, looked acutely uncomfortable. "William Armstrong was an easy target. At the time, he and my daughter were involved in a fading but volatile romance, and it was easier for me to blame Armstrong than accept the fact my daughter might have chosen to leave. I dedicated everything I had to proving Armstrong guilty of a crime we now know he didn't commit."

McKnight stepped in. "There was never any concrete evidence against Armstrong, but a good cop is trained to never quit. To keep looking. Evidence often surfaces long after the fact to solve cold cases. We wanted to give the congressman his daughter back. We wanted justice."

"I have my daughter back now," Manning said. "And now it's time for justice." He paused, a dramatic effect no doubt left over from his days in the state legislature. "William Armstrong had nothing to do with my daughter's disappearance. She left of her own free will, the exact same way she returned. I'd like to take this opportunity to publicly apologize to Armstrong for the difficulty he's endured over the past seventeen years."

Jess stared at the television. Surprise pounded through her, making breathing difficult. Manning finished his statement and took a few questions, but the words blurred together. Something about his daughter, and time, and healing.

"Well, what do you know," she said to the second puppy, a black Lab named Clyde. "I didn't think Manning had it in him."

But joy swamped her that he did. Liam deserved to be vindicated. He deserved his happy ending.

She'd not seen him since the afternoon at Kirby's when she'd fulfilled her promise to him. She wanted to remember him as she'd last seen him, holding his daughter. The image had the power to warm her heart and break it clear in two.

Emotion clogged her throat. Determined not to succumb to it, she returned her attention to the puppies happily destroying a stuffed hot dog. She'd spent entirely too much money at the pet store, particularly if Bonnie and Clyde were going to shred everything she bought, but giving the abandoned pups a home filled her with warmth. They were so innocent. Full of life and vitality, gratitude. Their antics made her smile.

She was sitting there watching them strew white stuffing all over her floor when the doorbell rang.

Jess stood and stretched, moved cautiously to the door. Reporters had hounded her the day after the showdown, but the past two days had been fairly quiet. Still, she looked out the peephole before pulling open her door.

The sight awaiting her knocked the breath from her lungs.

Liam.

Her heart surged, staggered. With the setting sun at his back, he stood on her front porch, all tall and strong, dressed in black jeans and a dark gray Henley shirt. The lines of his face were more relaxed than she'd ever seen them. Salt and pepper whiskers covered his jaw. And his eyes... The midnight-blue that had warned of a storm on the horizon was lighter, like a bright spring afternoon after the rain and thunder had blown away. The diamond stud winked from his ear.

The real William Armstrong, she knew. The wickedly sexy man who not only believed mountains were made to be moved, but who moved them. Liam.

Her mouth went dry. She thought about pretending she wasn't home, but she'd told him she didn't run anymore, and she didn't. Pulling open the door, she offered him a tight smile.

"Liam," she said politely. "This is a surprise." And the Grand Canyon was just a little erosion.

His gaze was unreadable. "Is it?"

"I didn't expect to see you again," she said with a well-practiced indifference. Not like this, anyway. Here. In her condo. On the news, in the tabloids…she'd never fully get away from William Armstrong in the public domain. But here, on her doorstep, that was different. More intimate. He stood close enough to touch.

"Is that what you want?" he asked quietly.

The question jarred her. The man couldn't read her mind. "Now's not a good time," she said, glancing over her shoulder to make sure the puppies hadn't carried their destruction further than their toys.

"That's an awfully cold greeting for the man you made love with lock, stock and block just a few days ago."

She looked at him and reminded herself to be strong. To tear a page from his book and let herself feel nothing. "A different lifetime, Liam. One that's over now."

"Is that what you want?" he asked again. "Why you left?"

Her defenses crumbled a little more. What she wanted had nothing to do with what was good for her. No matter how much she loved this man, she absolutely refused to share her life with a man who wouldn't share his heart.

"I—"

"Hey, Dad!" The energetic voice came from the driveway. "Is she home?" Molly came charging onto the porch, followed by a laughing Emily Armstrong clutching a funky purple leash. A bright orange bandanna adorned the dog's neck. "Oh. Hi."

A smile sprang from Jess's heart and touched her lips. The teenager looked wonderful, her long dark hair loose and flowing around her flushed cheeks, her blue eyes sparkling. She bore no visible signs of her ordeal. "Emily. It's good to see you."

Liam dropped an arm around his daughter's shoulders. "Detective," he said, "Emmie wanted to officially meet the woman who saved her life."

Jess tried to keep her expression blank. She refused to wince. But it was hard, so hard, when her heart bled and hope crumbled into dust.

Granite, she reminded herself. Liam hadn't come here to see her. He'd come here because of his daughter. Because of the case. Just like all the other intimacies they'd shared.

"That's very sweet of you," she said to Emily, "but I didn't save your life. Your dad did."

The girl smiled. "That's not what he says."

"Oh?"

"He says he never would have gotten through this without you." A twinkle lit her eyes. "And trust me, for my dad to say something like that, it must be true."

Startled, Jess glanced at Liam.

"You showed me the way," he said in a husky voice. "Now can we come in for a few minutes?"

Jess blinked. *No. Absolutely not.* "Yes. Yes, of course." She'd been staring, she realized. Searching those amazingly blue, inscrutable eyes of his for a hidden meaning behind his words.

Inside, Molly made a beeline for Bonnie and Clyde. The

puppies barked rambunctiously, prompting Molly to begin eagerly licking them. The Lab's frantically wagging tail just barely missed a cup of hot cocoa on the coffee table.

Jess couldn't help but laugh.

"New friends?" Liam asked.

She reached for a box of treats and shook three into her hand. The dogs immediately sat and gazed at her, swishing their tails eagerly. "They needed a home," she said simply. She left out the part about love. "I had one to give."

"The fish weren't enough for you anymore?"

The quietly spoken question hit a little too close to home. She glanced at Liam, reminding herself not to read too much into his words or give him too much with her answer. "Sometimes there's no such thing as enough."

"How old are they?" Emily asked, breaking the tension. She'd picked up the female puppy and held her against her chest. Liam's daughter was even more striking in person than in her pictures, Jess realized. Because of her vitality. The energy and happiness she radiated. In many ways, she looked like her father, with all that dark hair and those moody blue eyes, her height, but the features looked softer on her. More feminine. She was a real knockout.

Jess could see why Adam Braxton had fallen hard.

She could also see why Liam had growled protectively.

"Twelve or thirteen weeks," she answered. "The shelter wasn't sure. They were found abandoned along White Rock Lake."

"They're so sweet!" Emily gushed. "Dad, I think Molly needs a friend," she said quite emphatically, gesturing to where Molly was bathing Clyde's ears.

Liam grinned. "Oh, do you?"

"No one should be alone," the teenager said sagely.

Jess winced, glancing from father to daughter. A decided undercurrent zinged between them.

A knowing grin lit Emily's expression as she glanced at Jess. "My dad's told me a lot about you."

She smiled. "He told me a lot about you, too."

"That's why I wanted to meet you." Emily returned Bonnie to the floor, laughing when the pup licked her hand. "You gave my dad a fair shake. You listened to him. You helped him. And for that I wanted to say thanks."

Jess marveled at the girl's maturity. She was clearly wise beyond her years, reinforcing what a terrific job Liam had done raising her, especially since he'd pretty much been raising himself, too.

"She was just doing her job," Liam said.

Emily shrugged, eyed her father, then picked up the purple leash. "I think Molly wants to go outside," she said, smiling at Jess. "Would it be all right if I took her and the puppies into the back yard?"

No, Jess thought wildly. *I don't want to be alone with your father. There's nothing left to say, and the silence is too damning.*

"Jessica?" he asked.

Her gut screamed mischief, but when she glanced at her eagerly wiggling puppies, she realized she had no choice. Motherhood was a new adventure for her, putting her needs aside in favor of those younger, less able. "They do seem to want to go."

"Cool." Emily led Molly across the room, Bonnie and Clyde bounding behind her. When the door opened, a blast of cold air rushed in, but when they went outside, all the oxygen seemed to go with them. The air thickened, the silence turned deafening, and Jess was left alone. With Liam.

Just looking at him hurt. She could hardly meet his gaze without remembering the sight of him over her, under her, inside her. The glow that had been in his blue eyes, the lust she'd mistaken for love, the need she'd thought was for her rather than just the release of his body.

He was looking at her, too, his expression completely unreadable. She'd seen a similar expression on the face of the department's lead hostage negotiator.

She didn't know why that thought made her heart strum harder, deeper.

But then the moment shattered, and Liam swore creatively, strode across the room. She stiffened, completely unprepared for him to pull her into his arms and flush against his body. He muttered something between an oath and a prayer and just held her, running one hand along her back, into her hair.

Jess stood completely still. The smell of sandalwood and smoke permeated her senses like a heady drug, triggering the urge to let go and simply melt into this man. The steady thudding of his heart echoed through the quiet room. The warmth of his body seduced. God, how she'd wanted this. Dreamed of feeling his arms close around her. Longed for it. Even that first night, when she had more reason to doubt him than to love him, she'd been drawn to him. She remembered the feel of his body beneath her hands when she'd frisked him, all that hard muscle and angry male.

She'd known then how dangerous the man was.

She just hadn't paid a lick of attention.

Emotion streamed through her, and she figured it was a good thing Liam was holding her. Otherwise she might shatter.

"God, you feel good," he whispered. The husky words caressed the side of her neck. "It's okay to feel me, too, Jessica. It's okay to hold me back."

She winced. She hadn't known words could weave through her, tighten around her heart. But she couldn't do as he wanted. She just might never let go.

Liam pulled back and looked into her eyes, framing her

face with his big hands. His thumbs gently brushed along her cheekbones. ''Always the tough one, aren't you?''

She blinked furiously. Being tough had always made her proud, but somehow, when Liam uttered the word, when he looked at her like that, she felt like she was failing some critical test. ''Why are you doing this? This isn't a good idea—we've already said all there is to say.''

''For such a good detective, you couldn't be more wrong.''

''You have your family back now, Liam. Emily and Heather. The three of you need some time—''

''No.'' He was happy his daughter would have a chance to get to know her mother, but the woman's return had no impact on Liam's life, other than the sweet taste of vindication. ''Emmie and Heather are going to start counseling to repair their relationship, but there's nothing between me and Heather to repair. Never really was. That's a big part of why she left. She'll always be a part of my daughter's life, but she doesn't own my heart. Not like you do.''

He saw her eyes widen and heard the sharp intake of breath but had his fingers on her mouth before she could speak. ''Shh.'' He drank in the way she was watching him, the courage in her wide amber eyes, the fire. She was fighting him, he knew. Protecting herself. He'd let her down badly. She was brave and strong, and Liam wanted nothing more than to show her she didn't have to be so tough. That he could be there for her. That he could help carry the load.

The past three days, without her, had been hell. He'd thought seeing her might help, but when she'd answered the front door, the need had turned sharper than before. Cut deeper. He didn't think it would ever be sated.

''I was wrong,'' he said, opting for the tactic that had never failed him in business. Brutal honesty.

She blinked. ''About what?''

He wanted to hold her but knew he needed to give her

the words, the truth, before he gave her his body. "I thought I knew how badly I needed to see you, but I was wrong."

She tried to push out of his arms, but he wouldn't let her go. "Liam—"

"Have you ever wanted something so badly you hurt? That you know without it, your life will never be the same?"

"Liam, don't do this."

Outside, his daughter the matchmaker glanced toward the window and grinned at him, gave him a thumbs-up, then vanished around the corner.

Liam couldn't help but smile. When had she gotten so darn smart? "When Emmie was gone, I didn't think anyone could strike out at me anymore. Lash any harder. Cut me any deeper. I didn't think there was anything else of value to take. But when I realized you could be in danger—"

She lifted her hands to his and pulled them from her face. "I was just doing my job."

"Your job. I tried that line, too," he told her. "I told myself that's all it was, that the draw I felt to you was only because of that. The investigation. Because you were as dedicated to finding her as I was. That once she was home, everything would go back to the way it was before. But I was wrong."

Finally, he had her attention. She looked like he'd suddenly begun to speak Swahili. "Wrong?"

He slid his hands around her waist to the small of her back, where he pressed her against him. "My daughter is home now, and I can see her smile, touch her, hold her, but it's still not right. I've still driven by your house every morning, every evening."

He heard the small gasp, saw the thaw deep in her eyes. It was like sunshine glimmering on a frozen river, tiny cracks giving way to a tide of water. "You were right, Jessica. About everything."

Her lips twitched. "About you being a pigheaded, insensitive—"

On a growl, Liam blocked the words by putting his mouth to hers until he felt her lips quit moving. Then he pulled back and narrowed his eyes. "You never said I was pigheaded."

"Oh?" She looked at him speculatively. "Then what was I right about?"

Liam couldn't believe it. Here he was pouring out his heart and soul to her, and she was teasing him. God, he loved this woman. "You're enjoying this, aren't you?"

Her smile widened. "You better believe it. Detectives live for the moment when evidence overwhelms even the best defense."

"And just what is it you think I was defending?"

"Your heart, Liam. That part of you that's been hurt too many times before." A soft light glowed in her eyes. "But I'm not going to hurt you. I love you too much."

A growl broke from his throat, and he pulled her against his body. "You are one amazing woman."

"I'm Wallace Clark's daughter."

The fact no longer scraped. "Your father was doing his job," Liam said, and realized it was true. "He was doing what he believed in. But in trying to take my freedom, he gave me my future. I can't fault him for that."

"That sounds an awful lot like forgiveness," she said, and lifted her arms to curl around his neck.

"Full circle," he told her, loving the smell of apples and baby powder that was all Jessica. "From that very first night when you didn't let me break into Braxton's house, I knew you were special. I knew you were different." He paused, drinking in the sight of her, knowing it would never be enough. "I don't want to be an island. Not if that means living without you."

Her eyes filled. "Are you suggesting a bridge?" she asked. "Geological realignment?"

"Whatever it takes." He pressed his lips to hers again, then pulled back and smiled. God, she was amazing. "You said you would find my daughter, then walk away. Case closed. But I can't let you do that."

Awareness dawned in her gaze like a vivid sunrise after a long, dark night. "What are you saying?"

"I love you. That if you'll give me another chance, I want to share my life with you."

Her answering smile nearly blinded him. "Do you have any idea how much I love you?"

"If it's at least a fraction of how much I love you, we've got one hell of a future ahead of us."

She pushed up and kissed him. "Now this is what I call a much more satisfying way to close a case."

"Actually," he said, slipping a hand into his pocket and fingering his mother's wedding band, "it's just beginning."

Epilogue

Darkness blanketed the house. Silence. No light greeted Jess in the kitchen, none in the foyer. The dogs didn't come bounding down the hall to greet her. Puzzled, she set her keys and purse on the table and made her way up the curved staircase.

From all appearances, no one was home.

The sudden racing of her heart made no sense but didn't surprise her. Not anymore. Strong emotion inspired strong reaction. She started to call out, but instinct held her back. Eighteen months had passed since Liam had come home to a similar scene, and after all this time, emotion still choked her throat. She hated to imagine what it must have been like for him to stand on the threshold of losing what he loved most. His child.

Find my daughter, Jessica. Don't make me sorry I trusted you.

Liam's words from the very first night escorted her across the quirky loft area to the closed door. Soft light slipped from the gap above the carpet. She remembered putting her hand on the glass knob so long ago, remembered the husky voice taunting about what awaited on the other side.

Just my big, unmade bed.

And like that cold night when her life had changed, her heart strummed harder, deeper.

I don't think you want to go in there, he'd said.

But she did. So very much her heart ached with it.

Bracing herself, she turned the knob and eased the door open, stepped inside. Felt the breath back up in her throat.

No matter how long she lived, how many times she discovered similar scenes, the sight awaiting her would never cease to steal her breath.

Liam lay atop the thick comforter of their big bed. Dark gray sweatpants covered his long legs. Their three-month-old daughter napped on his bare chest. He had one hand resting on her tiny back; with the other, he gently stroked her soft cheek. Her little head rested over his heart. Jess may have carried Caitlin for nine months, but other than her mouth, she was the spitting image of her father, dark hair and all.

Together, they looked more than just content. They looked perfect.

Jess felt her heart swell, her throat clog.

"I told you she'd be here any minute," Liam told his daughter, then looked at his wife and smiled. "Our girl's hungry."

And if Jess knew her husband, he was, too. The word *satiated* didn't exist in his vocabulary.

Her breasts responded instinctively, growing heavier in anticipation.

"Why the grin?" he asked.

She crossed to him but stopped a few feet from the bed. With his dark good looks and enigmatic eyes, that tall, powerful body of his, she'd thought Liam drop-dead sexy from day one. Never in her wildest imaginings would she have guessed that creating a child with him would amplify the effect.

"Do you have any idea what it does to a woman to see her husband and child like this?"

A tender light gleamed in his eyes. "I hope it makes you want to join us," he said, extending a hand toward her.

Emotion swamped her. She closed the distance between them and sat on the side of the mattress, one hand instantly finding her daughter, the other her husband. She couldn't touch them enough. Before they'd come into her life, she hadn't known it was possible to feel so much at one time. Love and hope and joy. Amazement. Contentment. Desire.

"You're leaking."

Instinctively, Jess glanced at her blouse, but Liam lifted a hand to her cheek, where he wiped a tear from beneath her eyes.

"Hormones."

Their daughter cooed and squirmed, prompting Liam to lower his hand from Jessica's face to her chest, where he slipped a button through its hole. "Best not to keep Caitlin waiting."

Her breasts tightened. Tingled. She longed to draw her daughter to her chest, feel her tiny mouth latch on. "Impatient, isn't she?"

Liam laughed. "We Armstrongs know a good deal when we find one." He eased her down on the bed beside him and unfastened her bra, released one heavy breast. "Speaking of which, while you were gone, Miss Caitlin informed me she's a bit lonely now that Emily's gone down to UT. She'd like us to get to work on a brother or sister as soon as possible."

"Is that a fact?" Jess asked, loving the prospect of expanding their family. She reached for her daughter, who instantly latched on and began to suckle. Amazing how quickly life could change. Time moved on. Emily had entered the University of Texas, where she was majoring in psychology. Heather was piecing together the fragments of her life. Kirby was serving time. And Liam…

For too long, he'd held himself apart from the world, unable, unwilling to share. To let himself care for anyone other than Emily. To make himself vulnerable. To need. But the seeds had been there all along, waiting for the right time to grow. Now free, he loved with the same single-minded intensity he did everything else. She couldn't imagine any man being a better father or husband. She couldn't imagine feeling happier. More loved.

She found fascinating the circumstances that had brought them together. Life had a strange sense of humor, but she wasn't complaining. The night really was darkest just before dawn erupted in a tapestry of hope and promise.

Glancing at him, Jess found him watching her. Just watching her, those amazingly blue eyes of his heavy-lidded and hypnotic. "I could spend forever just like this," he rasped. "Do you have any idea how much I love you?"

That was easy. "You show me every day."

He leaned over and pressed his mouth to hers, kissed her while their daughter continued to suckle at her breast "Rest assured. The best is yet to come."

*   *   *   *   *

Watch out for exciting new covers on your favourite books!

Every month we bring you romantic
fiction that you love!
Now it will be even easier to find your favourite
book with our **fabulous new covers!**

We've listened to you – our loyal readers, and as of
August publications you'll find that...

We've improved:

- ☑ *Variety between the books*
- ☑ *Ease of selection*
- ☑ *Flashes or symbols to highlight mini-series and themes*

We've kept:

- ☑ *The familiar cover colours*
- ☑ *The series names you know*
- ☑ *The style and quality of the stories you love*

Be sure to look out for next months titles so that you can preview our exciting new look.

▼ SILHOUETTE®

0704/RE-LAUNCH/SILH

SILHOUETTE®
SENSATION™

AVAILABLE FROM 21ST MAY 2004

SHOOTING STARR Kathleen Creighton

As long as the safety of innocent victims was at stake, Caitlyn Brown ha
vowed to break the law. Unfortunately for her, CJ Starr was committed
to upholding it—so why did it have to hurt him so much when he turne
her in to the police?

LAST MAN STANDING Wendy Rosnau

The Brotherhood

Elena Tandi knew that street soldier Lucky Masado could shed light on
who her family really was. But she couldn't have forseen the passion sh
would have for him, or her desire to stand by him in his final battle.

ON DEAN'S WATCH Linda Winstead Jones

Reva Macklin wasn't going to let anyone jeopardise the safe haven she
had found for herself and her son. But she hadn't bargained on the
pleasure of Dean Sinclair's embraces. And this undercover officer had
secrets of his own…

SAVING DR RYAN Karen Templeton

The Men of Mayes County

Maddie Kincaid was alone with her two small children when she went
into labour. She found rugged, handsome doctor Ryan Logan to assis
her delivery—and then he made her an offer she couldn't refuse…

THE LAST HONOURABLE MAN Vickie Taylor

Without Del Cooper's help Elisa Reyes knew her unborn child had n
future. She had every reason to hate him—but that was before she
accepted his honour-bound proposal and he unleashed all her pent-u
desires…

NORTHERN EXPOSURE Debra Lee Brown

When a rock slide left photographer Wendy Walters and game warde
Joe Peterson stranded in a frozen Alaskan wilderness, they had to fin
their way to safety before danger—or their mutual attraction—caugh
with them.

AVAILABLE FROM 21ST MAY 2004

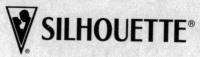

SILHOUETTE®

Intrigue™

Breathtaking romantic suspense

ROCKY MOUNTAIN MAVERICK Gayle Wilson
HER SECRET ALIBI Debra Webb
CLAIMING HIS FAMILY Ann Voss Peterson
ATTEMPTED MATRIMONY Joanna Wayne

Special Edition™

Life, love and family

SHOWDOWN! Laurie Paige
THE SUMMER HOUSE Susan Mallery & Teresa Southwick
HER BABY SECRET Victoria Pade
BALANCING ACT Lilian Darcy
EXPECTING THE CEO'S BABY Karen Rose Smith
MAN BEHIND THE BADGE Pamela Toth

Superromance™

*Enjoy the drama, explore the emotions,
experience the relationship*

A BABY OF HER OWN Brenda Novak
THE FARMER'S WIFE Lori Handeland
THE PERFECT MUM Janice Kay Johnson
MAGGIE'S GUARDIAN Anna Adams

Desire™ 2-in-1

Passionate, dramatic love stories

SCENES OF PASSION Suzanne Brockmann
A BACHELOR AND A BABY Marie Ferrarella

HER CONVENIENT MILLIONAIRE Gail Dayton
THE GENTRYS: CAL Linda Conrad

WARRIOR IN HER BED Cathleen Galitz
COWBOY BOSS Kathie DeNosky

SILHOUETTE SPOTLIGHT

Two bestselling novels in one volume by favourite authors, back by popular demand!

These innocent beauties seem like unlikely sirens, but could two powerful men resist their seductive charms?

Available from 21st May 2004

Available at most branches of WHSmith, Tesco, Martins, Borders, Eason, Sainsbury's and all good paperback bookshops.

Spence Harrison has to solve the mystery of his past so that he can be free to love the woman who has infiltrated his heart.

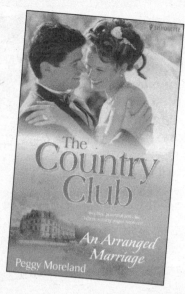

The employees of the Lassiter Detective Agency are facing their toughest case yet—to find their secret desires.

Diana
Palmer

MOST WANTED

❤ SILHOUETTE®

MJO29D

FREE!

4 Books
and a surprise gift!

We would like to take this opportunity to thank you for reading this Silhouette® book by offering you the chance to take four more specially selected titles from the Sensation™ series absolutely FREE! We're also making this offer to introduce you to the benefits of the Reader Service™—

★ FREE home delivery
★ FREE gifts and competitions
★ FREE monthly Newsletter
★ Books available before they're in the shops
★ Exclusive Reader Service discount

Accepting these FREE books and gift places you under no obligation to buy; you may cancel at any time, even after receiving your free shipment. Simply complete your details below and return the entire page to the address below. **You don't even need a stamp!**

YES! Please send me 4 free Sensation books and a surprise gift. I understand that unless you hear from me, I will receive 6 superb new titles every month for just £2.99 each, postage and packing free. I am under no obligation to purchase any books and may cancel my subscription at any time. The free books and gift will be mine to keep in any case.

S4ZEE

Ms/Mrs/Miss/Mr ....Initials ....
BLOCK CAPITALS PLEASE

Surname...

Address..

....

....Postcode ....

Send this whole page to:
UK: The Reader Service, FREEPOST CN8I, Croydon, CR9 3WZ
EIRE: The Reader Service, PO Box 4546, Kilcock, County Kildare (stamp required)